EVERYTHING HE COULDN'T

NEWBERRY SPRINGS SERIES

BOOK TWO

HARLOW JAMES

ISBN: 9798878990639

Cover Designer: Abigail Davies
Editor: Melissa Frey

To those of us who strive to grow every day, to manage grief and abandonment, and tread through waves of change...

In the words of Brene Brown, "What we don't need in the midst of struggle is shame for being human."

"When thinking about life, remember this: No amount of guilt can change the past, and no amount of anxiety can change the future."

Unknown

CONTENTS

Prologue 1
Chapter 1 15
Chapter 2 39
Chapter 3 51
Chapter 4 69
Chapter 5 83
Chapter 6 103
Chapter 7 117
Chapter 8 136
Chapter 9 154
Chapter 10 173
Chapter 11 196
Chapter 12 219
Chapter 13 239
Chapter 14 277
Chapter 15 293
Chapter 16 302
Chapter 17 313
Chapter 18 334
Chapter 19 350
Chapter 20 361
Chapter 21 375

More Books by Harlow James 387
Acknowledgments 389
About the Author 393

PROLOGUE

Evelyn

Six Months Ago

"Nice of you to finally show up."

"I'm here, aren't I?" John Schmitt, the man whose baby I'm carrying, stumbles through the door to my townhouse. Avoiding my eyes, he walks over to the couch, the stench of alcohol seeping from his pores. He's almost an hour later than the time we agreed to over text—but like he said, at least he's here.

As I watch him plop down onto my sofa, reality slams into me for the hundredth time in the last twenty-four hours. The same reality that I'm not sure the man sitting before me will ever be ready to face.

We're having a baby in less than a month, and John is nowhere near prepared to be a father. Motherhood wasn't something I'd planned on at twenty-seven, either, but having sex means risking pregnancy, and we both took that risk. Although it seems I'm the only adult between the two of us who's coming to grips with the shift in my life—in *our* lives—that has already occurred.

I place my hands on my hips while I battle whether to lay into him or cry, knowing that my hormones will probably let the tears win eventually. "So, what was it tonight? Tequila? Whiskey?"

A scoff leaves his lips as he rests his head on the back of my sofa, closing his eyes with his face pointed up toward the ceiling. "Vodka, not that it matters. Why do you care?"

"Why do I care? Because we're about to have a baby, John, and the last thing I need is a drunk, deadbeat dad for our daughter."

His head pops up, and he glares at me. "I didn't ask for this, Evelyn."

I throw my hands up in the air, my heart rate rising exponentially as I stare at him. "And you think I did? How many times are we going to have this same argument?"

"As many times as you bring it up!" He tosses his hat onto the cushion beside him. "This was just supposed to be sex. A good time, you know? I didn't want to have kids, at least not right now."

His words sting, but this isn't the first time he's said them, so each time the pain hurts a little less. "Well, apparently you didn't pay attention during sex ed, because pregnancy is a natural consequence of having sex, John." My hands find my bump, rubbing circles over the spot where our daughter just kicked me. And I swear she knows there's turmoil in the air around her tonight.

"I'm just not fucking ready for this. I'm trying, but . . . my entire life is about to change, and I . . ." He brushes his hands through his hair. "I'm not ready."

"Yours is not the only life that is about to change. In case you've forgotten, this is affecting me, too." Shaking my head at him, I finally admit, "But I'm beginning to wonder if this would just be easier if I did it alone." My heart pounds as my admission rests between us, but the words have been on the tip of my tongue for weeks. It finally feels good to let them have a voice.

But my declaration gains his attention again. "You want to do this alone?"

My eyes burn, but I hold back the imminent tears that will fall at some point this evening. I called John over to make plans about the birth, seeing as how he's been avoiding the conversation for months. But now, with four weeks to go, we can't ignore the fact that our daughter will be here sooner rather than later. And if his drunken state and inability to focus on anyone but himself are any indication, he's still not prepared to face reality.

"I've been alone in this so far, so how would it be any different once she's here? Relying on myself is basically what I've been doing since I told you I was pregnant, John.

You haven't even accompanied me to one of my doctor's appointments. This little girl deserves a father who loves her and wants her, and if you can't be that man, then maybe you shouldn't be in her life at all."

This relationship, if you can call it that, was over months ago the second those two pink lines showed up. But I won't deny this man knowing his daughter, if that's what he truly wants—if he can finally accept and commit to it.

Launching from the couch, he trips over his feet but catches himself before he falls. Standing right in front of me, his eyes flick back and forth between mine. "I don't want that."

The first tear decides to fall at that very moment, but not because I'm sad about my circumstances and not because I feel sorry for the man standing in front of me.

No, that tear is for my daughter who I've promised to protect from anyone who won't support her, stand up for her, and love her unconditionally the way parents are supposed to love their children. The way my parents proved they didn't know how to do.

"Then man the fuck up. She's coming, whether you're ready or not. But I won't let you resent her, I won't let you toy with her emotions, and I sure as hell won't let *you* let *her* down her entire life, John. So either be in it fully or not at all."

He lifts his hand, tucking my hair behind my ear. "I'm sorry, Evelyn. This wasn't supposed to happen."

"Well, it did." I gently push his hand away, not sure if his gesture is the alcohol talking or his true remorse for the emotional turmoil he's put me through for months. Being pregnant and fighting with your baby's father is not something I would recommend or wish on my worst enemy.

"Please, don't touch me." Hurt flashes across his eyes. "You and I can remain civil as long as the drinking stops. But if this is how you're going to deal with this, I don't want you around, John. In fact, don't bother coming back here at all until you've sobered up, pulled your head out of your ass, and have committed to being a father. If you can't do that, you're not welcome in my or your daughter's life. And I promise that I will do everything in my power to make sure you *never* hurt her."

His jaw clenches as he stares at me, intensity swirling in his blue eyes, eyes that once sparkled and reeled me in with his charm, sexiness, and confidence. Now, they just seem dull, lifeless, and sad.

And that fact makes another tear fall as my hands tremble with nerves.

"I have to get some sleep. I have a shift tomorrow," he finally says, ordering an Uber on his phone while avoiding the ultimatum I just gave him, which doesn't surprise me. But I mean it. I will not let him hurt her—or me—anymore.

I didn't expect the fairytale with him. That was never what our relationship was about. All I was looking for at the time was some fun, and John Schmitt is the *definition* of fun. We spent plenty of time indulging in each other, laughing and living a carefree existence, and things were easy and simple before I got pregnant. Now, I'm not sure that the word "simple" is in either of our vocabularies, especially as I watch him walk out to the car that just pulled up to my townhouse.

John Schmitt is not a bad man, but he's a man who's making choices at the moment that are affecting people besides himself. And I hope to God he realizes that in the next four weeks, or who knows how much worse this could get once our daughter is born.

"I'll talk to you later, Evelyn," he says as he opens the door to his ride, but I call out to him before he slides into the back seat.

"Don't bother unless you're ready to go all in, John. I'm serious. Your life is about to change, and you need to accept it or don't even think about knocking on this door," I say with more conviction than I currently feel. The words I'm speaking are truly how I feel, but nerves rattle my spine as I stand there and watch them sink into his brain.

With a nod of his head, he settles into the back seat, and I watch the taillights glare against the dark night sky as the car speeds away.

Little did I know that John Schmitt would never return to my townhouse again after that night, and not because he didn't *want* to be a father.

It was because he *couldn't*.

~

Walker

Six Months Ago

I reach up and tug on the collar of my shirt. I fucking hate wearing a suit, especially for a reason like this. Not only do I feel like I'm choking because of the shirt, but the palpable tension in the air is suffocating me as well.

The walls of people standing around are all looking solemn and crying as they stare at the ground and absorb the preacher's words while my best friend's body lies cold and dead in a casket. Their eyes occasionally land on me with a look of remorse I'm not sure I can take much more of.

This is my fault. I couldn't save him. And there's nothing I hate more than not being able to save someone.

John Schmitt, known to everyone else as Schmitty, is dead. And I'm the one responsible.

I knew we shouldn't have gone into that blaze, but he and I have tackled much worse fires than that one. We had to make sure the building was clear, that there wasn't a family that couldn't get out in time. And even though I saw the hesitation on the chief's face, he trusted us to come out alive.

It's not every day that an apartment complex catches on fire, especially in a town like Newberry Springs. But it happened, and I, wanting to do what my training prepared me for, insisted that we check out the building and make sure everyone got out okay.

Little did I know that the only person to die that night would be the man who trusted me with his life, the man who followed me into the blaze when we shouldn't have risked it in the first place.

And now, as I stand here holding my breath because it's easier than feeling knives scrape my lungs each time I inhale the suffocating sadness filling this place, I let the guilt wash over me. Because not only did my best friend die, but he's leaving behind a child, a child who will never know her dad.

My eyes find Evelyn, her head hanging low in her black dress that drapes beautifully over the bump carrying her daughter, and I fucking hate myself—for making her cry, for taking away her child's father, and for wishing that it were *my* child she was carrying instead.

"Let us bow our heads and pray," the preacher says, directing everyone to mimic the movement before reciting yet another passage from the Bible. But he may as well be speaking German because the last thing I can focus on right now are his words.

The chilly wind whips through the cemetery, making this cold and wintry December day in Newberry Springs, Texas, even more unbearable. A shiver runs down my spine as I watch a flock of birds fly through the air, fighting the wind to get to their destination. For a moment, I sympathize with them. Navigating my life this past year has felt a lot like the fight those birds are in right now.

The sun peeks out from behind the clouds for just a few moments, bathing the grass where the casket lies in a ray of light before disappearing just as quickly as it arrived, in the blink of an eye. Just as fast as John lived and died, like the snap of my fingers.

Movement to my right pulls me back to the service, my shirt growing tighter around my neck as I count down the minutes until I can leave and drown my sorrows in some whiskey. It is what John would have wanted, after all, a toast to him in his honor since the man did love to drink and have a good time. Although the last time we spoke, he was talking about giving up alcohol altogether.

Thinking back on his promise gives me the distraction I need to get through the next twenty minutes.

~

"You look like shit," I tell my best friend as he shuts the door on his locker and spins to face me, leaving the two of us alone in the locker room at the fire station.

"Well, I feel like shit, if it's any consolation." Schmitty runs his hand through his hair before putting his Newberry Springs Fire Department ball cap on his head, completing his uniform.

It's the beginning of our shift on a Friday night, which means this could be a quiet night or a night from hell. There's usually no in-between.

"Hungover again?" I ask through clenched teeth, already knowing the answer since this has been John's MO since Evelyn told him she was pregnant, a detail I try not to focus on too much for fear that it will drive me insane.

"Yeah," he admits, avoiding my eyes.

"Isn't that getting a little old, man?"

He eyes me now, defensiveness registering in the tension of his shoulders. "You act like you haven't been drinking with me."

"I didn't say I haven't. But seriously, man, I'm getting a little worried. You put away so much more than I do on any given night, that's for damn sure. And I sure as hell wasn't with you last night. I know you can drink more than the rest of 'em, but sooner or later, you're gonna have to stop. You can't be doing this when the baby gets here."

He narrows his eyes at me, spewing his frustrations at the drop of a hat. "Why do you care? It's not like you're the one who's about to have a kid."

And that response has me gearing up for an argument just as fast. I cross the room like a bullet leaving a gun, slamming my best friend against the lockers behind him, letting all of my anger, frustration, and gut-wrenching anxiety fuel my reaction. "Are you fucking kidding me? Why do I care, John? Because you're my best fucking friend! And for the past eight months, I've been watching you bury your denial about your kid being born under copious amounts of alcohol. How about that?"

"Fuck you, Walker," he spits out as I feel a few of the other guys move into the locker room, investigating the confrontation

brewing. "You have no idea what this is like," he continues, trying to shove me off.

*But I just push against him even harder. "You're right, Schmitty. I don't have a fucking clue, but I do know this—*you *are not a fucking coward. You are John mother-fucking Schmitt. You've jumped out of a fucking airplane, and you run into burning buildings as a* job, *for crying out loud." I watch my best friend's eyes begin to well with tears. "You are brave and bold, loyal and strong as an ox—and* not *a fucking coward." Lowering my voice, I say, "And I know without a doubt that you are not the type of man who's not going to be there for his daughter." I stab my finger into his sternum. "That's not who you fucking are."*

"I'm . . . I'm scared, man." His voice squeaks as the admission leaves his lips, but it wouldn't take a rocket scientist to determine that was his problem. Hell, I've known that for months, but what the fuck was I supposed to say without accidentally admitting that it's been torture for me watching him and Evelyn together—and now, even worse, watching her grow and carry his child?

So instead, I've picked him up when he calls from the bar. I've even gone with him when he's asked, ordering water when he thought we were having shots of vodka. And I've stood by patiently, waiting for him to acknowledge that, even though he thinks he's not ready to be a father, he can totally do this. And that little girl will be lucky to have him as her dad.

All the while, I lie in bed at night wondering how I ended up in this position, lusting after a woman that my best friend drew in first. And what's worse? She was in my life the whole time. For years, I never acknowledged I might want more with Evelyn.

Hell, even though I'm a firm believer in soulmates and all that shit, no woman has ever made me consider if I'd found mine—until the night my best friend pursued Evelyn right in front of me.

And now look where we've all landed.

"It's okay to be scared, fucker," I say, removing my arm from his chest. "But it's time to stop drinking yourself to death, man. Evelyn needs you. Your daughter needs you. Hell, this entire station needs you. And I fucking need you, John." And I need you to be the man I know you are so I don't have to fucking punch you in the face for being a piece-of-shit dad, *I add in my head.*

"I know. Fuck." He pinches the bridge of his nose as he gathers himself.

Over my shoulder, I call out to our audience. "Get the fuck out of here. I'll be in the kitchen shortly to feed you assholes. Give us a minute, will ya?"

As the resident chef on shift, no one eats until I cook the food. But right now, my best friend needs me, so those fuckers can wait.

Snickering filters down the hall as Drew, one of the other crew members, calls out to us. "Just wanted to make sure I wasn't going to have to pull you off of him, Walker!"

Shaking my head, I turn back to my best friend. "You good?"

Taking in an unstable breath, John stares right at me. "Yeah, man. I'm good. You're right. Evelyn's right. I need to stop fighting this and just accept it, focus on what I need to do. I have no idea what that is, but I can learn, you know?"

I smack his shoulder before leading him down the hall. "Exactly. No one knows how to be a parent when your kid is born. You learn as you go. Promise me that you're not going to let those girls down, man."

"I promise." His words are wobbly, but I'll take it.

"Good. And just so you know, I, for one, can't wait to watch the shitshow of you figuring this all out, especially watching you learn how to change a fucking diaper."

We share a laugh as we make our way toward the kitchen where the rest of the crew is waiting for us.

Little did I know, that was the last laugh—and the last fight—I'd ever have with my best friend. Because two hours later, he'd be dead.

CHAPTER ONE

Walker

Present Day

"Well, if it isn't my favorite brother-in-law!" My brother's wife, Kelsea, saunters up to me, tossing her towel over her shoulder as she leans against the bar between us. It's Friday night, and I need a beer—or maybe five—before I head home.

"Good to know I still beat out Forrest."

"Well, when he was helping us remodel our bathroom, he was the favorite. But today, I guess I'll let that be you." Her crooked, teasing smile gives me a comfort that I need today, more than I'll let on. But that's why I decided to stop by my brother's brewery on my way home this evening.

My twin brother, Wyatt, expanded the Gibson family ranch business when he opened up this brewery and restaurant nearly three years ago. After earning his MBA, he returned to our hometown and used his shiny new degree to build this booming establishment. And Kelsea, his best friend since we were kids, was right there alongside him while he did it.

Kelsea grew up with us. Our parents acted more like her family than her own since her mother left both her and her dad when she was ten. Her father is a truck driver, so he was often gone for long stretches of time, and she would stay with us during those weeks. She and Wyatt always had a special bond, though, not unlike the one I have with my twin, but the two of them also developed feelings for each other as time passed.

Last year, I got sick and tired of watching them avoid their more-than-obvious feelings, so I convinced Kelsea to fake date me to make my brother jealous. And when I tell you I thought my brother was about to burn the world down when I touched her, I'm *not* exaggerating. Everything worked out well, though, since they got married last May and just celebrated their one-year anniversary. I'd say my meddling was worth it.

"Then why don't you get your favorite brother-in-law a beer, please? It's been a rough day."

She flashes me a sad smile, knowing exactly why today is hitting harder than most other ones, and reaches for a glass. "Sure thing."

I watch her pour me a pint of my favorite blonde ale that my brother brews here himself, and then she slides the glass over to me. "Thank you."

"Of course. So how are you holding up?"

"I can't believe it's been six months," I say, staring at my beer instead of into her eyes. Kelsea has always been easy for me to talk to. When you've known someone your entire life, they can read you better than anyone, and Kelsea inherently knows when shit is bothering me. I don't even try to hide it from her anymore. Besides, she's best friends with Evelyn, so I'm sure she's aware of how hard today is.

"I know," she replies, her pout flashing at me for just a second.

"How's she doing?" I ask, knowing damn well Kelsea knows who I'm asking about.

"She's okay. It's been a rough week. Kaydence isn't sleeping well, so I've been trying not to pry too much because she's already on edge. And you know Evelyn. She's not one to tell people when she's struggling. So honestly, I'm not sure how today is hitting her. I was going to stop by her shop tomorrow to get my baby snuggles in while attempting to surreptitiously make sure she's not crumbling."

Evelyn owns a fashion boutique in our small town that has done very well since she moved here about nine years ago. She sells an array of women's clothing, accessories, and shoes. I've only been in there a few times, but she always has something new for the women of Newberry

Springs. Even my mother keeps up with the new items she has in stock.

"Okay. That's good, I guess."

Kelsea reaches over and places her palm on top of mine. "You know, you could check on her yourself if you're that concerned."

I pull my hand away from Kelsea's. "The last person Evelyn wants to see is me, Kelsea."

"That's not true, Walker." Kelsea straightens her spine. "She's hurting, too, you know."

I lift my eyes and see my sister-in-law staring down at me with a chastising glare. "Yeah, because of me."

"No, *not* because of you. When are you gonna accept that Schmitty's death was not your fault?"

"When it stops being true."

Before Kelsea can give me her rebuttal, my little brother by two minutes interrupts our conversation. "Hey, look. It's the ugly twin."

Rolling my eyes, I drain half my beer before replying. "Stop stealing my lines."

"Well, with the five o'clock shadow on your face, your hair sticking up on the ends telling me you're in dire need of a haircut, and the bags under your eyes, I'd say that you're definitely less put together than I am right now."

I glare over at him. "I just got off work."

"You worked today? Really?" Wyatt asks as his brow pinches together.

"Thought it was better to keep my mind as busy as possible."

"Yeah, I guess. I just thought—"

"I don't want to talk about it anymore, all right?" I cut him off, draining the rest of my beer before sliding the glass back over to Kelsea. "I'll take a refill, please."

"You sure?" she asks.

"Yup. Less talking, more drinking. That's my motto for the evening." I toss my eyes over to my brother. "You got a problem with that?"

I can see his need to argue with me, but when his shoulders drop, I know he understands my request. "Nope. But give me your keys." He waits with his palm outstretched.

I dig into my pocket, slam the key ring into his waiting hand, and then reach for the beer that Kelsea sits right in front of me. "There you go. Now, go take care of your brewery, and I'll let you know when I'm ready to go home."

Wyatt sighs, kisses Kelsea on the temple, and walks away as he shoves my keys into his pocket.

"He's worried about you," Kelsea whispers as she wipes down the counter in front of me.

After I gulp down half my beer, begging for the alcohol to take effect and dull the ache in my chest—one that I'm not sure will ever go away now—I say, "Yeah, well, I'm worried about me, too."

~

"I wish I had grass," I say as I run my hand across the lawn outside of the brewery, resting my ass on the ground since it seems easier than standing right now.

Summer nights are the best when the sun goes down and the air gets that slight chill in it, offering a reprieve from the heat and humidity of the day. And after several beers, lying down in the grass sounds like the perfect way to enjoy the crisp air.

Flopping all the way down onto the lawn, I start making snow angels, or grass angels, if you will.

"It's so soft."

The crunch of gravel under shoes alerts me to my brother's presence, but I close my eyes and keep fanning my hands and legs in and out.

"It's time to leave, Walker."

"Just five more minutes."

"Nope. You've had your fun, but now, I have a business to close. I promised Kelsea I would be home at a reasonable hour tonight, and the last thing I want to do is piss off my wife."

"You have a wife." I hiccup and then giggle at the sound. "And you know who you should thank for that, right? Me."

"Yeah, yeah. I know." He hunches over and reaches for my hand, halting my movements and forcing me to pop my eyes open. "You finally helped me see reason. And tonight, I'm gonna do the same for you."

All of the joy I was just feeling instantly deflates as reality slams back into me. Unfortunately, the world around me also begins to spin, so I try my best to focus on not vomiting up the six beers I took down in a relatively short amount of time and take my brother's hand as he helps me up.

"I'm good. Really. I don't need a lecture."

"I don't give a shit what you think you need, Walker. But let's get you home first before I lay into you."

After Wyatt helps me to his truck, I buckle my seat belt then lean my head against the window, closing my eyes in hopes that the spinning will stop. I must fall asleep on the ride home because the next thing I know, the sound of a slamming car door makes me jump up, disoriented and even more nauseous than before.

"Am I home?" I ask as Wyatt opens the passenger side door and helps me out, throwing my arm over his neck to help me walk. It's not entirely necessary, but I'm not going to turn down leaning against him right now. It actually feels kind of nice to lean on him, if I'm being honest.

"Last time I checked, this is where you live." He slides the key into the lock and opens up the door to my townhouse. The two-bedroom space is enough for me, seeing as I'm single, and it's close to the fire station.

Flames. So much heat. Where the fuck is Schmitty?

I blink repeatedly to try to cast the images of that night from my mind as Wyatt closes the door behind us. I stumble over to the couch. Shutting my eyes as I rest my head against the back of the couch doesn't help, either. In fact, it just gives more life and color to the nightmare I know will haunt me once I pass out.

"Walker." The cut of my brother's voice makes me wince. "Fucking look at me, Walker."

Lulling my head to the side, I open my eyes to find my twin staring down at me, his arms crossed over his chest. It's crazy how two people can look so much alike but be so different.

Wyatt has come a long way in the past year. From denying his feelings for his best friend to going all in. I'm proud of the man he's become, how loyal and steadfast he is in everything he does. But right now, that determination of his is about to be unleashed on me. And that makes me resent it.

"What's up, little brother?" I hiccup again, annoyed that they just seem to be appearing randomly. "You know, it's funny. You're younger, but right now, you look so much taller than me."

"That's because you're sitting down, asshole."

"No need for name calling, Wyatt. But sticks and stones and all that." I wave him off.

He bends over and gets in my face. "Are you happy with yourself?"

Flashing him my best grin, I say, "I'm always happy with myself, Wyatt. I'm a happy fucking guy."

"Really? Could have fooled me."

"Well, then you must not be paying attention. I mean, I

get it. You're married now. Happy. *You* get to be with the woman you love. That's gotta be nice."

"It *is* nice, Walker. And if you'd take a second to stop drinking, you'd realize that you could be happy, too. Maybe you could even be with—"

I shove him out of my face, warring with the anger that's bubbling up in my gut now. "I don't get to be happy, Wyatt. Not anymore."

"Fuck that, Walker." He runs his hand through his hair, shaking his head as he stares at the ground. When he lifts his head and locks eyes with me again, he lets out months of frustration. The only reason I know that is because the look in his eyes is the same one I give myself when I stare into the mirror every day. "Drinking away your guilt isn't going to help you. When are you going to realize that? Schmitty is gone. He's not coming back. And it sucks. It really fucking does. It was a horrible accident, but you can't keep blaming yourself, man."

"Then who am I supposed to blame, Wyatt?" I shout, letting the alcohol fuel my reaction now. My brother is ruining my damn buzz, and the last thing I wanted to do was face all of my shit today.

"No one! It was *no one's* fault. You take the risk of dying every time you run into a fire, Walker. That's what you signed up for, and that's what Schmitty signed up for, too. He wasn't naïve. Is it tragic that he died? Yes. But you know what's more tragic? You wasting your life away, drinking yourself sick thinking it's going to change anything. That's fucking tragic." He takes a few steps closer to me and plops down on the couch beside me. And when he reaches over and places his hand on my shoulder, I fucking lose it.

All of the anguish, the guilt, the anger—it all rushes to the surface. Tears cloud my vision, and I slump forward, bracing my arms on my knees as I hang my head and break apart. "I couldn't fucking save him, Wyatt. He has a daughter, and I couldn't fucking save him for her."

Strong arms pull me from the flames, but I fight them. John's still in there. And he won't survive if I don't go back in.

He rubs my back, pinching my neck and breathing deeply as I choke on my sobs. "I know, Walker. I know. But keeping this weight on your shoulders isn't good for you. It's been six months, and while I know it's still fresh and will always affect you, it's time to start to move on."

"How? How do I move on knowing that I was the last one to see him alive? Knowing that because of that night, his daughter doesn't have a father. That Evelyn—"

"Have you talked to her?"

I simply shake my head. If they gave out gold medals for avoidance, I'd have collected them all. I'd definitely be the fucking champion in that sport. Over the past six months, each time I've run into Evelyn, it's felt like being stabbed in the chest repeatedly, each wound reopening again after feeling like it had finally started to heal. Because she's close with Kelsea and has even helped out on my parents' ranch from time to time, I've found it impossible to avoid her completely. But when I see her, a simple head nod of acknowledgement is the only thing I've been able to muster. And even that feels monumental.

"What am I supposed to say? 'Sorry that you're a single mom? Sorry I couldn't save the man who didn't mean to get you pregnant in the first place? Sorry that he never got the chance to prove to you that he really wanted to be a dad, despite how he was acting?'" I twist my head to face him. "The night he died, he promised to try to be there for them. He was going to talk to Evelyn after our shift. But . . ."

"He never got the chance to," Wyatt finishes for me. I bob my head in agreement. "The entire situation sucks, man. But instead of wallowing, why not figure out a way to honor him? Why not try to be there for Evelyn the way he couldn't?"

"I'm not sure she'd even want my help, Wyatt."

"You'll never know if you don't ask."

"Fuck." I throw myself back against the sofa and drag my hands down my face, wiping away tears and snot in the process. "I'm so tired of feeling like my chest is being cracked open."

"I know. And I'm tired of driving you home after you've drunk yourself stupid. Something has to change, Walker. It's time to try to heal the wounds that Schmitty's death has left instead of making them worse."

"I don't even know where to start."

"You'll figure it out. And I bet it will come to you when you least expect it." With another slap on my shoulder, he stands and moves toward the door. "In the meantime, take a fucking shower. You stink."

"You sure you're not just smelling yourself?"

He shrugs, but then the corner of his mouth tips up. "Maybe, but I have my hot-ass wife waiting for me at home to help clean me up if that's the case."

I grimace. "Please refrain from sharing details of the sex you have with Kelsea. The woman is like my sister, after all."

"She *is* your sister now, technically. But I can't help it, man. I'm fucking happy."

"You're welcome, again."

He nods and opens the door. "I know. You meddled in my life, and I will always be grateful. But now, it's my turn to do the same to you. Talk to Evelyn, Walker. I'm telling you, it just might be what you need to start healing and move forward."

As the door shuts behind him, my heart rate picks up. I know that speaking to Evelyn will only bring up other emotions I've been trying to avoid, ones I've been shoving down since the first night I realized that maybe the woman I'd always seen as a friend had the potential to be more.

Too bad she saw my best friend first.

"Are there any biscuits left?"

My mother glances at me over her shoulder as I enter

the kitchen at the ranch. "Just took a fresh batch out of the oven."

"Excellent." A small sliver of joy runs through me as the comfort of home sinks in.

Coming over to the Gibson Ranch a few days a week always helps ground me, and since I spent yesterday nursing my hangover and beating up my body in the gym as punishment, I have even more work to catch up on over here today.

When my brothers and I were little, my parents started building this ranch, fostering my mother's lifelong dream of owning a farmhouse that was more of an experience than a farm, which came to fruition through years of hard work. Now, their property not only houses up to thirty guests at a time, but they host weddings and company events, take part in cattle farming, and offer horseback riding lessons to families, which is my area of responsibility.

I plant a kiss on her cheek and then find the basket of biscuits on the counter, reaching in for a fresh one. If my momma is famous for one thing, it's her biscuits. The reviews online for the Gibson Ranch are almost guaranteed to mention the delectable balls of dough, and she takes tremendous pride in that—as well as in keeping her secret recipe tucked away in her brain until she can pass it along to her future daughters-in-law. The generational tradition started with her grandmother, and she takes it very seriously.

Kelsea is the first recipient, of course, but the pressure for me and my older brother, Forrest, to add two more daughters-in-law to the family is always lurking under the surface of any conversation with our mother.

"You're here a little early today," Momma says as she flips the burner on the stove and moves the pot of jam over to the counter to cool.

"Well, I have a lot to catch up on."

"Everything okay?"

"It will be," I offer, not wanting to make my mother worry any more than I need to. My parents obviously know about what's happened in my life over the past six months, but my brother hasn't advertised my drinking binges to them, and I'd like to keep it that way.

"I got the jars!" Kelsea calls out as she enters the kitchen, setting the box she's carrying on the counter. "Oh. Hey, Walker." She walks over, gives me a quick hug, and then goes right back to extracting each glass jar from the box.

Every week, Kelsea and Momma make jam, spice blends, and mixes to sell at the farmers market in town. Wyatt and I usually take turns working the market with Kelsea, but lately, I haven't been very helpful—mostly because Evelyn sets up her booth for her boutique right next to ours and that would mean having to face the woman I'm not ready to mend my friendship with just yet.

I'm working on that in my head. Slowly. It's . . . a work in progress, we'll say.

"Hey, Kels. You ladies look busy, so I'll get out of your hair."

"If you stay on the other side of the counter, you won't be in the way, so there's no need to leave so soon." My mother winks at me. "I feel like I've barely seen you lately. Where have you been?"

Kelsea eyes me discretely behind her curly blonde hair. She knows what I've been up to, but I know she won't share that with my mom.

"Just busy with work. And tired. My body needed some rest yesterday, so I took the day off from everything."

"Those days are needed sometimes. Although, days off just make me antsy and restless anymore. I figure I'll just sleep when I'm dead," my mother says with a wave of her hand in the air.

Kelsea and I both laugh because the running joke is that my mother never sleeps. She's always either cooking, cleaning, or tending to her flowers outside. But the pride she takes in the ranch is contagious, too, which is why my brothers and I have a stake in the property and business as well.

"So, since you had a day of rest, does that mean you're going to join me at the farmers market this week?" Kelsea says with a tilt to her lips.

"Well . . ."

"It *is* your turn, after all." She cuts me off before I can come up with an excuse.

I clear my throat and then cast my gaze toward my

mom, who's busy placing the Gibson logo stickers on the jar lids. "Yeah, I'll be there."

Kelsea's eyebrows pop up. "Good. That's . . . great."

My mother lifts her eyes and bounces them back and forth between the two of us. "What's going on, you two?"

"Nothing," we say simultaneously.

"Have you forgotten that I've raised you both your entire lives, so I know bullshit when I see it?" She places her hands on her hips and arches a brow. My mother rarely cusses, so our secrecy must be striking a nerve with her today.

"Nothing's going on, Momma." I round the counter, place another kiss on her cheek, and then do the same to Kelsea. My sister-in-law's eyes widen in an attempt to have a silent conversation with me, but I ignore her. I'm sure she's going to corner me later to interrogate me before I leave. "Look, I've got a lot of work today, so I'm going to get to it. But if any bacon magically becomes available soon, please let me know."

Momma reaches out for me, locking her hand around my wrist before I get too far. "You know I'll save you some, Walker. Now, are you *sure* you're okay? You look tired, honey."

"I'm okay, Momma. I promise. I love you."

She squeezes my arm and then releases me. "I love you, too, son."

Kelsea flashes me a tight-lipped smile, and then I head out back toward the stables to the right of the house.

The crunch of the dirt and hay under my boots brings me a peace I should have searched out the day before yesterday instead of trying to find solace in beer. Alas, I'm back to where I should be, tending to my horses and doing good old-fashioned hard labor as a form of therapy.

It's still early in the morning, but the sun is already unforgiving as I trek across the land, eager to get to work and sweat out the anxiety still resting in my chest after the other night. It felt good to tell Wyatt how I feel, but now that I've said it out loud, those fears have a voice. I'm still debating if I want to listen to them.

But as I walk into the stables, the backside of my older brother catches my eye and pivots my focus once more. "What are you doing here on a Sunday?" I ask Forrest as he twists to face me.

"Dad wanted me to come take some measurements for the addition to the stables." He hooks his tape measure onto a loop of his tool belt and places his hands on his hips. My brother is the only one of us who has dark hair like our father, and he towers over Wyatt, my dad, and myself. We used to joke that mom had an affair with the mailman and that's how Forrest came to exist, but one night, it made her cry, so we stopped.

My older brother owns his own construction business, something he started after dropping out of college. He worked for a construction company for a while and then took it over when the owner retired and sold it to him. So when something of that nature needs to be done around the ranch, or more recently at Wyatt and Kelsea's house, he's the one we call.

"Hyacinth is pregnant, so that makes sense," I say, referencing the female horse we just confirmed is expecting.

He nods. "Yeah, and Dad said you might be looking to purchase a few more yearlings in the coming months."

The smaller horses tend to do better with the young children who come in for lessons, and since we sold a few horses last year, the idea of buying a few more to replace them makes sense. The yearlings will be close to three years old, which is just about when they can learn to be ridden. "That's right."

"So we need more stables then, correct?"

"I'm pretty sure you just answered your own question."

He scoffs and turns his back to me again, returning to his measuring. "Heard you tied one on at the brewery the other night," he mutters over his shoulder, writing a few numbers on a notepad as he moves across the space. The smell of horse manure and hay infiltrates my nose as I follow him to the door that leads out to the training pen.

"And where did you hear that?"

"From me," Wyatt answers for him as he walks up to us from the barn adjacent to the stables. He takes his ball cap off his head, brushes back the dirty-blond hair that matches mine, slicking it with his sweat, and then replaces it once more.

"Thanks, asshole. I'll be sure to spread *your* business around next time to repay you."

"I heard about it from Javi, actually, before our brother opened his big, fat mouth," Forrest interjects as he stares up at the side of the barn, assessing the structure.

Javier Montes is one of Forrest's construction managers at his company, and he tends to visit Wyatt's brewery quite often, so the likelihood that he saw me there is high.

"And I'm pretty sure you inserted yourself into my love life last year, so payback is a bitch, isn't it?" Wyatt clarifies.

"This isn't my love life, though," I counter. "It's different."

"Still doesn't change the fact that you're being irresponsible and avoiding reality," Forrest replies.

Scoffing, I turn to my older brother. "Me? Avoiding reality? That's rich coming from the king of denial." My older brother is better at keeping his feelings locked away than any of us.

"What's that supposed to mean?" he argues.

Wyatt steps in before the two of us start fistfighting like we've done many times before. "Relax, Walker. Forrest is just concerned, that's all. Don't worry, I told him I drove you home and gave you the hard dose of reality you needed."

"Yeah, it was just like Dad scolding me for every idiotic thing I did growing up."

Forrest laughs. "Don't worry. Dad still does that to me, and I'm thirty-three. But here's the tougher question, Walker," he asks as he changes his stance, crossing his arms over his broad chest. "Why were you drinking? What is it that you were trying to forget?"

"Do I really need to answer that question?" I ask as my heart rate climbs, knowing that my brothers aren't stupid. They know these last six months have been unbearable, but after the other night, I'm done drinking to cover up the pain. I need to find a healthier outlet.

"I think you do. It doesn't have to be out loud, but you need to be aware of the dark path you're headed down if you continue at this rate. Schmitty died, and Evelyn is single again." He clears his throat and then drops his chin. "Trust me, as someone who's been there. Alcohol doesn't make the self-loathing go away."

I close the distance between us and point a finger at his chest. "My situation is different, and you fucking know it. I'm not drinking to cover up a broken heart. I lost my best fucking friend—"

"Okay," Wyatt says, sliding between us and pushing us apart. "Let's stop this little debacle before Dad comes over here and makes us clean up cow pies for the rest of the day." That used to be our punishment when we were younger and wouldn't stop fighting with each other. "Everyone is angry, and everyone has shit they need to deal with, apparently. But instead of fucking arguing about it, why not support one another?" Wyatt turns to me. "The drinking has to stop, Walker. I think we can all agree on that."

"I fucking know. I'm done, okay?" I say as I step away

from my brothers and adjust my cowboy hat on my head. Even though we all have ball caps with the ranch logo on them, I still prefer wearing my Stetson when I'm with the horses.

"Good. And Forrest?" Wyatt faces him now. "Don't lecture Walker about his love life when yours is nonexistent."

"Yours was, too, up until a year ago," he mumbles.

"I know. But now, I'm fucking content, and call me sappy, but I'd like to see you two get there, too."

"I know it would make your mother happy," our dad says as he walks up to us. After his health scare last year—a tumor pressing on his optic nerve—he's dialed down the work he does on the ranch, but he still likes to see that things run smoothly. Plus, bossing everyone around is his favorite pastime.

Stopping next to Wyatt, he places his hand on his shoulder. "You did well diffusing that, son. See what having a woman in your life will do to you?"

"Make you want world peace?" Forrest asks sarcastically.

"Make you want to be up in your brothers' business?" I add.

"Or how about helping the people you love realize that happiness is a choice, and you two need to start making better ones," our dad corrects us both, and Wyatt nods in agreement. "Walker, get going on those stables. You're behind since you took yesterday off."

Hanging my head, I reply, "Yes, sir."

"And Forrest? If you don't have those measurements to me by the end of the day, I'm going to take my business to another company."

Forrest rolls his eyes. "Okay, Dad. Good luck getting the same price I give you."

"I'm serious, you two. You're lucky your mother doesn't witness these fights. She's worried enough about the both of you. No sense in making her scared you're going to beat the shit out of each other, too."

"Wouldn't be a contest," Forrest tosses over his shoulder at me, accompanied by a wink as he follows Dad toward the barn.

"In your dreams, big brother!" I call after him, letting myself relax after the tension of the earlier conversation dissipates.

But even though my brothers drive me crazy and my father can be overbearing at times, I'm grateful we have each other. It's not easy going through life alone, and lately, I've realized that more than ever.

"So you're going to the farmers market this week?" Wyatt asks, pulling my attention back to him as we stride side by side back into the stables.

"I see that your wife has already shared the news with you, then?"

"She was just as shocked as I am."

"Well, there's no sense in avoiding it forever. Like you said the other night, it's time to move on." Just the thought of seeing Evelyn again makes my throat tight, but I swallow down the lump and remind myself that I'm doing this to help my family.

"You can try to talk to Evelyn then."

"Uh, I'm not going to attempt *that* conversation at the farmers market, Wyatt."

"I'm not saying to jump straight into talking about Schmitty, man. Just be friendly. Check in on her. Offer to help her set up her booth or something." He shrugs. "Start slow, and build your friendship again."

I blow out a deep breath. "Yeah, I guess I could do that."

"And *then* you can confess your feelings for her," he jokes as I shove him to the side.

"Shut the fuck up, Wyatt."

He chuckles, tossing his arm around my neck. "I'm just joking. You know I need to date her first to make you jealous, right? That would be the ultimate payback."

"I think your wife would murder you."

"Nope. She loves me. And she loves *you*," he says, more seriously now. "And seeing you and Evelyn talk again just might make her even happier than I already make her. So this is a good thing, man. Take it one day at a time, but I'm proud of you. You're taking the right steps."

"God, I hope so," I mutter out loud but more to myself, wondering if my brother's suggestion of just trying to talk to Evelyn is as easy as it sounds.

And as I take a ride on my horse, Barricade, later that evening while the sun sets and lights up the sky in oranges and pinks that would make any grown man stop and stare, I wonder if starting small really is the key to breaking down the fences between me and Evelyn or maybe finding some peace by making sure that she and Kaydence are okay.

I guess I'll find out on Thursday.

CHAPTER TWO

Evelyn

"And here's a coupon for twenty percent off next week." I flash said coupon to the customer before placing it inside her bag and then handing her purchase to her.

"Thank you. I'll definitely be back."

"Excellent. Have a great day!" I wait for the young lady to leave my boutique before letting my smile fall and plopping down into my chair behind the counter. Kaydence naps peacefully in her Pack 'n Play next to me, so I take this downtime to enjoy the quiet.

Luna, the boutique I opened in Newberry Springs

almost nine years ago, is flourishing, and I couldn't be happier. Especially since that means I don't have to stress about supporting my daughter and myself.

Being a single mom wasn't ever an ambition of mine, but one thing I've learned about life is that things rarely work out the way you think they will. And even though this is by far the hardest thing I've ever done, I can't help but feel I'm handling it like a goddess.

Well, at least that's what I try to convince myself—and more importantly, other people—of on a daily basis.

Late at night, when my daughter finally falls asleep, my life looks more like crying into my pillow, reminding myself that being alone is better. Not having to depend on anyone else is the smart decision. I just wish that realization hadn't come at the cost of my daughter never knowing her father.

The chime above the door rings, alerting me to another customer. But when I see the curly blonde mane of my best friend bouncing toward me, I relax in my chair once more, knowing I don't have to put on the dog and pony show for her.

Before Kelsea speaks, I place a finger over my lips, warning her to be quiet since Kaydence is sleeping. A little noise doesn't usually faze her, seeing as how she sleeps at the boutique almost every day, but after a rough night last night, I'm hoping she'll take a longer nap so I can rest a little while longer.

"She's still sleeping?" Kelsea whispers as she approaches

us, peering over the side of the Pack 'n Play, admiring my little girl. I catch myself doing the same thing from time to time. Remembering that life has more meaning now that she's here gets me through the rough days and nights, even though most of the time it feels like I'm drowning.

"Yeah. She had a rough night."

"Teething?"

"I'm pretty sure. She's a little over five months, so it sounds about right, according to what I've read in books and online. But I'm telling you, having access to any and all information on the internet as a new mom is not a blessing." I point up at her. "I was up the other night going down a rabbit hole of horror stories from new moms that made me feel both relieved that I'm doing a pretty damn good job and horrified about the things that can happen to a baby right under your nose."

Kelsea's shoulders drop as she smiles at me. "First of all, you *are* doing a phenomenal job, Evelyn. You're freaking rocking this motherhood thing, and you're doing it fashionably dressed as well." She gestures to my outfit, an olive-green paisley-printed sundress that accents my post-baby body, a body I'm still getting used to.

"Gotta dress the part of fashion boutique owner, you know." I wink at her.

"But second of all, promise me no more late-night internet surfing, okay? You don't need an excuse to worry more than you already do."

An insurmountable mountain of anxiety has developed

in my chest since I had Kaydence, and from what I've heard, that's normal. I now have this tiny human to care for, a life other than my own that I'm responsible for. It's natural to feel overwhelmed by everything I have to worry about. And Kelsea is the only person I've opened up to about that. She's the only person I trust.

When I moved to Newberry Springs nine years ago, I'd lost faith in everyone close to me. I felt like the shell of an M&M—thin, fragile, and ready to break the second I came under any pressure because I didn't know who was waiting around to shatter what strength I had left.

Leaving home was the only option I'd had. When your own parents don't have your back, how on earth are you supposed to depend on them for survival? Or for anything, for that matter.

So, I took the trust fund my grandmother left me, packed up my Toyota Corolla, and headed north to a small town I knew my parents would never be caught dead in. The mixture of farm life and small-town living in Newberry Springs reeled me in, and one day, I crossed paths with a curly-headed blonde at the supermarket. She crashed her cart into mine while we were both drooling over the baked goods displayed in front of the bakery. We shared a laugh, I told her I was new in town, and the rest is history. Little did I know that she needed a friend at that moment in her life just as badly as I did, and that's who we became to each other.

She's my person. And that will never change.

I flash her the Boy Scout salute. "I promise to stay away from new mother horror stories."

"That's all I ask." She takes a seat in the other chair I keep behind the counter and then leans forward. "Now, be honest with me. How are you doing? This week was . . ."

"Yeah, I know," I say, cutting her off, not needing to be reminded of how long it's been since that horrible night, the night I got the phone call from Kelsea, of all people, that John had died. "I'm . . . I just think I'm still coming to grips with it, you know?"

"There's no timeline for grief, Evelyn. It's normal to feel an entire array of emotions, and sometimes, they come back when we least expect them to."

Kelsea's mother left her behind when she was ten, just up and left her at Wyatt's parents' house while her father was on the road, driving one of his routes for his trucking business. So she's no stranger to loss, and having a parent you can't depend on is something we have bonded over intensely throughout the years.

But even she doesn't know what I said to John the day before he died. She doesn't know the guilt I carry around because of it. I don't want her to look at me differently, and I sure as hell don't need anyone to give me pity if they find out how responsible I feel.

"I know. I guess it just hits me the hardest when Kaydence hits a milestone or on the nights she won't stop crying and I have no one to hand her off to." Although I don't know that there ever would have been given the way

John was acting before he died. He wasn't exactly chomping at the bit to be a father, so things would probably be the same as they are now. But deep in my heart, I want to believe that he would have seen the light once he saw her.

"Honestly, I'm just tired. But I'm realizing that I can actually function pretty well on three-to-four hours of sleep now, so that's a plus."

Kelsea chuckles and then leans back in her chair, crossing her arms over her chest. "That's about what I get nowadays, too, especially when I stay up late editing pictures."

My best friend started her own photography business a little less than a year ago after she attended a photography program the winter before last in New York. I am so damn proud of her for chasing her dreams, especially because she felt like she couldn't. It was a big ol' dramatic thing, but luckily, she got everything she wanted out of it.

"How is your schedule looking by the way? We need to do Kaydence's six-month pictures soon. And are we still on for Friday?" My Friday nights used to consist of going out drinking and dancing with my best friend when she had the night off from the brewery. Now, they consist of eating junk food and drinking wine once my daughter falls asleep.

"I have a Sunday evening, two weeks from now, saved for your sunset pictures, as requested. And I will be there with pizza on Friday night, just like you wanted."

"I guess it does pay to have friends who are extremely talented and love me, doesn't it?" I tease her.

She smiles back and then sticks her tongue out at me. "It does. Now, if only I could cut back hours at the brewery to truly focus on my photography, I'd be all set."

"Wyatt is still working you, huh?" I joke.

"No, it's me. He's told me to stop, but part of me just loves being there." She shrugs. "My heart belongs to that place, just like it does to the owner. Plus, it's how I see so many people around town. And I swear, I see Walker there more than any place else."

Just the mention of Walker makes my pulse speed up. Wyatt's twin brother was best friends with John, and I know that his death affected Walker just as much as it did me, but differently. The thing is, I wouldn't really know how he's doing because he doesn't talk to me. He hasn't since the funeral, and I'm not quite sure what to do with that, so I haven't done anything. Besides, I'm far too tired and focused on my own life changes to be worried about his.

"He was actually there on Friday," she continues, bringing up the six-month anniversary of John's death again.

"Well, I'm sure a beer or two probably could have helped me get through that day as well."

Kelsea's face goes flat. "He's hurting, too, you know . . ."

"I'm sure he is, but I don't have the mental capacity to

worry about him right now," I bark out a little more harshly than I intended.

Kelsea winces. "I know. I just think maybe you two should talk. He's supposed to be at the farmers market this week, actually."

My stomach instantly twists. "Good for him. It's about time he helps again."

Every week, spring through fall, our town holds a farmers market for local growers to sell their produce and local businesses to show off their products. I set up a booth right next to the Gibson Ranch one so I can hang out with my bestie, and either Wyatt or Walker usually helps her. Lately, though, it's only been Wyatt or Kelsea managing it all by herself. But that's not my problem to deal with.

"Evelyn . . ." she starts, but I hold up my hand to stop her.

"Enough about Walker." Needing to shift the focus back to her, I say, "Let's get back to that husband of yours. How is married life treating you? Still blissfully happy?" It's hard to believe that she and Wyatt got married over a year ago now. Life has changed so much since then, and not just for me. But I truly am so damn happy for her that *her* life is working out the way she wanted.

Kelsea's smile is hard for her to contain. "Yes, things are perfect. Well, not perfect, but perfect for us. In fact, we're talking about kids."

That little detail has me launching myself up from my chair. "What? Are you serious?"

"You're going to wake your daughter," Kelsea chastises me, reaching out to yank me back down to my seat. "Not anytime soon, but we're talking about *when* we want that. I still want to get my business off the ground. In fact, I have a few weddings in the next three months at the ranch. If I can nail those, I know it will help my portfolio, and word around town will spread. And I want to establish a client base before I take some time off."

My excitement deflates a little, but I get where she's coming from. "So not super soon then . . ."

She shakes her head, her smile reassuring. "Probably within the year. But with the way Wyatt has been screwing me lately, who the hell knows if it will take that long."

"Hell yes, girl!" I pump my fist in the air. "Ugh. You're so lucky to be married. All of that regular sex must be nice. The last time I got fucked was before I found out I was pregnant."

Her cheeks turn pink, which instantly makes me laugh. Kelsea was never a very sexually experienced or uninhibited person, especially before she married Wyatt. He's definitely brought her out of her shell, though, and she's much more open to talking about sex now than she was years ago. But it still makes me laugh that she gets embarrassed when I talk about it bluntly.

"It *is* nice," she says, reaching for my hand. "And maybe you'll have that one day, too."

Rolling my eyes, I scoff. "Doubtful. I come in a package now, Kelsea. It takes a special type of man to accept that."

There's a twinkle in her eyes. "I bet he's out there."

"Well, if he is, he's gonna have to come to Newberry Springs to find us, because I'm not going anywhere." I wave my hand around my shop. "My store is here. You're here. That's all I really need." My heart twists a little in my chest as if trying to tell me that something's missing, but I ignore it just like I do other feelings I don't allow to come to the surface.

Kaydence coos from her crib, alerting us to the fact that she's awake now. I move to stand, but Kelsea pushes me back down and reaches for my daughter, brushing her hair flat as she picks her up. "Who wouldn't want this little girl in their life?" She croons as she bounces Kaydence in her arms.

A rush of pride runs through me as I stare up at my daughter. She may not have been planned or expected, but my life is so much better with her in it. And then that pang of guilt follows my happy moment, swirling together to let those mixed emotions rest in my stomach like they always do.

"Exactly." Kelsea presses a kiss to Kaydence's forehead just as the chime above the door rings.

I stand from my chair and greet my new customer, a young man I don't think has ever entered the store before. But he doesn't even glance around at the clothes or the array of purses or jewelry I have to offer. No, his eyes are set right on me as he stalks toward me, my heart hammering with awareness.

Kelsea moves to the side when he approaches the counter.

"May I help you?" I ask, my voice shaking a little.

"Are you Evelyn Sumner?" the man asks, his eyes hidden by the bill of his baseball hat.

"Yes . . ."

"Great. You've been served," he announces as he drops the manila envelope from his hands on the counter before me and then turns and walks right back out of my shop just as quickly as he came in. My eyes stay forward, blinking slowly as my brain tries to catch up with what just happened, and my stomach feels like it's about to jump out of my mouth.

Kelsea scrambles over to where I'm standing, still holding Kaydence. "Oh my God, Evelyn. What is that?"

Her voice pulls me out of my trance as I reach for the envelope and slide my finger under the sticky seal. "I don't know."

Kaydence begins to cry as I struggle to extract the papers with shaky hands.

"Do you have a bottle for her?"

"Yeah, there's one in her diaper bag. In the back." I hear Kelsea's footsteps move away from me as I finally get the papers free and scan the words as fast as I can.

Once I realize what's in front of me, my stomach drops right back down, nearly hitting the floor. I gasp, covering my mouth with my hand as I reread the petition for custody in my hands.

"What is it?" Kelsea asks frantically, holding the bottle in Kaydence's mouth as she peeks over my shoulder.

"It's a petition for custody," I reply much more calmly than I feel.

"What? From whom?"

I swallow down the knot in my throat and then turn to face her. Her blue eyes are as wide as saucers, and I swear I can hear her heartbeat.

Or maybe that's mine.

"It's from Schmitty's parents," I answer her then brace myself to utter the rest. "They want Kaydence. They want to take my daughter from me."

CHAPTER THREE

Walker

"You ready for the next box?" Kelsea asks me from the bed of the truck she's currently standing in. She's staring down at where I'm standing near the tailgate. "Or are you just going to stare at her all day?"

"I wasn't staring," I say as I direct my attention back to Kelsea, pretending as if Evelyn doesn't exist yet again. But I can't. As soon as I saw her stroll up to our tents at the farmers market, pushing Kaydence in her stroller, my nerves were shot.

She's so freaking beautiful, more so than I remember

because it's been so long since I've seen her. But now she has that motherly figure and presence to her, making her even more confident and protective than she was before—because she's responsible for that little girl, the one I haven't allowed myself to take a peek at yet since she's sleeping soundly in the stroller.

"Could have fooled me. You can say hello, you know," Kelsea teases me as she hands me the last box of jars filled with jam.

I set them on the ground under our display table and then twist to face my sister-in-law again. "She's busy."

Evelyn is in the process of setting up her booth, just like the two of us are. I've seen her do this a million times, but today, she seems a little more frazzled than normal. If I've learned one thing about Evelyn Sumner in the years I've known her, it's that she's good at putting up a front. She has subtle cues that can alert someone to the fact that her usual confidence is shaken, and I guess I'm one of the lucky ones aware enough to pick up on them.

For instance, she tucks her long, blonde hair behind her ear when she's nervous, just as she's doing when I cast another glance over at her right now. She will also chew on her fingernails when she's deep in thought. And just as the thought flies through my mind, her thumb finds her mouth, and she nibbles on the nail.

But her surefire tell is her eyes. They get brighter somehow, which is difficult, seeing as how the woman has sky-blue eyes that light up whenever she's around people. But today, they seem almost clear and busy as her attention darts all around her as if she's expecting someone to pop out and scare the shit out of her, like she's in a goddamn horror movie.

"Do you need anything?" Kelsea asks her as she hops down from the bed of Wyatt's truck and walks under Evelyn's tent.

Evelyn tucks her hair behind her ear again and then plasters on a fake smile. "No, I think I'm good. I feel like I'm forgetting something, but it may just be that I haven't eaten yet."

Kelsea shakes her head. "That's no good. You gotta take care of yourself, Momma." And just that subtle acknowledgment that Evelyn is a mother now causes me to cast my eyes over to Kaydence again as she sleeps soundly, oblivious to the chaotic world around her.

People from all over town are starting to arrive as the hour approaches eight. The market stays open until noon, which is perfect, considering the sweltering heat will deter people from remaining outside by then.

"I've got an extra breakfast sandwich my mom made this morning," I offer, since she made me two but I was too anxious to eat them both.

For the first time all morning, Evelyn's eyes meet mine. "Are you sure?" And my body forgets how to function when our gazes connect.

Fuck. Just breathe, Walker. "Yeah. I wasn't that hungry this morning."

"Well, if you're not gonna eat it . . ."

"I insist." Walking back over to the truck, I take a deep breath, feeling like the hard part is over. I spoke to her. We said more than two words to each other. That has to be a good sign, right?

Jesus, Walker. You sound like some teenage boy afraid to talk to his freaking crush.

When I return, Kelsea is grinning from ear to ear. I roll my eyes, hand Evelyn the sandwich, and then shove both of my hands in my pockets, drawing my shoulders up to my ears. "It might not be very warm anymore, but . . ."

"No, this is perfect. Thanks, Walker." Evelyn gives me a small smile that makes my heart jump. Fuck, even the smallest things from this woman still do something to me.

Avoiding her since Schmitty died wasn't just about my guilt—it was also about the self-loathing I felt for harboring feelings for the woman my best friend was seeing. I know they weren't very serious, but when they found out Evelyn was pregnant, it felt even worse to be pining after her.

And the kicker is, I never saw her that way until Schmitty claimed her, even if their relationship seemed casual.

After eight years of being friends, it took one man to step in and make me see reason, make me realize that the girl I'd always been around but never really noticed was actually a knockout—strong, smart, determined, and freaking beautiful. Gorgeous. All the wet dream adjectives combined.

Maybe I just never allowed myself to see it. Maybe because she was Kelsea's best friend, I told myself she was off-limits. And maybe since she was always single and never seemed to seek out a serious relationship, it never mattered to me that she was unattached, too. Because I lived my life the same way.

But that night at the Jameson—the honky-tonk we went to for Schmitty's birthday more than a year and a half ago—that night changed everything. Suddenly, that twinkle in her eyes was directed at my best friend. Her boldness was laced in the words she spoke to *him*, not me. And even though I was there to make my brother jealous by fake dating Kelsea, my eyes followed Evelyn all night long, almost as if I was watching her slip right through my fingers.

And she did.

She fell into *his* bed, *his* arms, *his* life.

And then she got pregnant with *his* baby.

That's why being near her is so hard. That's why I've been avoiding it—because I was afraid that seeing her again would bring back all the feelings I've been pushing down since she started seeing my best friend.

I was right. They're all back now—with a vengeance.

"You know what? I think you need some coffee, too!" Kelsea exclaims. "Lord knows I could use another cup."

Evelyn moans as she takes a bite of the sandwich and

nods her head. "Yes, please. Kaydence does not believe in sleeping through the night yet, and she has a tooth that is finally breaking through. Last night was another rough one."

Hearing her struggle with her new life makes my chest twist, and a desire I'm unfamiliar with starts building in my stomach. Fuck, I wish there was something I could do to help her. But is that overstepping? Is it wrong to want to help her after what happened?

"You've got it." Kelsea turns to me. "You mind watching the booth while I run over to the Roasted truck?" she asks, referencing the coffee shop that brings their mobile truck to the farmers market each week.

"Sure. Grab me something, too, will you?"

Kelsea nods. "Yup. I'll be back, you two." She winks over her shoulder at me and then traipses off, leaving us alone.

"God, I forgot how good your mom's biscuits are," Evelyn mumbles around the last bite of her sandwich, crumpling up the foil and tossing it in the trash can behind her.

"They're addicting, for sure."

"Thanks again for that." She pats her stomach. "I feel better."

"No problem at all."

We don't speak another word to each other for a while as customers approach both of our booths. Evelyn helps customers sort through the clothing items she brought with her today from her store, and I sell an entire box of jam within thirty minutes.

My eyes keep darting around, waiting for Kelsea to return. But knowing her, she probably got held up talking to someone. That girl knows everyone around town, and more often than not, these days become networking opportunities as well, a chance for business owners to support one another and cross-promote, if possible. I know Kelsea has also been using her connections to help get her photography business off the ground, which I respect wholeheartedly.

A lull in customers has me looking over at Evelyn again. Her eyes are focused on Kaydence, who's still sleeping in the stroller.

"She's beautiful," I mumble, but Evelyn hears me.

"Oh. Thank you."

"She looks just like you."

"Really?" She pops her head up and smiles at me, disbelievingly so. "I see John in her."

Just the mention of his name makes my heart rate pick up. I take a few steps closer, peering into the stroller to get a good look at the baby girl I wish I could protect from the shitty parts of life, especially since she experienced them even before she was born. And I'm partially to blame for that.

"Nope. That's all you, Evelyn. John's ugly mug can't take any responsibility for how gorgeous that little girl is. She's got your nose, your long eyelashes, even that blonde hair."

Evelyn stares at me. "I guess maybe I *try* to see him in her."

Our eyes meet, and suddenly, it feels hard to breathe. "Evelyn . . ." I start, not sure what to say but knowing I need to say something.

"Excuse me?" A voice to my right pulls my attention away from Evelyn, and suddenly I remember that I'm here to do a job. "I'd like to buy some jam, please."

Evelyn tucks her hair behind her ear and returns to her booth as I help out my next customer. A few more people trail in behind her, and even Evelyn makes a sale before she turns back to me. "Where the heck is Kelsea?"

"I don't know. Three coffees sure are taking a while, huh?"

Evelyn purses her lips. "Yeah, they sure are. And I need to use the bathroom."

"Go ahead," I say. "I'll look after your booth."

"That's not what I'm worried about." Her eyes dart to the stroller. "The baby . . ."

"Oh." Without taking a second to consider what I'm offering, I say, "I can watch her, too."

Evelyn's eyes widen. "Are you sure?"

No. I'm not fucking sure. But what am I supposed to say now: Just kidding?

"We'll be fine. She's sleeping, right?"

Evelyn looks between me and her daughter repeatedly. Finally, she sighs and says, "Okay. I'll be right back." With a point of her finger in my direction, she saunters off, giving me the perfect view of her backside, the ass I've admired far too many times. And I'm suddenly reminded of how incredible it is—especially because Evelyn has a little more cushion back there after having Kaydence, and in my opinion, that just makes her sexier.

Wondering if anyone caught me staring, I direct my attention back to our booths, making sure everything is in place. I put a few more spice blend bags and jars of jam on top of the table, filling in the space left from the last items I sold. I put Evelyn's cash box under her table in a box so it doesn't get swiped by someone walking by. And I even start loading some empty boxes in the bed of the truck to take back to the ranch.

But then the unthinkable happens. Kaydence begins to cry.

I abandon the box in my hands, letting it fall to the ground as I rush over to the stroller and see the blonde-haired cutie wailing as if a small breeze just pissed her off.

"Hey, it's okay. It's okay." Not sure what else to do, I reach in and unclip her from the harness, thinking maybe the restraint is making her uncomfortable. But all she does is cry harder. So I do what feels natural—I lift her up and cradle her in my arms, holding her as best I know how.

I haven't held a baby before. Fuck, the only kids I'm around are the ones I teach horseback riding to. But those kids are far bigger than this little girl in my arms right now.

I must be doing something right, though, because her

crying starts to subside, and then she's staring up at me as we walk around.

"Hey, there," I say, speaking to her as if she can carry on a conversation with me. Her eyes widen as she takes me all in, and then one of her little chubby hands reaches up and smacks me in the face. "Whoa. Hey. I'm just doing what you wanted, Kaydence. You didn't like being in there, so I took you out. Your mommy will be back soon, but in the meantime, you have to settle for me, all right?"

A gummy smile graces her lips, and then she lets out a squeal I take as a win. "That's right. We're good, huh? Wanna go for a walk?" I ask her, dipping under the top of the tent covering our booths. I begin to bounce her as we stroll slowly down the street lined with booths on either side.

People wave to us as we pass. I even hold up her hand and pretend she's waving back to them, which makes everyone involved smile. Kaydence kicks her legs and coos as we keep moving farther away from the Gibson Ranch tent, but I don't care. She's smiling and happy, so as far as I'm concerned, people can steal as much jam as they want if it keeps this little girl from crying again.

Something takes hold in my body, a sense of purpose that hits me so hard, it almost knocks me over. And as I stare at the baby girl in my arms, I *do* see my best friend staring back at me. It's subtle, like the shape of her lips and the flecks of gold in her green eyes, eyes she got from John, for sure.

But something else is hitting me, too—I just can't put a finger on what it is.

And I don't have time to figure it out, because Evelyn comes running up to us frantically with tears in her eyes and shaky hands. "Oh my God! There you are!" She rips Kaydence from my arms and holds her to her chest, closing her eyes as she breathes her in.

"Hey. Everything is fine. She woke up and was pissed, so I took her out, and we started walking. It seemed to calm her down."

When she opens her eyes and looks up at me, I see a terror in her blue irises I've never seen before. "I thought she was gone. I thought that they took her."

Instantly, my brows draw together. "Who the fuck would take her? You asked *me* to watch her, remember?"

"I know, I know. I just . . ."

"Who would fucking take her, Evelyn?" I ask through clenched teeth. And the words she mutters next nearly knock me on my ass.

"John's parents. They're contesting custody."

"What the actual fuck?" I'm back under our tents sitting down after Kelsea finally returned with our coffees. And I'm not stupid. Given how half of hers is gone already, I'm sure she was biding her time before returning to our booths, thinking that giving Evelyn and me a chance to talk would be best. And maybe it was ten minutes ago.

But since then, my head is fucking spinning over how much has happened since I arrived at the market this morning.

"It's crazy, right?" Kelsea asks. She's looking down at me from where she stands taking another sip of her coffee.

I'm holding mine between my legs while I hunch forward, but the last thing on my mind is taking a drink. "I don't get it. Why on earth would they do this?"

Evelyn kisses Kaydence's head again, still holding on to her since she took her from my arms moments ago. "I don't know. I haven't seen them since the funeral. They never contacted me after she was born. I never thought to reach out because I got the sense that they didn't approve of John having a kid with a woman he wasn't going to marry. But why now? Why six months later?"

Shaking my head, I stand from my chair. "Maybe I should talk to them?"

"No," Evelyn pleads as Kelsea shakes her head. "Not until I get a lawyer. I don't want them to be able to use anything against me, Walker."

"She's right," Kelsea agrees.

"So who's your lawyer? Do you have someone in mind?"

"I don't know yet." Evelyn gazes at the ground. "I haven't called anyone yet. I guess I'm still coming to grips with this. It hadn't hit me completely until I came back and saw my baby girl was missing." Tears fall down her cheeks again. "I really thought she was gone and it was them."

"I'm sorry, Ev. I wouldn't have walked away if I knew it would freak you out."

"It's okay. It's not your fault. You didn't know."

"But maybe this was a wake-up call that you need to do something soon, Evelyn," Kelsea interjects. "You don't know their reasoning for this petition, and until you do, you're going to be on pins and needles."

"I know," Evelyn agrees, breathing in her daughter again.

"I have a buddy, Chase, who's a lawyer," I offer. "His office is in town. I can give him a call."

"You don't have to do that," Evelyn says. "I can handle this on my own."

Her rebuttal instantly makes me angry. "I know you can, Evelyn. But you don't have to. Please, let me fucking help any way I can."

She bites her bottom lip and then nods reluctantly. "Okay."

"Do you want to go home?" Kelsea asks her best friend. "I can finish manning your booth . . ."

Evelyn stands and places Kaydence on her hip. "No, I'm good. The distraction will probably be best, anyway."

"I think I might take off then," I tell Kelsea. "I need to call Chase, and there are a few other things I need to take care of." Honestly, I have nothing else going on at the moment, but my mind is spinning with this new information, and now I'm in fix-it mode.

That's what I do. If there's a problem, I need to fix it. And when I can't, it fucking kills me. Hence the purgatory I've been in for months since I let my best friend die on my watch.

"Okay. No problem. I can hold down the fort," Kelsea replies.

"I know you can." Stepping around her, I stand in front of Evelyn. "I'm sorry again. But I promise, I'll call Chase, and we will figure this out."

She stares up at me, her eyes turning brighter the longer we look at each other. "I can figure this out on my own, Walker. This isn't your problem."

Her argument pisses me off even more than I was earlier. But I tame my reaction so I don't let all my cards show just yet. "*Yes, it is*. I know John's parents. Something's going on that *you* don't know yet. And until you do, you're not getting rid of me, Evelyn, whether you like it or not. I'm not going to let you fight this alone." Without waiting for her to reply, I march off to my truck, hopping into it once I get there, and take off for Chase's office, calling him as I drive to let him know I'm on my way.

When I arrive, he greets me at the door. Chase Gunerson and I graduated from high school the same year. We grew up together, which is true of most people in this small town, but we were good friends who played football together and shared many of the same classes. Chase moved away to go to law school but decided to set his practice up in our hometown since most lawyers set up shop in Lexington, the next town over. It's far bigger than Newberry Springs, so it makes sense. But I've never been more glad to have a friend nearby, able and willing to help in this situation.

After he pulls up the court records, he leans back in his chair and winces. "It doesn't look good, man. John's parents are contesting physical custody on the grounds that Evelyn is an unfit mother. This says there is evidence to support the claim, but that won't be shown until we set up a mediation."

"Fuck. So what is she supposed to do?"

"Well, the courts tend to favor the biological parents, so she has that on her side. But even though she's a single woman on her own, she has no priors or anything on her record that would show her to be an unfit parent. So I'm guessing his parents must have found something they thought they could use against her to get their way."

"I can't fucking believe they would do this."

"Did they know about the baby?" he asks, steepling his hands in front of his face.

"I'm sure they did. John wouldn't hide something like this from them. Although, he wasn't exactly acting like himself before he died." My best friend had not been acting like the man I'd always thought he'd been thanks to his impending fatherhood. But I'm pretty sure he would have told his parents they were going to be grandparents. At least, I hope he did. "Honestly, I'm not sure. I could barely get him to talk to me about it before the end, so who knows."

And as soon as you finally got him to see reason, the unthinkable happened.

"Well, Evelyn is going to have to fight this tooth and nail, but I'll do everything in my power to help her." Chase's confidence makes me feel a tiny bit better.

"I know you will."

He stares off into the distance. "You know, if she were married, this would be a little easier, at least."

The mention of marriage has me intrigued. "Why?"

"Because two-parent households are golden in family court cases. A judge will be hard-pressed to split up a family unit, that's for sure."

Marriage? That's fucking bullshit. Evelyn is basically being punished because she's a single mom—and not by choice, I might add.

Chase and I catch up a little bit more before I leave. But his words continue to swirl around in my brain for hours as I do my laundry and get ready for my next forty-eight-hour shift. At my station, we work forty-eight/ninety-six, which means forty-eight hours on duty, ninety-six hours off. It's grueling some weeks, but I enjoy the long breaks away from work.

If John were still alive, this situation wouldn't even be an issue. I'm sure he never planned on marrying Evelyn, at least not because they were having a kid together. But if he were still alive, I have a feeling his parents wouldn't be trying to take a child away from her mother.

I've known Mr. and Mrs. Schmitt almost my entire life, and I know they have slightly old-fashioned values. So maybe when they found out about the baby, they were pressuring John to do the "right thing" and marry Evelyn, even though he wasn't in love with her—at least, that's what he led me to believe. Getting married definitely sounds like something they would suggest, which makes me ponder how I can help Evelyn get out of this situation unscathed.

And then it dawns on me.

It's insane—asinine, really. But it just might work.

John can't be here to take care of his daughter and help Evelyn. But I can. And I think I know how I can do that.

So before I head to the station for my shift, I decide to take a detour and drive a few minutes out of my way to Evelyn's townhouse, hoping she won't shut the door in my face when I explain my proposition.

I plaster on nerves of steel as I knock on her front door and wait for her to answer. And when she does, she appears to be caught just as off guard by my presence as I am by this crazy idea.

But I have to at least try to make things right.

"Walker?" she asks, holding Kaydence on her hip. The scent of food wafts out of the open door into the night. "What are you doing here?"

"I have a solution to your problem."

"What problem?"

"Schmitty's parents. I . . . I think I know how to fix this."

She hikes Kaydence further up on her hip. "I told you, this isn't your problem to fix, okay? I know you're just trying to be nice, and I was trying to appease you by agreeing, but—"

"Goddammit, Ev. Will you just listen to me?"

She sighs and then arches a brow at me. "Fine. What is it? What did you drive all the way over here to ask me?"

Before I can chicken out, I utter the words I only imagined asking once to the love of my life. But maybe this time, God and John will forgive me for taking a chance on this woman, helping her while also finding out if these feelings of mine are only one-sided. So I say what I came here to say.

"Evelyn . . . I'm here to ask you to marry me."

CHAPTER FOUR

Evelyn

"What the hell did you just say?" In this moment, I'm grateful my daughter can't talk yet, because I'm sure she'd repeat the one word in that sentence that she shouldn't.

"Marry me, Evelyn." Walker's eyes plead with me as I stand there trying to figure out if he's joking.

"Stop messing around, Walker," I say through a laugh, shifting Kaydence to my other hip. The first time he uttered those words, I nearly dropped her out of shock.

"I'm not messing around, Evelyn. Take my last name. I can't fix this entire mess, but I can give you this."

Shaking my head at him, I yank him inside my house and shut the door. "Walker, this isn't funny. I don't know if you're drunk or what, but—"

He holds up his hand to stop me. "I'm not drunk. I'm dead serious, Evelyn. I met with Chase today."

"What? Why?"

"I couldn't sit around and wait for something else to happen with John's parents. I had to act. I had to know what we're up against."

I'm fuming now. "Goddammit, Walker. How many times do I have to tell you that this isn't your battle to fight?"

"I fucking know that, Evelyn!" he shouts back at me, startling Kaydence. And just as I expect, she starts to cry. "Shit, I'm sorry," he tells her in a soothing voice as she clings to me and he buries his hands in his hair. "Fuck, I keep messing this up."

"I think we both need to take a few moments, gather ourselves, and then perhaps call an ambulance—because you've clearly hit your head." Marching into the kitchen, I turn off the burner on the stove and then grab a pacifier for Kaydence. Once I get her calm, I reenter my living room to find Walker pacing. "Okay, you need to start from the beginning."

"Okay." He nods and then takes a deep breath. "Chase said that although the courts tend to favor the biological parent in cases like this, Mr. and Mrs. Schmitt must have something on you to think they could contest custody and win. He said if Kaydence was in a two-parent household, it would be no contest. So I decided we should get married."

"*You* decided?" My brows pop up while I'm simultaneously wondering what the hell John's parents found out about me. My skin crawls with nerves. "Just . . . like that?" I ask with a snap of my fingers. "Walker, we haven't exactly spoken much in the last six months, so forgive me for being flabbergasted by the idea that you speak to me for the first time today, and then, only a few hours later, you're asking me to marry you."

He runs a hand through his hair again. "Fuck, I know, Evelyn. And I'm sorry. But honestly? I didn't know what to say to you, so I just didn't say anything." His entire body tightens. "John died when he was with me, and now you're all alone, and I—"

"What happened was not your fault," I say, knowing deep down that I hold responsibility for John's death more than anyone else. Walker and John were just doing their job the night he died. That isn't on Walker. It's a risk they both take every time they enter a burning building. But the last words I said to him before he left the night before about not returning? I'm still sick to my stomach over it. "But the two of us getting married? My God, that's just crazy."

"No, it's not. It's perfect. We can say we bonded over our grief and fell in love." His voice is much more resolute now than it was a few moments ago. "We can move in together and put on a united front. The last thing this little girl needs is for her world to be turned upside down any more than it already has been, Ev. Please," he says, wincing. "Please, let me help you."

"We can't, Walker. It's not right." All I can do is shake my head as my heart pounds wildly. "Do you know what it's like to walk around town and have people stare at you with nothing but pity in their eyes? To see a little girl that resembles her dad but who will never meet him and see her mom struggling to worm her way out of sadness and regret? And you know why? Because the last thing I said to my child's father is that I hope he figures out how to be the man she's going to need or maybe he just shouldn't be involved at all."

"What?"

"I basically sent him to the fire to die, Walker," I admit on a shaky breath. "I told him not to bother coming back to me if he wasn't going to step up and quit his partying ways. I told him to grow up and start acting like an adult because his life was about to change. Little did I know that those words would ring true for all of us."

Walker just stands there blinking at me for an ungodly amount of time, and guilt leaves my body in the form of tears.

"I can't take any more gossip surrounding my life, Walker—people's opinions on how I had a baby by one man and then married his best friend right after he died might just be too much to bear. I can't handle the speculation."

"Then let me handle it." He cuts me off, taking a step closer to me as his posture becomes more resolute. "Let *me* take the blame. Tell everyone that I'm the one who pursued you, that I stepped up because John couldn't, and then we fell in love." I can see him visibly swallow, as if those words caused a lump to form in his throat. "You're not the one to blame for what happened to John, Evelyn. I am." He points a finger at his chest. "I knew we shouldn't have gone into that blaze, but I wanted to be the fucking hero. My pride got in the way, and it cost my best friend his life. You didn't kill him, Evelyn. I did."

His words feel like a sledgehammer to my heart.

No wonder this man has been avoiding me. He's so convinced that John's death is his responsibility. And while I appreciate him trying to right the wrong he thinks he's liable for, I don't think that us getting married is the solution. It could just make matters worse.

My bottom lip trembles as my eyes fill with tears again. "God, Walker . . . we are so fucked up."

I don't mean for my words to make him laugh, but they do. Walker shakes his head at me as we chuckle through our emotions. "Then let's be fucked up together and get you through this. This doesn't have to be forever. If you want a divorce down the line . . ." He clears his throat. "I can give you that. But for right now? This little girl needs you and *only* you. And I can't stand the thought of her not having her mom *and* her dad. So let me help you. Please . . ." He takes another step closer to me, the heat of his body enveloping me.

The light from the ceiling fan makes his brown eyes lighter, highlighting the ring of gold around his irises as he stares down at me. I've never noticed that before, or the scar above his eyebrow, or the slight tint of red in his facial hair, probably because he's usually clean-shaven. But the scruff on his jawline tonight gives him an edge that almost portrays him in a different light.

Walker is not an unattractive man, but something about the way my body is reacting to him right now should be a warning in and of itself. Or perhaps it's just been so long since I've felt the touch of a man that my vagina is getting frisky from the proximity of this one.

"Can I think about it?" I finally manage to squeak out, my eyes bouncing back and forth between his as his do the same.

"Of course. But don't take too long. Time is of the essence. I set up a meeting with Chase for tomorrow afternoon. We can go together, and he can talk to you more about what to expect in this process. But Evelyn, I think this might work in both our favors."

That little admission has me tilting my head at him. "What do you mean?"

"Let's just say I have my own selfish reasons for doing this, but most importantly, we need to do this for Kaydence." He reaches out to stroke her cheek and then tips his chin at me before heading for the front door. "We'll talk tomorrow," he says right before he leaves, and the breath I didn't realize I was holding exits my lungs right along with my intelligence as I momentarily consider that this might just be a good idea after all.

~

"So, when is the mediation?"

"In two weeks," Chase replies as I sit across from him at his desk. After I closed down the boutique for the day, I raced across town to make this late-afternoon meeting. Walker was already here waiting on me. The way he stood in front of the office with his arms crossed over his chest as if he were guarding the entrance waiting for us to arrive made that uneasy feeling come over me again as I hopped out of my car.

But now, the scent of his cologne is what's distracting me from what Chase is saying.

Has Walker always smelled this good?

"So I'm going to have to sit across from them and look them in the eye as they tell me why I'm not fit to be a mother?"

"Not exactly. Most of the talking will be done between

me and their attorney. But yes, you will need to be in the same room as them."

"And you really think that us getting married could help?" I ask Chase, avoiding Walker's eyes as I feel him turn to look at me.

Chase shifts in his seat. "As your attorney, I can't advise you to marry for legal purposes such as this. But I will say that two parents tend to send a stronger message than one."

Walker nudges my shoulder with his. "See?"

I move away from him as I shift Kaydence to my other thigh. She's chewing on a teething ring, which has kept her quiet through this intense discussion, thank God. "I shouldn't have to do this. She's my daughter."

"You don't *have* to do anything," Chase clarifies, casting his gaze over to Walker and then back to me. "But it couldn't hurt. Again though, I have no idea that this idea of yours even exists, Walker, all right?" He points a finger across the desk just as Walker mimes zipping his lips.

"Okay. Thanks for the information. And for taking on my case."

"My pleasure. I'm here if you have any questions, and I'll be in contact as the mediation approaches to make sure that we agree on how we want to approach this."

The last hour has been filled with so much legal jargon, I'm surprised my brain is still functioning. But in two weeks, I'm going to have to face the people who want to take my child from me—her *grandparents,* for crying out loud—and somehow defend my ability to mother her.

What the hell has happened in the last few days of my life?

Walker stays behind to discuss something with Chase, but he catches up to me before I settle into my car. Kaydence is already buckled into her car seat, and the air conditioning is running, cooling off the interior.

"Evelyn!" He runs over to me.

"Yeah . . ." The furrow in his brow has me letting out a sigh. I just feel so defeated right now, not to mention confused.

"Have you made a decision yet?"

"Not yet, Walker. This isn't me deciding to color my hair or what to make for dinner tonight. This is a huge choice . . ."

"I know. But the sooner we do this, the better. The timing will look suspect anyway, but we can go to the courthouse on Monday and argue that we already had plans to marry before you were ever served the papers." He reaches out and grabs my hand, his caress comforting, even though it shouldn't be. This man is asking me to marry him under false pretenses. This man hasn't been in my life for the past six months—the hardest six months of my life.

And now he's trying to swoop in like Superman and save the day, like getting married isn't a big fucking deal?

"I'm sorry. I'm still trying to wrap my head around this, Walker."

His shoulders deflate. "I know. Is there anything I can do to help make the decision for you?"

"Just . . . give me some space? Please?" I hate pushing him away right now, especially with the hurt in his eyes. But I can't think with him around me. I need time to process this, maybe make a pros and cons list, for crying out loud.

He shoves his hands in his pockets and nods. "Okay. I'll be waiting, then. Have a good night, Evelyn."

I watch him walk back to his truck and then make my way inside my car to drive home. And even though I said I want to be alone, what I really need is my best friend right now. So I call her as I drive.

"We're still on for dinner, right?" I ask her as soon as my Bluetooth connects to her call.

"Yes. Why? Do you want to cancel?"

"Oh, hell no. I need your company now more than ever."

"Is everything okay?"

"I'm not sure yet. But make sure you bring wine, please. I feel like I'm going to need a lot of it."

"Evelyn, you're scaring me," Kelsea whispers as I hear a door shut in the background.

"Well, I'm a little shaken up, too, right now, Kels. I think . . . I think I might be getting married next week."

"He asked you to marry him?" Kelsea's eyes bug out as she stares across the couch at me. Kaydence is playing on the

floor with a few toys, and I'm down on the floor with her, trying to keep my glass of wine away from her hands so she doesn't swat at it and spill it everywhere.

At least it's white wine so it won't leave a nasty stain on the carpet if she does.

"Yup. Like it was no big deal." I take a sip of my wine and then stare up at my best friend. "This is crazy, right?" Kelsea attempts to hide a smirk behind the rim of her glass, but I catch it. "What was that look for?"

"What look?"

I point up at her. "The one where you seem like you have a secret to tell me, but you know you shouldn't." Narrowing my eyes at her, I say, "Kelsea Anne Gibson, are you hiding something from me?"

She clears her throat and then sighs. "No, Evelyn. But honestly, and it pains me to say this, I think Walker may be on to something with this idea."

"Wow. Okay. You've definitely had too much wine already." I roll my eyes at her and then take down more of my own alcohol.

"It's not the booze talking. It's the fact that Walker hasn't been the same since that night, and neither have you," she explains, a tenderness in her voice. "Maybe the root of this decision is to help you keep Kaydence in your custody, which I don't see changing, anyway. But also, perhaps this can be a way for you two to reconnect, remember how to be friends."

"I mean, we weren't super close before this, but . . ."

"How bad could it be, Evelyn? It's Walker. You know him. He's the same guy he was before, but he's different now, too."

"Yeah, but things have been so weird with him since John died."

"Then maybe this is a chance for you guys to support each other through that grief. You haven't really had a chance to process that, you know? He died, and Kaydence was born a month later. And maybe he needs this, too, as a way to make up for his own guilt. You two are the only ones who are tied to John's death in similar ways. Let him help you."

My best friend looks at me as though the answer is so simple. But deep down, I know nothing about this is simple. I'm talking about marrying my dead baby-daddy's best friend. His parents are trying to take my daughter away from me. And the man who's offered to marry me is more of a stranger to me now than he was just a year ago.

But losing my daughter—my living, breathing flesh that changed my world for the better, even though my life is not nearly as carefree as it was before—that is just not an option.

So I do what any self-respecting mother would do in this situation—I commit to protecting my child and myself. I make a decision that I may end up regretting, but I can't risk her grandparents taking her away from me. She's too important.

"I can't believe I'm agreeing to this," I mutter as I tip back my wine glass and drain the rest of the liquid.

"So you're going to do it?" Kelsea sits up taller in her spot on the couch.

"I can't lose her, Kels. I can't lose my daughter."

"I know, Ev. And you won't. But now, you have Walker to help you through this."

"Why can't I just marry you?" I whine, making Kelsea laugh.

She holds up her left hand, showing off her beautiful diamond ring and wedding band. "Sorry, girl. I'm already taken."

"Ugh. And I only like dick, so that won't work."

"Yeah. And no offense to you, but I'm not giving up Wyatt's dick. Sorry." She shrugs.

Chuckling, I say, "I don't blame you. Good dick is hard to find."

"Well, Wyatt and Walker are twins, so . . ."

I hold my hand up between us. "Uh, no. This will be a sexless marriage, my friend."

"That's surprising coming from you. Come on . . . aren't you just a teensy bit curious about Walker's skills?" She brings her index finger and thumb together in front of her, leaving just a little space between them.

"Do I miss sex? Yes. But doing that with Walker will just muddle this already fuzzy relationship we're entering into. No. I think it's just better that we remain friends who don't have sex during this marriage. Besides, it's not like we're going to be married forever."

Kelsea flashes me that smirk again. "Okay. Whatever you say."

And even though I don't want to admit it, it sounds like my best friend doesn't believe me. I'm not so sure that I believe myself.

CHAPTER FIVE

Walker

I toss the last bale of hay onto the stack inside the barn and wipe the sweat from my forehead. Thank God for the work on this ranch to help me fight off these nerves.

I'm getting married tomorrow, and even though this was my idea, I cannot shake the feeling that I'm making a life-changing decision in less than twenty-four hours. But when I got the text from Evelyn last night that said she agreed to my proposition, something in me shifted. For the first time in six months, I feel like I have a purpose again. I don't feel like I'm wandering aimlessly, wondering what the entire point of life is.

Death has a funny way of making you wake up and realize that living requires effort. It requires the choice to make each day count. And now that I'm past the point of drowning my guilt in alcohol, I get to focus on changing someone else's life for the better: Evelyn's and Kaydence's.

My brother was right, although I'd never admit that out loud to him—at least, not yet. Channeling my grief in a positive way may just be the key to working myself out of the darkness that has surrounded me since that night, even though the memories from that evening are bright and prominent every day, thanks to the flames I barely escaped.

"Need any help?" Wyatt asks me, gathering my attention as I twist around to face him. He strides toward me in his signature Gibson Ranch tee, matching ball cap, Wranglers, and Ariat work boots. It's Sunday, so that means all three of us boys will be on the ranch at some point throughout the day to put in our time.

"I just finished. I still need to brush Hyacinth and Mulberry, but then I was gonna take Barricade for a ride before I head home."

"The horses look good, Walker. When's your next lesson?"

"Not for a few weeks. I kind of pushed back some dates because I wasn't in the right state of mind, you know?" It's been months since I've given any horseback riding lessons, but as the weight on my chest has lifted over the past week,

I know I'm ready to get back to normal as much as I can—at least to my *new* normal.

He nods and then pops his cheek out with his tongue. "Speaking of not thinking rationally, a little birdie told me that you're getting married tomorrow . . ."

Fuck. I guess Kelsea spoke to my brother before I had the chance to. Doesn't surprise me, but still, I was going to approach him about this later. Although, I'm sure Kelsea spoke to Wyatt about it since Evelyn probably asked her to be her witness for the ceremony. "Well, that little curly-haired birdie would be correct."

Wyatt shakes his head at me. "You're going to marry Evelyn? What the hell are you thinking, man?"

"So I guess you don't want to be my best man, then?" I ask as I cross my arms over my chest and mimic his stance. I'm sure we look like one of those pictures where a person tries to find the differences between the two sides even though they look alike to the naked eye.

"Walker, talk to me. What the fuck is going through your head?"

"I'm thinking that I couldn't save my friend, but maybe I can save his daughter from growing up without her mom *and* her dad." Or that maybe I could finally do something about the longing I've felt for Evelyn over the past year and even longer.

But I'm not ready to face that prospect just yet.

"Kelsea told me about the custody petition. But

marriage? Do you think that's a good idea given how you feel?"

"How I feel is irrelevant," I say, brushing him off as I turn to walk away from him.

But he follows closely on my tail. "The hell it is. You've had a thing for Evelyn ever since her and John started fooling around—don't try to deny it. Kelsea and I are both aware. And now, you think that marrying her is going to make that all go away? Are you thinking with your head at all? Or are you letting your dick do the thinking?"

Spinning around, I get nose to nose with him and stare straight into his eyes. "I'm thinking with my fucking *heart*, Wyatt," I seethe, trying to control the rage I feel as my brother asks me the questions that he should, the ones I know he's bringing up just to make sure that my head is a factor in this choice.

But I also feel like he's not listening to me, either.

"For the first time in the past year, I feel like I'm making the *right* decision. I *have* to do this. I can't stand by and watch that little girl's life be decided for her yet again. And Evelyn doesn't deserve this. She's a great mom. So yeah. Maybe I still find her stunning and intriguing, and she also may drive me a little crazy with frustration. But that's not what this is about. I'm doing this for the girls. I'm doing this for John. And maybe . . . I'm doing this a little bit for me, too."

Wyatt studies me for a minute before he relents with a

sigh. "I hope you know what you're getting into. This has disaster written all over it, man."

"Well, you're married now, so how hard can it be?" I joke, grateful that we both seem to unclench at the same time.

"I'm serious, Walker. What happens now? Are you two going to move in together?"

"Yeah. We talked a few things through last night." Particularly, we agreed to continue this arrangement until the court decides final custody, and then we'll choose when to divorce. And I am going to move into Evelyn's place since that's where Kaydence is, making things easier on her. No sense in uprooting their life even more because this was *my* idea, after all.

Oh, and there was Evelyn's no-sex *and* no-women rule, which I countered with no men. The last thing we need is any speculation that the marriage isn't real by either of us dating or sleeping with other people. And I've gone over a year without sex, so I know I can last a bit longer, easily.

Plus, the idea of Evelyn with any other man makes my blood boil, so I know it will be easier on both of us if we're celibate.

"You're really doing this?" my brother clarifies.

"I am."

Wyatt sighs and stares up at the sky. "What time do I need to be at the courthouse tomorrow, then?"

"Ten in the morning. And don't be late."

~

My heart is racing as I check my reflection in the glass display case on the wall for the thousandth time. Straightening my tie, I bounce on my heels, waiting for Kelsea and Evelyn to arrive with Kaydence. I'm wearing a suit again for the second time in a year, but this time, it's in celebration of something—well, at least it feels like this is a win-win for everyone involved.

"Worried about how you look for your fake marriage?" my brother whispers in my ear before I shove him away.

"This isn't fake, Wyatt. It's as real as it fucking gets. Chase had to call in a favor to Judge Carlson so we could get married today instead of waiting the seventy-two-hour waiting period for a marriage license."

"Did you guys draw up a contract of some sort?" he asks under his breath as people stroll by us, headed to various courtrooms down this hall.

"What? Why would we do that?"

"Because if this is real, and you divorce one day, you realize that Evelyn is entitled to your income, net worth, etcetera, right?"

"I don't give a shit about all of that," I say as I wave him off. "Besides, she more than deserves it for my part in all of this. And if it means that Kaydence is taken care of, then she can have whatever she wants."

My brother mutters beside me. "Jesus Christ. You are so in over your head."

"Yeah, but at least I see a light on the surface that's beginning to look a little brighter as we speak." As the words leave my tongue, Evelyn appears from around the corner, gliding toward me in a white sundress, and just the sight of her makes the world stop. My eyes zero in on only her.

Thin straps trace her shoulders, and the top of the dress exposes her entire collarbone. The fabric drapes over her figure, cinching in at the waist to highlight her curves and hips, and she has a ring of baby's breath around her head. The rest of her long blonde locks frame her face in curls.

I wore a suit and tie, knowing we needed to play the part, but seeing her dressed like this—ethereal, angelic, and more beautiful than I've ever seen her—has me frozen in place.

Fuck. Maybe this wasn't such a good idea since the deepest part of my soul wishes this were real, with feelings involved and all.

But hell, it's too late to back out now.

Focus on Kaydence. Focus on that little girl not losing her mom. That's why you're doing this, remember?

Kelsea catches me staring, and she arches her brow at me as the three ladies approach me and my brother. So I do my best to pretend I wasn't just drooling, shove my inappropriate and startling reaction down as far as I can, and remember that I'm doing this to help John and his daughter.

Are you sure you aren't trying to help yourself to Evelyn, too, though?

"Evelyn, you look—"

"Sorry, we're late." She cuts me off, reaching toward Kelsea for Kaydence. "This little one spit up on her dress, so we had to change her last minute."

Smiling at the little girl in a mint-green dress, I reach out and stroke her cheek. "Could have fooled me. She looks perfect," I say before turning to lock eyes with Evelyn. "You both do."

I might imagine it, but I swear a tinge of pink graces her cheeks, and then Evelyn turns her focus to Wyatt. "Are they ready for us?"

"Yup. All set," I answer for him, irritated that she's avoiding me in this moment. But soon, she won't be able to. I'm going to be around every day, which is both a blessing and a curse. But I can survive this. Life has handed us all some pretty shitty cards lately, but look at us bluffing like we've got this in the bag.

The truth is, I don't know if this will help or hurt Evelyn's case, but my gut is telling me the former is more likely. So, with an extended elbow, I wait for Evelyn to weave her arm through mine after handing Kaydence back to Kelsea and then lead her and our friends into the courtroom.

The ceremony is quick, but it's legit. I even bought her a ring, a white-gold band with small diamonds on it, and a plain band for myself. Evelyn lets out a small gasp when I place it on her finger but refrains from chastising me in front of the judge and my brother. Kelsea smiles the entire time across from me while snapping a few pictures, like the entire arrangement was kismet and she can't contain her excitement. And my brother keeps taking deep breaths while he holds Kaydence, huffing them out like a bull getting ready to strike.

When the judge pronounces us husband and wife, I brace myself for the part that really has me tied up in knots—because I know that kissing Evelyn could make this entire situation worse for me. But I can't *not* kiss her. It would be strange and awkward, so I pull her into my chest by her waist and cup the side of her face with my hand.

"Walker . . ." She gasps as I lock eyes with her.

And then I do something I've been thinking about for over a year.

I place my lips on hers, gently at first, feeling her out. But the warmth of her mouth against mine encourages me to press for more. And then Evelyn meets me halfway, leaning into the kiss, and it's as if the feelings I've shoved down for this woman all rush toward the surface and crash around me like a tidal wave.

I momentarily debate pushing my luck by licking the seam of her lips and begging for her tongue to touch mine, but the last thing I want to do is maul this woman in a courtroom in front of a judge, my brother, and my sister-in-law. So I reluctantly pull away, popping my eyes open to find Evelyn's still closed.

My heart is pounding so hard, I swear everyone in the room can hear it, but my world just shifted beneath my feet. Suddenly, all of this became so real, and a rush of determination barrels into me.

I have to make this woman mine.

But what if she doesn't want me back?

When Evelyn finally opens her eyes, her blue irises meet mine, and they widen with shock.

"Yay!" Kelsea exclaims, clapping Kaydence's hands together as Wyatt still holds her while reality slams back into us. But it doesn't take long for the little girl to get the hang of it and start clapping all on her own.

"Congratulations, you two," Judge Carlson says as I reach over to shake his hand.

"Thank you, sir." And then I turn to my bride—correction, *my wife*. "You ready?"

"Uh-huh," Evelyn mutters as she gathers herself, taking my hand, and we walk out of the courthouse together, our lives forever changed by the previous moment.

"So what is next on the agenda, newlyweds?" my brother teases as we gather by our trucks and Evelyn's car. "Care to stop by Mom and Dad's and let them offer you their congratulations?"

My stomach instantly drops. "Fuck."

"Yeah, didn't think that one through, did you?"

Evelyn swats my arm. "You didn't tell your parents we were getting married? Oh my God, your mother is going to kill me!"

"Sorry. I was a little too busy trying to make sure we went through with this before the mediation in two weeks," I say while knowing that my mother's reaction to this will be far worse than the scolding Evelyn is giving me right now. "It's going to be okay, though . . ."

Wyatt snorts. "Yeah. All right."

Kelsea steps up and smacks the back of Wyatt's head, and in that moment, I think I love my sister-in-law even more. "Wyatt. You're not helping." Rolling her eyes at my brother, she purses her lips and then turns to face me again. "Don't worry about Momma G. Yes, she will be shocked, and Randy will have something to say as well, but they know Evelyn. I'm sure they'll understand your reason for keeping this under wraps."

"No, Kels," I interject. "My parents can't know this was arranged. You and Wyatt are the only ones."

Her brow furrows. "Then what are you going to tell them?"

"That we were seeing each other in secret and finally got tired of hiding our relationship." That's the reasoning I came up with last night to explain the sudden marriage when people ask. I just haven't had a chance to run that past Evelyn yet. Curious to hear her thoughts, I twist to gauge her reaction. "You okay with that?"

"Uh, yeah. I think that sounds good," she manages to squeak out as Kaydence claps her hands again, making us all laugh. And then she lets out a noise that sounds like an owl hoot.

"See?" I ask with a smile. "This little owl thinks so, too." Kaydence continues to hoot and then reaches out for me.

"She started making that noise yesterday. I'm not sure where she picked it up from," Evelyn explains as I intercept Kaydence, feeling a peace come over me as she reaches for my face and squeezes my cheeks together. And then I steal a glance at Evelyn.

Her eyes are locked on us, but there's something behind those blue orbs—gratitude, reverence, and uneasiness, like maybe she's unsure about what comes next.

All I know is, these girls are my responsibility now, and I refuse to let anyone down ever again.

The last thing I wanted was to leave Evelyn and Kaydence right after the ceremony, but I was due at the station for another shift. Thankfully, the chief had agreed to move my schedule around since I had to take off a day early for our meeting with Chase on Friday, and one of the guys had been willing to switch with me for tonight.

When I leave to go home the day after tomorrow, I'll be driving to Evelyn's townhouse, not my own. Most of my necessary belongings are in the bed of my truck, but the big stuff is staying at my townhouse for the time being. I'm actually thinking about renting out my place for now since I won't be using it. Evelyn says she has a guest bed for me to use, and she already has furniture, so there's no use in bringing any of that with me. And a fully furnished place will make it easier to draw in a renter.

"What's for dinner tonight, honey?" Drew, one of the other crew members and someone I consider a good friend, walks into the kitchen and leans over the pot on the stove, inhaling deeply.

"Chili, sweet cheeks." Stirring the concoction in front of me, I turn over my shoulder to meet his eyes. "With cornbread."

"Fuck, that sounds good." Drew moves toward the fridge, takes out two cans of Coke, and passes one to me.

"Well, it's my mother's recipe, so you know it will be."

"My mom never taught me how to cook," Drew whines.

"That wasn't an option for me and my brothers. Momma insisted we know how to fend for ourselves, even though that woman lived and still continues to live in her kitchen."

Growing up on a farm that became a bed and breakfast meant that we had to learn many skills over the years about maintaining a house and running a business. But our mom also wanted us to be able to step in and help in the kitchen as well. So one day a week, we would take turns making one of the meals for the day. I usually got dinner since my mornings were spent with the horses, but now that I'm the resident cook at the firehouse, I'm grateful my momma made me learn. And that sound of someone enjoying something you cooked for them never gets old.

"Maybe I need to meet your momma," Drew jokes.

"Sure. And then you can meet my father and his shotgun, too."

Drew cackles and then takes a seat at one of the stools around the counter. "So what's new with you since I last saw you? You seem to be in a better mood lately."

Oh, you know. I just got married today.

"I guess I decided I need to make some changes," I reply instead.

"Like what?"

"Well, for starters, I'm moving."

"Why?"

"I . . ." I debate momentarily about telling Drew about today, and then I realize it's going to be common knowledge eventually, so there's no sense in delaying the inevitable. Everyone is going to know sooner rather than later—that's how things work in small towns. "I got married today, so I'm moving in with my wife."

Drew gives me a deadpan gaze before blinking, pulling himself out of his shock. "Excuse me . . . did you just say you got *married*?"

"Yup." I turn back to the pot on the stove. "So if you know of anyone who might want to rent my townhouse, let me know."

"Hold the fucking phone!" he shouts just as Tanner and Brad stroll into the kitchen.

"What's going on?" Brad asks as he pulls his own drink out of the fridge. The oven timer goes off, signaling that the cornbread is done, so I move to extract it from the oven while Drew fills in our colleagues.

"Walker got married."

"What the fuck, man?" Tanner yells. "I didn't even know you were dating someone."

"Well, we were kind of keeping it under wraps," I explain, using the same reasoning I told Evelyn I would this morning.

"Who is it?" Drew prods. "Who the fuck would marry you?"

Spinning around to face my coworkers, I brace myself for the first reaction from other people to this news. And this one is gonna hit harder, I know it—because they all knew John, too.

"Evelyn."

The three of them go silent, staring at me for far too long before Drew blows out a breath. "Holy fuck."

"Yup. So I'm a married man now." I flick the burner on the stove and then declare, "And your dinner is ready, boys. Time to eat."

The inquisition from the guys at the firehouse that I expected to happen never did, making me feel unsettled throughout the rest of my shift. I anticipated shock, of course, but then I expected questions, lots of them.

But they never came.

And you know what? I didn't feel like they deserved answers, anyway, at least not right now.

Evelyn was right to be nervous about other people's reactions, but fuck everyone else. I am determined to keep my blinders on and remain dedicated to helping her through this battle with John's parents. That's the only thing that matters right now.

Well, that and getting some sleep, because I'm fucking exhausted.

When I pull up to Evelyn's townhouse, I blow out a harsh breath. Living with a woman is going to be a new experience for me, that's for sure. But living with a baby, too? I'm sure there is a shit ton I need to learn before we settle into a groove for the next few months.

It feels weird knocking on the door, since this will be my home for the foreseeable future, but I do anyway. Tanner said he was looking for a place when I mentioned my townhouse would be available for rent, so at least I have one less thing to worry about now.

Evelyn answers the door after a few minutes. "Hey. Sorry, I was in the middle of changing the baby."

"No problem." I move inside as she holds the door open for me, peering around since I'm not distracted like I was the last time I was here. Everything in Evelyn's home is comforting in neutral tones with small pops of bright color throughout, and as I stare around the space, I see not one but two pictures that focus on the moon. One is the moon surrounded by stars, and the second is the moon over the ocean, its light highlighting the ripples in the waves. Funny how I didn't notice that the last time I was here.

Her home is a stark contrast to the abundance of colors she dresses in or the hues that fill her boutique in the clothing she sells. This place feels like a home, and even though I know it will take time to adjust to living together, the atmosphere is welcoming.

"How was work?" she asks me, almost as if she feels that's what she's supposed to say. And I'm not gonna lie, it feels very 1950s housewife, but it's also kind of nice to have someone ask that besides Kelsea. She always checks in on me when I stop by the brewery after a shift, but I've never had that from someone else, let alone a woman I'm in a relationship with—if that's how we're classifying it right now.

"It was fine. Long. Uneventful, which honestly, is the best type of shift." The eventful ones are the ones where I see shit that haunts me in my dreams.

"I'm glad, then." Kaydence is resting on her hip like it's her favorite place in the world, but her eyes are locked on me. I reach out and grab her wrist, making that owl call to her that she made the morning of our wedding, and I'm awarded with a baby giggle that instantly makes me smile. "Well, let me show you to your room."

I follow Evelyn upstairs to the guest room, knowing I'd be a fool to press my luck right now about us staying in the same room to keep up appearances that the marriage is real. But we can have that discussion later, and while we're behind closed doors, just the two of us, I guess it doesn't really matter. Right now, I need sleep, even though my body is wired just being near this woman.

And then that memory of our kiss two days ago slips right back into my mind for the hundredth time.

Evelyn opens the door to my room, and I enter right behind her. The queen-sized bed is positioned in the far corner. There's a small dresser in here and a nightstand, but that's it.

"I know it's not much, but I mostly just had this here for Kelsea before she and Wyatt got together." She shrugs. "It hasn't been used in a year, obviously. But there are clean sheets on the bed."

"It's more than enough, Ev. Thank you. I'm a guy. We don't need a lot of space or art on the walls." That's when I catch one picture on the wall next to the closet—another picture of the moon.

Evelyn lets out a nervous laugh. "The dresser has some of my clothes in it, but if you need more space, I can move them."

"I'll be fine." I peer into the closet, knowing I can always hang up clothes if I need to. I'm one of those rare people who actually enjoys putting away laundry.

"Okay." Evelyn stares at the floor and then finally lifts her gaze to mine. "I didn't get a chance to thank you since the wedding," she says as I drop my duffle bag on the bed and then turn to face her.

"You don't have to thank me. I should be thanking you."

"How do you figure?"

I close the distance between us and then stare down into her eyes, thinking yet again about that kiss, wondering what she would do if I did it again.

But what would my reasoning be?

You're so damn gorgeous that I can't stand the thought of not putting my lips on yours . . .

Being married to you feels like a dream that I always wondered about . . .

I can't believe this is real, so I had to make sure it wasn't just a fantasy . . .

"Because you're the one who's welcoming me into your life, Ev. You didn't have to. I know you're strong enough to fight this on your own, but you're trusting me, and . . ." I battle with how to explain what I'm feeling. "It just means a lot to me."

"Oh. Well, you're welcome?" she says as more of a question, making us both laugh. "But honestly, Walker . . . it feels good to have someone to lean on for once." Her admission must catch her off guard, given the way her eyes widen.

Kaydence decides to clap at that very moment, breaking the moment between us and bringing a smile to my face again. If there's one thing I will cherish out of this, it's getting to be surrounded by that baby girl's joy, something I didn't realize would help me more than I thought it could. I thought that seeing her would make my heart hurt more, but as it turns out, I feel the opposite. Being near her almost makes me feel like John is here, too, like it's okay to smile and laugh again, like I don't have to feel guilty for feeling happiness instead of grief.

"We'll let you get some sleep," Evelyn says as she turns for the door.

"Yeah, I'm beat."

"Help yourself to anything in the house. I'm not sure when you'll wake up, but I leave for work around eight."

"I might be up by then."

"Okay." Her smile is fast and small. "Goodnight, Walker."

"Goodnight, Evelyn." I shift my eyes to Kaydence. "And goodnight to you, little owl."

Kaydence squeals, and then the two of them leave me alone in my room. I change out of my uniform, brush my teeth in the bathroom across the hall, and then plant myself face down in the mattress, desperate for sleep.

The same nightmare that visits me multiple times a week doesn't greet me this time. Instead, I have another type of dream—the kind where Evelyn's legs are wrapped around my head and my face is buried between her thighs.

Funny how that dream keeps me up just the same until a cry from the other room wakes me up for real.

CHAPTER SIX

Evelyn

"Shhh, baby girl. You gotta stop crying." Kaydence wails even louder in protest. "You're gonna wake up Walker," I whisper in her ear as I bounce her around my room.

The first night of sharing a residence with my husband of less than three days, and I'm already freaking out that he's going to regret this decision.

I knew that living with him would be a challenge, but the fact that my daughter wakes up in the middle of the night at least twice didn't cross my mind as an issue until she started crying ten minutes ago. Luckily, there's been no movement from his side of the hall, so maybe he sleeps like a rock and this won't be a problem. But with the way she's crying right now, it's only a matter of time before he wakes up.

My God. What was I thinking? I knew this would be a mistake. He's going to realize what he got himself into, and then I'm going to be a divorcée from a fake marriage that's actually real, one I got myself into to show two people I don't even know that I'm fit to be a mother.

Jesus, I have issues.

And if the man decides to stick this out for some asinine reason, I can't get used to having him here. It will just make things more difficult when this ends. And admitting to him that it feels good to have him to lean on cannot happen again. I can't believe I said that out loud, but my mind has been spinning in a blender since I agreed to this farce, and today made it even worse.

I can't count on people. I've learned that one too many times in my life, and I'm not about to make that mistake again. Letting Kelsea in nine years ago nearly killed me, but my gut told me she was safe. My gut around Walker is a freaking mess, and so is my brain and my heart, so I know damn well that my intuition cannot be trusted right now.

That kiss. It didn't even dawn on me that we'd have to kiss during the ceremony until the judge signaled for us to do so. And at that point, I couldn't deny him. That would have been suspicious.

But then his lips touched mine, and my heart fluttered.

My stomach bottomed out, and the warmth of his mouth reminded me how long it's been since a man touched me. The worst part is that the last man who touched me was his best friend.

God, this can't get any worse.

"Is everything okay?" Walker's voice pulls me from my thoughts as I spin to see him standing in my doorway, shirtless.

Holy shit.

I knew Walker was fit, but I had no idea that a man could have that many abs. Like, how many are there? I'm afraid to start counting because then he'll realize what I'm doing. But this man—he's deliciously fit, muscular, and toned in ways that usually have to be photoshopped, serving to remind me of sex and what it feels like, and I end up wondering what it would feel like to have *his* weight on top of me.

I bet he looks droolworthy in his bunker pants with those suspenders stretched over his massive shoulders. And shirtless. *Yes . . . he needs to remain shirtless.*

"I'm so sorry," I whisper, bouncing Kaydence as she continues to cry. It has to be her teeth. She's been a drooly mess, and I can see her bottom tooth fighting to break through her gums.

Walker rubs his eyes and steps further into the room. "It's okay." His dirty-blond hair is in disarray, and his eyes look glassy. The poor guy needs rest, and his new roommates are disrupting that.

"This is what it's like with a baby around, FYI. Sorry."

He glares at me. "Stop apologizing, Evelyn." Smoothing down Kaydence's baby hairs, he speaks to her. "What's going on, little owl? What's got you so upset?"

She hiccups on a sob and then lets out a cry that slices right through my heart. "She's teething."

"Oh, shit. That has to be painful."

"It is. I already gave her teething tablets and rubbed Orajel on her gums, but . . ."

"Do you mind if I take her?" he asks, reaching out for her. Before I can answer, she lunges for him, and he cocoons her against his chest. "Thatta girl." He walks away from me, bouncing her in his arms, whispering something in her ear, and I can't stop staring.

Is this what it would have been like if John had been around? Would I have been watching *him* comfort our daughter, or would I have still been alone?

Those questions keep me up at night as much as my daughter does.

Instead of asking myself more questions, I watch Walker calm my baby. "Have you tried ice?" he asks as he faces me again, wandering around the room as Kaydence continues to cry but at a much lower volume, thank God.

"No . . ."

"Maybe that would help."

"It can't hurt to try."

Walker leaves my room, giving me a chance to get my heart rate under control and slip a bra on. The oversized t-shirt I'm wearing probably hides my modest B-cups fairly well, but there's no need to provide any opportunities for Walker to see my boobs. Those types of situations need to be avoided at all costs.

My legs carry me down the stairs, and when I enter the kitchen, Kaydence is silent, sucking on a washcloth wrapped around an ice cube. In fact, she seems to be gnawing on it, perfectly content now in Walker's muscular arms.

Lucky girl.

Crap. The lines of Walker's biceps are distracting me too much. He needs to put a freaking shirt on.

"Whooo, whooo," Walker croons in a low decibel like an owl as he holds my daughter.

Oh my God. This is too much, too fast. My heart can't take much more of this.

"I've got her," I declare as I race toward them and pull her from his arms, willing my heart and libido to calm the fuck down.

"Oh. Uh, okay. She was fine, though."

"No. It's all right. You can go back to bed now." I turn my back to him, not being able to watch the confusion on his face because I know I'm acting irrationally right now. But dammit. This is exactly what I need to avoid, his help—accepting his help, wanting his help, asking for his help.

I've been doing this on my own for the past six months, and I can still do it that way even if he's living here. Walker may be helping me with this custody battle, but that's all he can help me with. We can't blur the lines of what this is. I won't be able to survive that.

"Evelyn . . ."

"Just go back to bed, Walker. You're not her dad." I watch my words slice right through him, and I've never wanted to retract my words so quickly in my life. But they do the job, because his face hardens, his jaw clenches, and then he marches off, leaving me alone once more until my daughter finally dozes off to sleep.

"Don't take this the wrong way, but you look exhausted," Kelsea says as I slide into the opposite side of the booth at Rose's Diner on Friday afternoon.

"I want to be offended, but I'm just too tired to care." After getting Kaydence settled into her highchair, happily snacking on a few puffed crackers, I turn my attention back to my best friend.

"Not sleeping well with Walker in the house?" she asks, a hint of amusement in her voice.

Narrowing my eyes at her, I reply, "No. My daughter cut her first tooth, so we've had a few rough evenings. But hopefully she'll sleep better tonight now that the little bugger poked through." However, the guilt over how I reacted with Walker the other night is not helping me sleep, either.

I know he was just trying to help, but it was overwhelming. Between his lack of a shirt and the way he so effortlessly soothed my child, my ovaries woke up from their deep slumber and nearly jumped out from under my skin. *My* body became hyperaware of *his* body and the gentleness he had with my baby. So I did what I do best—push people away before they can hurt me. And I have my lovely parents to thank for that skill.

Yesterday, I avoided him, leaving before he came out of his room and keeping my distance in the evening. Luckily, he brought a few more of his things over from his place, like his TV, so he locked himself in his room, and I guess he watched that for the rest of the night. I don't even know if he ate dinner—that's how intentional we were about avoiding each other.

Deep down, though, I hated that he felt like he couldn't come out of his room. He lives with me now, and *I'm* the one who made *him* feel uncomfortable in his temporary home. And I have no one else to blame for that but myself.

"But how are things going for the newlyweds then?" Kelsea prods as she takes a sip from her iced tea. Rose, one of the waitresses, dropped off our drinks without us even asking. We come here so often that there's no need to go through that formality anymore—one of the perks of being regular customers at an establishment that doesn't see many new faces often.

"Don't call us that." I reach for my own iced tea and take a sip.

"Is it that bad?"

"No." I focus on my glass in front of me. "It's just . . ."

"What aren't you telling me, Evelyn?" The sternness of her voice has me popping up my eyes to meet hers. She arches a brow at me. "What's going on?"

Sighing, I lean back in the booth, slumping my shoulders. "We haven't spoken since Wednesday night."

"Okay . . . why?"

"Wednesday night, Walker came over after work like we planned," I explain as she nods. "But then, later that night, Kaydence started crying because of her teeth. I panicked when I realized she'd wake him up, which she did." I glance over at my daughter who smacks the highchair, demanding more puffed crackers. I shake the container for her, depositing a few more for her to grab, and then focus back on Kelsea. "I'm not used to worrying about her waking someone else up, you know?"

"Yeah. So was Walker mad or something?"

I shake my head. "The complete opposite. He was so understanding and helpful," I let out in a whisper. "He came into my room and asked how he could help. Oh, and he was shirtless."

Kelsea tucks in her lips to hide her smile. "I see. And let me guess . . . your lady bits liked what they saw?"

I peer around us before finally admitting, "I didn't realize he was so freaking ripped."

"Well, he's a firefighter that also does work on a farm and has been pretty athletic for most of his life. It's okay that you find him attractive, Evelyn. You're not dead inside.

You're a woman with needs, and pretty strong ones if memory serves me correctly."

I point a finger at her. "No. It's not okay. That's exactly what *cannot* happen. And it's Walker . . . it just feels . . . weird." Sighing, I continue. "Anyway, he took Kaydence from me, helped soothe her with an ice cube wrapped in a washcloth for her to chew on, and when I saw the two of them together, I freaked out." Just remembering the look on his face right now has me wanting to bury myself under a blanket of embarrassment and shame.

"What did you say?"

"I—I told him that he wasn't her father and that he could go back to bed."

Kelsea tilts her head at me, disappointment filling her eyes. "Evelyn . . ."

I toss my hands in the air. "I know, okay? I messed up."

"Walker is just trying to help you . . ."

"That's the thing, Kelsea. For how long?" I whisper, not wanting others around us to hear. "How long is he planning on sticking around? How long before he realizes that he doesn't want to be a father? How long before I let him in and then he crushes the trust I put in him?" The only person I would ever admit these fears to is Kelsea because I know she won't judge me. But it still makes me anxious to admit them.

"Walker is not your mom or dad or John or that bastard who scarred you for life nine years ago," she declares, reaching out for my hand. "I've known him my entire life, Evelyn. He's a *good* man with a *good* heart. And if he says he genuinely wants to help, then he means it. Look at what he did to help Wyatt and me. He knew the risk going into that, but he saw it through because he knew the outcome would outweigh the trouble. So you need to apologize to him and try to make this easier on both of you."

I go to argue with her, but she holds her palm up to my face.

"No. Listen. I know you're second-guessing this right now, and you have every right to feel everything that you are at this moment. But trust me . . . Walker is one person you *can* let in. You did it with me, and I promise, you can do it with him." My hand trembles at just the thought of it. "You need to apologize to him and make it right."

"I know. But Kelsea . . . he's really freaking hot."

She throws her head back in laughter. "Glad to know you're not blind. Not that I agree with you exactly. I mean, I *am* married to his twin, but Walker will always just be Walker to me."

"That's the thing—he always was *just Walker* to me, too, until the other night. And when he kissed me at the wedding . . ."

Her eyes light up. "I knew it. I knew I saw something there."

"It freaked me out."

"I can tell. But for right now, you need to focus on repairing your friendship with him, and then maybe, down the line, you can bone your husband and get it out of your system."

My mouth drops open. "Oh my God. You sounded like me just now."

She shrugs just as Rose comes by to take our order. After we tell her what we want, Kelsea continues. "Perhaps you're rubbing off on me, and we're switching places."

"I'm not sure how I feel about this," I say as Kaydence lets out a squeal, getting our attention.

"Don't worry about me. I'm happy, in love, and have everything I've ever wanted in my life so far. However, I feel like I should let you know . . ." She shifts uncomfortably in her seat. "Word got out that you two got married."

My eyes dart around us, and suddenly, I feel like I'm under a microscope. Sets of eyes cast our direction, and it may just be my mind playing tricks on me, but it feels like people are whispering among themselves after looking over here.

"What? How do you know that?"

"I heard some people talking about it at the brewery the other night."

I slap a palm to my forehead. "Just great."

"Hey. You knew this was going to happen."

"I know, but it doesn't make it any easier."

"I know that, too." She tugs on my hand, forcing me to look at her again. "You can't worry about what people are going to think, though, Ev. It's like Walker said—let him manage that."

"That's not fair to him, though."

"He knew what he was signing up for when he suggested this. He's willing to bear that cross to help you get what you want. But I guess you need to ask yourself this: What do *you* want out of this, Evelyn? Is there more to this arrangement than just fighting to keep custody of Kaydence?"

Her questions have me twisted up in my thoughts for the rest of the day until I get home later that night, convinced that I don't have to answer any of them right now. What I need to do is apologize to Walker and fix this tension between us before it becomes irreparable.

"Walker?" I call out as I step through the front door. I place my bags on the floor and then walk over to the playpen, depositing Kaydence inside with her toys while I search him out. But after traveling upstairs and back down, I realize there's no sign of him.

So I send him a text.

Me: *Hey. I just got home. Will you be here soon?*

It takes a few minutes for him to reply, but when he does, my urgency from before dissipates at his response.

Walker: *No, sorry. Went to the gym and then I'm going straight to Forrest's office. He needs some extra manpower for a few days. I might just stay with him to avoid having to drive back and forth.*

Well, shit. I would have known that if we'd been communicating instead of avoiding each other.

Me: *Oh. Okay.*

Walker: *Everything all right?*

Me: *Yes.*

That wasn't true.

Me: *No. I just . . . I wanted to apologize for the other night.*

The little bubbles dance along the bottom of the screen as I wait on pins and needles for his reply.

Walker: *Don't worry about it. I overstepped.*

Me: *No, you didn't. I overreacted.*

Walker: *It's fine, Ev. You're right. I'm not her dad. And I need to remember that.*

His words make my chest ache.

Me: *You might not be, but seeing you fill that role just overwhelmed me, Walker. That was all. You were trying to help, and I didn't react appropriately. I'm sorry. It's just hard for me . . .*

To what?

Let people in? See him with her? Realize that I'm looking at him differently?

Walker: *I sensed that. I get it. Don't worry about it.*

Me: *So are we good?*

Walker: *Yeah, we're good.*

Me: *I'll see you soon, then.*

Walker: *See ya then. Take care of my little owl in the meantime.*

My eyes find my daughter just as she makes that owl like noise while she smacks her playpen walls. And then I let out a sigh of relief, even though I don't feel much more at ease. But at least I said what I needed to, and now Walker knows that I overreacted and feel badly about it.

Honestly, I don't know that I'll feel one hundred percent better until I see him in person. Looks like it's going to be a long two days before that can happen, though —and as that realization hits me, I remind myself that I'm alone once again. That was exactly what I wanted.

Funny how I'm not so sure what I want anymore.

CHAPTER SEVEN

Walker

"What are you doing out here? I didn't even see you arrive." My father strides up behind me as I refill the water bucket in Barricade's stall.

"Am I supposed to check in with you every time I come over on a Sunday?"

"Am I not allowed to wonder why my son is changing up his routine?" he counters. He has a point. Typically, I walk through the house, say good morning, and *then* come out to the horses.

"Touché." I empty the bucket, place it on the ground,

and then twist to face him. "Just wanted to get a head start on my to-do list so the day runs smoother."

"You're refilling water buckets, Walker. That's something that has to be done every day, and someone else could do it easily."

"Okay . . ." I can't tell my father that the reason I'm here so early is because I'm avoiding my wife at home. At least, I'm not *ready* to tell him that.

"Does this have anything to do with the fact that you married Evelyn Sumner and didn't tell your parents?" he asks.

So much for withholding the truth a little longer. "Um . . ."

When his hands meet his hips, I know I'm in for it. "Do you realize that your mother found out from Tammy down at the market this morning? She didn't even find out from her own son but the cashier at the damn grocery store, Walker." The tone of his voice makes me feel sixteen again, back when I got caught making out with Stephanie Collins in the barn after dark. Except I'd rather face that ten times over than deal with the disappointment I'm about to face from my mother.

I avoided going through the house this morning when I arrived, which meant forgoing my mother's biscuits, too. But I knew I needed to burn off some nerves before I tackled this topic. That *is* part of the reason I came here today, to let them know about my recent life choices, but apparently my parents learned about them before I could step up.

Unfortunately, this is what happens in a small town, just like I anticipated.

"I'm sorry," I say, shoving my hands in my pockets. "I should have told you, but it all kind of happened so fast."

"You and Evelyn? Shit, Walker, we didn't even know you were seeing her."

"I know. No one did. We didn't tell anyone. And the marriage . . . just sort of happened."

He sighs, shakes his head, and then gestures for me to follow him. "Let's go have this conversation with your mother so you don't have to repeat it twice."

I follow him into the house, knocking the mud off my boots on the mat by the back door before I enter. And when I lift my head and find my mother standing at the island of her white-and-gray kitchen, dabbing under her eyes with a tissue, I know I fucked up.

But if this is the price I'm going to pay to help Evelyn and Kaydence, then I'll gladly accept it.

"Hey, Momma."

Her eyes slice right through me like razor blades. "Walker Bradley Gibson . . . how could you have gotten married and not tell me? Or your dad?"

"I'm sorry, Momma."

"No." She slaps her palm on the marble. "I need to know why. When did this happen? And how?"

I could tell her the truth, but Evelyn and I agreed that

Wyatt and Kelsea would be the only ones who would know.

Speaking of my brother, he and Forrest enter the house at this exact moment.

"Oh, good. Now the whole family is here to listen to your explanation of why you got married without any of us knowing," my mother declares.

"What the fuck?" Forrest exclaims. "You got married?" He tosses a look at my twin. "What is with all of my brothers getting married?"

"Some of us are in love, fuck face," Wyatt fires back.

"Wyatt!" My father yells, making the room go silent. My heart pounds in my chest as the five of us cast our gazes between one another. My mother is still crying, Forrest crosses his arms over his chest, Wyatt looks at me like we know a secret no one else knows—*because we do*—and my dad commands the room with his stance. "This is not the time to start more shit, you three," he finally says after enough time has passed to soothe some of the tension. "Now, Walker. Start explaining."

Taking a deep breath, I toss my Stetson on the dining room table and then run a hand through my hair. "Evelyn and I have been seeing each other in secret for months. I'm sorry I didn't tell you, but she was afraid of what people would think because of Schmitty, you know?" My mother's face starts to soften, so I know my explanation is starting to calm her down. "We bonded over our grief, and it just naturally turned into more. But I got tired of hiding, so I suggested we get married so other people's opinions wouldn't matter as much if they knew we were serious about each other."

Kelsea comes through the front door at that moment, nervously stepping into the tension-filled room. "Sorry. Is everything okay?"

"Did you know that Walker and Evelyn got married?" my mother asks.

"Uh . . . yeah." Kelsea casts her eyes down to the floor as Wyatt pulls her to his side.

"We both did," Wyatt announces. "We were their witnesses."

"Oh, mother of God!" Momma shouts, tossing a wooden spoon in the air. It finds the floor a second later with a loud clunk. "So apparently your father and I were the only ones in this family who didn't know about this?"

Forrest raises his hand. "I didn't know anything about this shit. Just want to clarify."

"Look. I'm sorry. I know I can't take it back, but I don't regret it. Evelyn and Kaydence mean the world to me." *Not a lie.* "Please don't blame her for any of it. It was *my* idea. I wanted her to be my wife. I was tired of hiding our feelings. And now that I'm living with them and everything is out in the open, I hope that you can just accept that."

My mother stares at me, letting out a shudder as she exhales. "I missed my baby boy getting married," she whines.

"I know. We can have a bigger ceremony if you want

to," I offer, knowing that the chances of that happening are slim considering Evelyn anticipates this marriage being temporary.

"We could do that. But . . . I guess I have another daughter-in-law then?" Hope resonates through her words.

"Yes, Momma."

"And a grandbaby?" Her eyes widen a bit as her voice softens. My mother loves children, and babies are her kryptonite. In fact, I don't know if she's even met Kaydence since Evelyn has been scarce since she was born.

"You do."

She huffs and then wipes under her eyes, gathering herself back to her matriarchal state. "Well, you'd better bring my new daughter-in-law to my house, then. I have to make sure she's of sound mind since she agreed to marry you without us knowing as well." Her smile tells me that everything is going to be okay, even though I know the inquisition isn't over. "We love Evelyn, Walker. You know that. So I just don't get why you felt the need to hide an important relationship from us?"

"I know. And again, I'm sorry. But with John passing . . ." I start.

"I think I understand a bit better now," my mother replies, cutting me off. And if there's any more reason to love my momma, it's that one right there. She's kept her watchful eye on me over the past six months. We haven't explicitly had a conversation about it, but she knows I haven't been myself since that night. So I think, deep down, she understands that I made some decisions she might not agree with, but she will find it in her heart to accept them.

"Does this mean Evelyn gets the biscuit recipe?" Kelsea interjects, making everyone laugh, except for Forrest. He just shakes his head with a slight grin on his lips and a roll of his eyes.

"Eventually. Right now, I need my heart to catch up to my head on this matter."

"I love you, Momma," I say as I walk over to her and pull her into my chest for a hug.

"I know you do. You love with your whole heart, Walker. You always have. So I know your heart must have been in the right place if this is the decision you made. I just wish you'd have let us be a part of it."

"I regret that, too, but I don't regret marrying Evelyn, Momma."

Little do they know just how true those words are, even though things have been less than easy since we said I do.

"Walker!" Kelsea shouts after me as I head back out to the barn.

I'm going to finish up a few things and then head home —my new home, that is. I can't hide from Evelyn forever, and now I really need to let her know about my parents' newfound knowledge of our relationship.

"What's up?"

She catches up to me, striding beside me as we enter the humid space. The horses neigh when we move into the barn, calling for our attention. But I can tell by the way Kelsea is acting right now that she needs my attention more. "That could have gone better, yeah?"

I shrug. "It went about as badly as I thought it would. I planned on talking to them today anyway, but apparently they found out this morning from Tammy at the market."

"Small-town gossip," she teases.

"Yeah."

"Is everything going okay with Evelyn?" she asks, but the tone in her voice says she already knows the answer to that question.

"Why are you asking?"

"I saw her on Friday for lunch. She told me about Wednesday night."

My stomach twists again, and a flash of irritation runs through my veins. "Oh. Well, I overstepped, so . . ."

She places her palm on my shoulder, stopping me in my tracks. "No, you didn't, Walker. You just have to understand how Evelyn is about accepting help."

"I'm starting to gather that it doesn't come easy for her."

Kelsea scoffs. "That's putting it mildly, and I hope that she works on that with you. But . . . she also told me something else about that night."

Curiosity strikes me. "What?"

"That you came into her room shirtless."

My brows pop up. "She told you that?"

"Yup." Kelsea's grin gets bigger. "And she also told me that it made her feel some . . . *things*." She bounces her eyebrows and chuckles. "If my best friend knew what I was about to tell you, she'd kill me. But . . . she reacted to that kiss, Walker. And the night you came into her room without a shirt on . . . She feels *something*, so you need to push it. See if the way you feel is the same way she does—or can with time."

I cross my arms over my chest. "Why are you telling me this, Kelsea?"

Kelsea mimics my stance. "Because I know you have feelings for her, Walker, and on the chance that Evelyn feels the same way, you need to take your shot at seeing if there's something real between you two. This is your opportunity to go after what you want."

My mouth gapes open, ready to reply, but Kelsea keeps speaking before I can say something in return.

"I saw it that night at the Jameson, the night that she started talking to Schmitty. It was there in your eyes, but I don't even think you had realized it yet. You *liked* her, and then as things between her and Schmitty progressed, you retreated. You started avoiding them, and Wyatt and I both agreed it was because you realized you missed your shot."

"Okay . . ." My heart is racing as I listen to my sister-in-law recount the timeline of my feelings for Evelyn, as if I don't know the details already myself. But it also alerts me to the fact that I haven't been very good at hiding those feelings from everyone else. Which then begs the question: Does Evelyn know how I feel, too?

"But then she got pregnant, and . . ."

"I don't think you need to finish that sentence."

She closes her lips and nods. "Sorry. But here's what I know. I love my best friend, but she's freaking stubborn, especially about getting close to people. I won't share the details of why because it's not my story to tell, but I will say this—if there is one man I could want for my best friend, it's you," she whispers as if it's a magical spell she's sending out into the universe.

I sigh and find the nearest bale of hay to sit on, resting my forearms on my knees. "Kelsea . . . I didn't do this to pursue her. I did it for Kaydence." Even though the thought of things becoming real with Evelyn has crossed my mind more than once at this point. Well, up until Wednesday night, that is.

"I know that, but now that you're in it, why not do something for yourself, too? Try to break down her walls, try to show her that she can count on you. She's never been able to count on anyone except for me, Walker. But you care about her, so chase her. Wear her down. One man's 'I wasn't ready' is another man's 'I knew the second I saw her.' You might not have known the minute you met Evelyn, but you've known for a long time that you want her as more than a friend. So now's your chance, Walker. Don't mess it up."

Hope blooms in my chest as my sister-in-law stares down at me.

Could this really be it? Am I going to sit back and appease Evelyn's desire to stand on her own two feet, using it as an excuse not to make her see that I'm the man she should be with? Or do I push back, prove to her that we could have something real, and hope to God that she feels that way, too, in the end?

"You're meddling," I say, arching a brow at her.

"Ha! That's rich coming from you," she fires right back through a smirk.

"I want her, Kelsea," I admit. "But after Wednesday night . . ." That look in her eyes as she reminded me that I'm not Kaydence's father flashes through my mind yet again.

"You took her by surprise. You came on strong and didn't even mean to." She squints as she contemplates her next words. "Think of Evelyn like a scared little bunny. You wouldn't run up to a bunny, Walker. You would approach slowly and show them that you mean no harm. And then, before you know it, you're getting bunny cuddles." She shrugs with the biggest smile on her face.

"I don't know whether to find that analogy of yours adorable or frightening. Are you sneaking up on random bunnies throughout the day now, Kelsea?"

She leans over and smacks my arm. "Shut up, Walker. You know what I mean."

Standing from my seat, I stare down at this girl who has

known me my entire life. But she also knows Evelyn better than anyone else, so I know she's speaking the truth. "You really think I should go for it?"

"I think you already want to, but you're trying to talk yourself out of it. That's the only reason you'd be here so early on a Sunday. You're avoiding her."

"You act like you know me or something."

"Or something." She winks at me. "Now go home, Walker. Wear down your *wife*." She emphasizes that last word with intention.

"Fine." I glance away, wrestling with an awareness growing in my chest by the minute. But then I reach out and pull Kelsea into me, squeezing her tightly. "Thank you," I whisper in her ear.

"Don't thank me yet. You have your work cut out for you, but I'm cheering you on. And let me know if you need any advice. I can give you some tips to get into her head."

"Conspiring against your best friend, babe?" Wyatt asks as he comes up behind us.

I release Kelsea and then glance at my brother. "Just helping me out with a few things," I clarify, shooting a wink at Kelsea this time.

"Sure. That sounds innocent." Wrapping his arm around her, he continues, "But keep your hands off my wife, okay? You have your own now. Why don't you go home to *her*?"

A delighted grin takes over my face as the wheels start turning in my head. Kelsea is right. If I don't use this marriage and time together to try to get Evelyn to see that she should be with me, I'd be stupid.

And so, with determination flowing through my veins again, I tip my chin and my cowboy hat to my brother and Kelsea, announcing before I take off, "Oh, don't worry. My wife is about to find out just exactly who she married, and I hope she can handle it."

"Hey." Evelyn spins to face me as I enter her house. It's been almost three days since we've spoken in person, and suddenly some of those nerves come back. But I push them down again and remember what Kelsea told me: Slowly approach the rabbit.

"Oh. Hi." A genuine smile graces her lips. "Uh, how was your day?"

"Well, I went to my parents' house today."

Realization dawns on her face. "Oh, shit."

"Yeah. Wanna sit?" I gesture toward the couch and take a seat on the opposite end from her. My eyes find Kaydence on the floor, chewing on a stuffed rabbit. *Oh, the irony*. I reach out and grab her free hand. "How's my little owl today?"

She flashes me a toothless grin that makes my heart melt. Fuck, this little girl makes me want this to work even more. *Baby steps, Walker.*

"Well, she finally cut that tooth a few days ago, so we've

been getting some decent sleep the past couple of nights." Nights that I've been staying at my townhouse, avoiding her. I wasn't really working with Forrest, like I said. I just wanted to give her some space, and I was able to deep clean my place before Tanner moves in this week.

"That's good."

Evelyn reaches out for my hand. Her touch sends a bolt of lightning across my skin, igniting that fire inside me once more, just like I needed her to. "I'm sorry again for that night, Walker. I've been dying to tell you that in person."

"I know, Ev. It's okay. There's going to be a learning curve to this relationship. We'll figure it out." *And I'm going to wear you down, woman. Just you wait.*

"I hope so." She clears her throat, winces, and then says, "So your parents know now, I take it?"

"Yeah. Momma didn't take it so well."

Evelyn buries her face in her hands. "Oh God. She hates me now, doesn't she?"

My parents have known Evelyn for years since she and Kelsea are so close. And last year when my father had surgery, she was there to help at the ranch while he was recovering. So she's not a stranger, but honestly, I'm not sure if that makes this situation better or worse. But Evelyn hasn't been around much since she had the baby.

"She doesn't hate you, but she sure as hell was pissed at me for not telling her I was getting married. And Wyatt admitted that he and Kelsea knew and were our witnesses, which just flabbergasted her even more."

Her head pops back up. "She's mad at you for marrying me?"

"No, for not telling them that we were in a relationship." Her brow furrows. "Remember, no one is to know the real reason for this marriage, Ev. Not even my parents. As far as they know, we've been dating for months, okay? Remember, that's what everyone needs to believe in order for this to work. We bonded over our grief, right?"

She gives me a timid nod and then whispers, "Do you ever think about him?"

My stomach lurches. "Every day. I miss him, Ev. He was my best friend."

Tears fill her eyes. "I wish things had been better between us before he died, Walker. I feel so guilty about it every day."

I reach over and pull her into me, encasing her in my arms. And fuck, does she feel good against my chest. I can feel her breasts press into me through our shirts. She smells like a vanilla cupcake, and the way she rests her head on my shoulder makes me want to lift her chin up and kiss her again.

But not yet. I can't scare her away again this soon.

So instead, I comfort her as a friend, the same way we've always been with each other, and pray that this will all change the way I want it to with time.

"I carry that guilt, too, Evelyn. But at least we know

we're not alone in that anymore." She hums. "Don't take this the wrong way, but it feels good to know someone else feels the same pain about Schmitty as I do."

"I know what you mean." She lifts her head and locks eyes with me. "If only you had reached out sooner instead of avoiding me," she teases, and fuck, I want to kiss that smirk off her face.

"I know. I'm sorry." I tuck a strand of her hair behind her ear, catching the small hitch in her breath that accompanies my touch.

"Stop apologizing."

Our eyes are locked on one another. "You started it."

Her grin builds, and then she pushes away from me, smoothing her hair back in place. Meanwhile, my heart pounds like a bass drum, and my dick is half-mast from holding her just now, so I won't be getting up from this couch anytime soon. "Okay, then. Well, you're home now, so welcome to the chaos." She fans her arms around the room. Toys are scattered everywhere, there's a load of clean laundry on the chair in the corner, and the kitchen table is covered with Kaydence's diaper bag and car seat.

"Hey, I actually prefer this. It beats living alone."

As she stands and walks away from me, she says, "That's all I've ever known."

I remain on the couch since the kitchen isn't too far away and Kaydence is right next to me. "Well, every four days, you'll get that again."

"You work forty-eight/ninety-sixes, right?"

"Yeah. I have to go back in tomorrow."

She nods. "I remember John doing that, so . . ." She shrugs, but all it does is remind me that this woman used to be with my best friend.

"I can try to stay out of your hair when I'm here, if that's what you prefer."

"No, Walker. It's fine. I'll adjust."

Kaydence lets out a squeal, reminding us that she's here. I lean down and pick her up, bringing her onto my lap and staring into those big green eyes of hers. "I can't believe she's almost six months old."

"I know. Kelsea is doing her pictures next week."

"Then I'll be there," I say as I blow raspberries against Kaydence's cheek.

"Oh. Uh, you don't have to . . ."

Standing from the couch, I turn my head toward Evelyn, who's watching me from the kitchen. "Don't you think it would be a little strange if your husband wasn't in her pictures?"

"I hadn't thought about it, honestly."

"Then it's settled. This needs to appear real to anyone looking in, Evelyn, including the court, if it goes there. And don't you dare try to argue with me about it."

She rears her head back, but she's almost smiling. "I wasn't going to . . ."

"Yes, you were. You had your rebuttal on the tip of your tongue, but don't bother. Which reminds me, I'm going to need you somewhere in a few weeks, too . . . as my wife."

She blinks a few times. "Okay. Where?"

"The fire station fundraiser."

Her eyes widen, and she wraps her arms around her waist. "I don't know if that's such a good idea, Walker."

"Everyone knows already, Evelyn. We can't hide forever, and it would look suspicious if I showed up without you."

She licks her lips nervously. "Okay. You're right."

"Those words are music to my ears."

Rolling her eyes, she heads back into the kitchen. "Don't get cocky, Walker. It's unbecoming of you."

Little do you know just how cocky I can be, woman. And I can't wait to show you.

"You hungry? I'm not much of a cook, and I'm used to just whipping something together for myself. But . . ." Evelyn says, changing the subject.

"I can cook," I interject.

"You can?"

"Yeah, I do it at the firehouse all the time."

She tilts her head at me, planting her hands on her hips as well. "How did I never know this?"

I shrug. "It's not something we've ever talked about, I guess. But I learned from my momma, so . . ."

"Oh, you must be one hell of a cook, then," she teases.

I blow on my knuckles. "I'm not too shabby." Still holding Kaydence, I walk around Evelyn into the kitchen and open her fridge. She doesn't have much, but I'm sure I can whip up something.

"By all means, have at it, then—if you don't mind."

My eyes dance across an assortment of veggies and some leftover chicken. "You like stir fry?"

"Sounds great."

I place Kaydence in her highchair, grab the ingredients from the fridge, and get to work. And that is how Evelyn and I fall into our new routine as husband and wife.

CHAPTER EIGHT

Evelyn

"Oh my gosh! That one was perfect!" Kelsea exclaims behind the lens of her camera, staring down at the window where she can see a preview of the shot. "Go ahead and relax while I glance through these and change my lens, and then we'll move to another location."

Relax? How the hell am I supposed to relax when Walker has been standing behind me, beside me, and around me for the past thirty minutes, touching my waist, smiling down at me like we're in love, and doting on my baby girl?

My heart and vagina can't handle much more of this.

I let out the breath I was holding and step away from him, needing the space before I spontaneously combust. Holding Kaydence in my arms, I stroll around the field we're in on the Gibson Ranch and watch the sun begin to set in the distance.

This past week has been . . . well, *nice* isn't the fanciest word to describe it, but that's how it's felt. Walker and I have slipped into a routine on the days and nights when he's home, helping us adjust to this new normal. The waistband of my shorts has grown tighter from all the delicious meals he's made for us, and having his help in the evenings has alleviated some stress from the bath-and-bedtime routine. My house is cleaner and more organized with his assistance and, believe it or not, I married a man who actually enjoys doing laundry. How the hell I managed that is beyond me.

But the worst part is, I *enjoy* having him in my house. There's someone to talk to, to share the monotonous moments of our days with, to tell stories to when something out of the ordinary happens in our ordinary little town.

Our friendship has grown and blossomed in the past seven days. But so has my attraction to him.

"Want me to take her?" Walker asks, closing the distance between us that I just created on purpose.

"If you want." I hand her off and then stroll over to where Kelsea is standing. "What's next, best friend?"

"Well, I want some shots of Kaydence under the tree,"

she explains, referencing a giant oak tree on the property, the one that she and Wyatt got married under. "But then I want a few of just you and Walker."

"What? Why?" My heart rate speeds up exponentially.

The corner of her mouth lifts. "Because generally when you do a family photo shoot, you do some of just the parents."

I narrow my eyes at her. "Kelsea . . ."

"Hey, it will be good for you. Help you get more comfortable with this whole situation, and you'll have photographic evidence for the court that the three of you are a family. Remember how important that is?" She arches a brow at me.

The impending mediation with John's parents has been rattling my nerves all week. This Friday, I have to sit across from them and listen to why they think I shouldn't be allowed to raise my own kid. Just the thought of that has my blood pressure rising, and not in the good way Walker's proximity does.

Wait. No. That's not a good reason, either.

"Let's go." Kelsea leads the three of us across the field to the oak tree, setting up a blanket on the ground to place Kaydence on. Getting shots of her proves tricky as she's just started to crawl and doesn't want to sit still anymore, but Kelsea gives me a small preview of some close ups of her face, her smile, and her eyes, and I fall in love with my baby girl all over again.

I never knew I could love another human so much. It's a

type of unconditional love that I wish my parents would have for me. But sadly, some humans never understand how to love another human being more than themselves.

"You ready for me?" Wyatt strolls up to us from over the small hill that blocks the tree from the main house.

"Hey, little brother. What are you doing out here?" Walker asks, reaching out to shake his brother's hand. And it always makes me laugh when he refers to Wyatt as his little brother, because they're twins. But apparently, Walker was born two minutes before Wyatt was, a fact he likes to remind him of every chance he gets.

"I was told that my baby holding services were needed," he says, looking at his wife.

"That's right. I can't take pictures of the two of you and hold a baby, as talented as I may be."

"You *do* have many talents," Wyatt says to her, bouncing his eyebrows.

"Way to keep it PG in front of the baby," I tease before handing her over to Wyatt and taking a step back.

"Perfect. Now, Evelyn and Walker, go stand by the edge of the creek." Kelsea directs us where she wants us and then, suddenly, it's just me and my husband, trying to pretend we're in love.

All I know is that I'm definitely in *lust* at this point, and that's difficult enough to handle.

But love? Not sure I'll ever find that at the rate I'm going.

Kelsea has us pose a few different ways, walking toward

and away from the camera and pretending to dance to get some candid shots.

"Who taught you how to dance?" I ask as Walker spins me into his chest and back out again.

"Momma. She made sure all three of us boys could move a woman around a dance floor since Dad used to dance with her all the time."

A rush of emotion runs through me. Walker comes from such a different family life, and I feel grateful *for* him that he had that—and a little bad for myself.

He's also had one hell of an example of love to look up to, and that proves to be yet another stark difference between the two of us.

Kelsea halts our movements, nods her head as she peers down at her camera, and then clears her throat. "Great. Now, Evelyn, I want you to stand face-to-face with Walker and peer up into his eyes."

"Excuse me?"

"Look into my eyes, wifey," Walker teases as he places two fingers under my chin and turns my head back to face him. Our eyes meet as he stares down at me and, instantly, it gets harder to breathe.

Walker has light-brown eyes that are more like pools of chocolate, smooth and irresistible. There's a playfulness in his gaze almost every day, even more so since we've been married, but I've noticed how much his eyes darken when he's angry or passionate about something.

And just as I think it, his eyes darken right before my eyes. That penetrating look of his is directed right at me.

"Perfect. Hold it right there," Kelsea declares as I hear the click of her camera. But that's the only sound that registers around us as we continue to stare at each other, the sound of my heartbeat in my ears growing louder with each passing second.

Walker moves his hand from under my chin to around my face, tilting my head up slightly as he cups my jaw. His fingertips singe my skin, making goosebumps travel down my arms. And then his other hand grabs me by the waist, pulling me into his body. "Come on, Evelyn. Pretend that you *like* me for a moment. You did marry me, after all." His smirk lets me know that he's trying to rile me up by suggesting that I *don't* like him. He's been teasing me about that since the night I went off on him.

"If you keep mocking me like this, pretending to like you is going to become much harder."

"But I'm your husband. The camera has to believe that we're in love."

"The camera can believe whatever it wants, Walker. We know the truth here."

His smile fades as Wyatt shouts from the side, "Give her a kiss, Walker!"

Kelsea laughs, but then Walker's grin builds in slow motion, long enough to let me prepare for what's about to happen.

But I'm still not ready for it.

His lips press to mine, just as soft as our kiss was when we got married, but then he pulls me into him harder and slants his mouth over mine, slipping his tongue just slightly between my lips. My knees threaten to buckle.

I want to pull away.

I should.

But the feel of his tongue has me opening up to him, fusing our mouths together, gripping the front of his shirt, drawing a moan from deep in his throat.

Or maybe that was me.

This kiss is not like the one we shared on the day we became husband and wife. No. There's an intensity behind the way Walker's mouth is moving over mine like he's trying to prove something, perhaps a theorem of how the world works.

And I think he's convincing us all with flying colors.

My body takes over as Walker and I battle for control with our tongues, tasting each other as if we're addicts—and that's exactly how I feel right now.

Addicted and in trouble.

A twig snaps beside us, jolting me back to reality, causing me to jump away from him and remember where we are.

My eyes bounce back and forth between his as Kelsea approaches us. "Um, yeah. That was . . ." Kelsea says, but I cut her off.

"Did you get what you needed?" Turning to face my friend, I swallow down both the lump in my throat and my libido and attempt to pull myself together even though my mind is a fucking mess.

"Yup. All set."

"Perfect." I rush toward Wyatt, grab Kaydence from him, and then head for the truck, leaving the three of them behind. And even though Walker and I drove here together in his truck, and I know he'll be over here in just a few minutes to drive us back home, I need some space for as long as I can get—space from the man who is waking up a part of me I had accepted would be dormant for a long time.

"Stop bouncing your knee."

I look down at my leg, stop moving it, and then glare at Walker.

"It's going to be fine, Evelyn," Walker whispers, reaching over and grabbing my free hand since the other one is holding Kaydence on my lap.

Our mediation is in ten minutes, and I feel like I'm about to pass out.

It's not so much the idea of meeting John's parents like this—it's more that someone in that room is going to see through the farce of this marriage, and then I'll really lose my child because I was trying to manipulate the legal system.

Before I can argue with him, Chase comes striding up to us. "You two ready?"

"No," I admit as I stand.

"Yes, we are." Walker places his hand on the small of my back, gifting me with yet another thing to worry about: the way my body responds to him.

Our picture session on Sunday is still on my mind—and more specifically, that kiss. Even though I walked away from him and our friends right after, he hasn't uttered a word about it since. Which should make me grateful, but all it's done is make me more uneasy.

But I can't think about that right now. I need to get through this meeting, and then I can regroup and process my feelings about how quickly my life has started to feel like it's spinning out of control.

Chase leads us into the mediation room first, and I'm grateful to find it empty. A large mahogany oval table sits in the center of the room with cushioned desk chairs placed all around it. We choose the seats on the side that faces the door, and while I have my back turned, digging in the diaper bag for something to keep Kaydence occupied, I hear the voices of other people enter the room.

When I lift my head, my heart nearly stops. Mr. and Mrs. Schmitt stand there next to a man who looks old enough to be my father, who I gather must be their lawyer. John's mother looks at me with no emotion in her eyes whatsoever until she glances at Kaydence in my arms. And then her bottom lip trembles, and she buries her face in her husband's chest. The atmosphere in the room becomes extremely uncomfortable as we watch her fall apart, but I try to remain neutral.

I can't imagine the grief she must be carrying, losing her only son. If I lost Kaydence, I don't know what I would do.

Suddenly, the severity of this situation becomes even heavier.

"Let's all take a seat," Chase advises, waiting for everyone to settle in. And while we do, I take the opportunity to steal a glance at Walker.

The playful man who has been living with me for almost three weeks now is nowhere to be found. In his place is the man I encountered at the farmers market that day we saw each other for the first time in months—withdrawn, devoid of joy, and sitting like all the guilt of the world is resting on his shoulders.

I reach over and take his hand from where it's clenched in his lap. His eyes lift and find mine in that moment, and when his lips lift for just a second, I remember that this situation isn't just about me.

I needed that reminder.

"Good morning," another man declares as he enters the room. Chase explained that another lawyer would be present as the mediator for the meeting.

Nerves rush through me, but Walker squeezes my hand. I let out a long breath.

The man takes his seat, and then the meeting gets

underway. "I'm Gregory Sullivan. I will be mediating this custody case. I've taken the liberty to review both parties' declarations, but I would like for the lawyers to speak on behalf of their clients first." He nods toward Chase, and then I'm holding my breath again.

"My client, Evelyn Sumner, is defending her right to custody on the basis of biological maternity. The child in question has been with her since birth and is thriving in her home environment. There is no need for her to be placed in an alternative living situation. Honestly, the grounds of this contestation are lacking at best."

Mr. Sullivan nods, taking a few notes.

The Schmitts' lawyer speaks up next. "My clients are petitioning for custody on the grounds of an unstable home life for the child. A rocky home caused by the lack of two parents, as well as the history of Miss Sumner's personal affairs during her employment at Ferguson & Associates, serve to provide reason that she may not be capable of making sound judgments in regard to parenting."

My entire body goes numb. *Oh no, they did not.*

They went to Ferguson & Associates and dug up information? Information that I thought would be buried so the firm's reputation wouldn't be jeopardized?

"First of all, her last name isn't Sumner anymore. It's Gibson," Walker declares as Chase places his hand on his arm, reminding him that he shouldn't be speaking.

Goosebumps break out over my skin from the tone of his voice.

"Yes. Evelyn and Walker recently got married, so a single-parent household is no longer a viable argument," Chase explains.

"And when did this wedding take place?" Mr. Sullivan asks.

"Almost three weeks ago," Chase replies.

Mr. and Mrs. Schmitt turn their eyes to their attorney. They share a few whispers, and then their attorney speaks. "So right after the custody papers were delivered?"

"We were dating long before that," Walker declares again, making the tension in the room grow.

"Cool it, Walker." Chase leans over and speaks through clenched teeth.

"Nope. Sorry. Can't do that. Not when these people"—he gestures toward John's parents—"are trying to take a little girl from her mother." He leans forward in his seat, glaring at them. "Why on earth are you doing this? John was my best friend. I spent time over at your house. You guys were like a second family to me. And you don't even know Evelyn," he says, lifting my hand and kissing the back of it. My heart lurches from the sweet gesture and from hearing him defend me.

I don't think I've ever felt protected like this before.

"I lost my son," John's mom says through tears. "I didn't even know he was having a child until a week before he died."

I instantly become nauseous. So John kept me and Kaydence a secret from his parents. They must have been in shock when they saw me at the funeral, and perhaps this ploy to get Kaydence is a consequence of that.

"They weren't married," Mrs. Schmitt continues. "They were going to have this baby out of wedlock, and now she's being raised—"

"—by two capable adults who are in love," Walker finishes for her. My pulse is racing so fast that a hummingbird's wings might be slower.

"Yes, it does seem that the argument about Miss Sumner being a single parent is void now," Mr. Sullivan declares, cutting through the back and forth between Walker and John's mom.

"But what about Miss Sumner's history with her former employer?" the Schmitts' lawyer protests.

"Mrs. Gibson," Walker corrects the lawyer yet again. And something about the way he keeps reminding everyone that we're married causes warmth and need to pool low in my belly.

"This is a former employer, correct?" Chase asks, ignoring his interjection. "Then why is it relevant? Mrs. Gibson has been self-employed for the past nine years." He darts his eyes over to Walker, who's gleaming now at the mention of my new last name—though technically I haven't changed it yet. What's the point in doing that if this is all temporary, anyway?

John's mom buries her head in her hands again. I can hear Walker grinding his teeth together beside me.

"All right," Mr. Sullivan says. "It seems we have some issues that need to be investigated further." He turns to me and Walker. "I'm not going to lie, the timing of your nuptials is concerning. And even though the argument from Mr. and Mrs. Schmitt is lacking, they do have some rights to the child from a biological standpoint." He flips through the papers. "Since their son is the biological father, his rights were terminated upon his death. However, as grandparents, they can petition for custody or visitation."

"Visitation would have made more sense. But full custody? I don't understand why you couldn't have just talked to me about this instead of going this route," I finally chime in, looking across the table at these people my child is related to. "You could have sought me out, and we could have discussed this civilly instead of getting lawyers involved."

Since my parents aren't in the picture and won't ever be if I have anything to say about it, I would love for my daughter to have some relationship with John's parents. But the fact that they're pushing for full custody makes me wonder if their intentions will ever be pure. Will they settle for a relationship with their granddaughter as grandparents, or will they contest custody again if I do something they don't agree with as a parent? Can they even contest again after doing it once?

"Evelyn," Mr. Sullivan warns. He takes a deep breath and then folds his hands in front of him. "Look. There is a lot of emotion in this room right now, so I need everyone to listen and stop talking." We all bend our heads down, taking our reprimanding. "I'm not a judge, but here is what I see as our best option. Both parties have forty-five days to come to an agreement about custody, or this will be put before a judge. I'd like to settle this without getting a judge involved, so here's what I propose we do. We reconvene in forty-five days, once everyone has cooled off and some evidence can be collected. First, to prove that the child is being raised in a stable environment, a social worker will visit Mr. and Mrs. Gibson's residence randomly within the time frame dictated here today. If the social worker deems the home to be unstable or if he or she sees signs of neglect or anything along those lines, he or she will document that as evidence. Second, Mr. and Mrs. Schmitt will be ordered to attend grief counseling, one session per week until we meet again. And more detailed evidence regarding their reasoning to deem Mrs. Gibson as an unfit parent needs to be gathered. And third, both parties will develop a visitation plan that would work for their schedules so we have something to discuss next time in the hope that a simple court-ordered visitation plan can squash this contestation. Do both parties agree to these stipulations?"

Chase turns to me, arching a brow.

"Yes, I can do this," I reply, wanting to argue but knowing I shouldn't.

Mrs. Schmitt nods. "Okay. Yes."

"Perfect." Mr. Sullivan stands from his chair. "I will be in touch with both attorneys with a date and copies of the agreement."

We watch him and the Schmitts leave before Chase turns to me and Walker. "Well, that went well."

"Are you kidding? I can't believe he's even entertaining the idea of letting this continue," Walker says as he grabs Kaydence from my arms and holds her to his chest, kissing her temple.

The sight makes my insides melt, but then I remember what just happened as well. "And now I have to be on the lookout for some man or woman to investigate my home? Randomly? Do you know what my house looks like most days with a six-month-old?"

"This is a good thing," Chase says, clearly trying to calm both of us down. "He saw the grief on John's mother's face."

"Margaret. His mom's name is Margaret," Walker clarifies, pain etched across his features. It must be difficult to watch two people you've known for so long act out of character. It reminds me yet again that this situation is painful for him, too.

Chase nods. "Whatever her name is, she is clearly grieving the loss of her son and is using this as a way to cling to the last part of him she has. The chances of them winning this if it goes before a judge are slim to none, Evelyn. This is going to work out in your favor, but for now, you just need to wait this out and play by the rules."

Walker comes up beside me. "It's just forty-five days, Ev.

Can you handle it?" he asks as Kaydence rests her head on Walker's shoulder, both sets of their eyes focused on me.

No. No, I don't think I can—not when the two of them together makes me question whether this could turn into something permanent.

But I shove that thought out of my head as quickly as it came.

"I can handle it. I don't think that I should have to, but I guess it could have gone worse."

Chase nods, smiling. "That's the spirit. I'll let you know about the date and time of the next meeting. Now, if you'll excuse me, I have a courtroom to get to for another case."

Chase leaves, and suddenly the room feels two inches big with just me, Walker, and my daughter in it.

"It's going to be okay," Walker soothes.

"You seemed angrier than I did just now," I retort.

"I am, but I'm trying to remain optimistic for *you*, calm for *you* instead of punching my fist through the wall like I really want to." He winks and then closes the distance between us. I stare up into his eyes just like I did five days ago while taking pictures, those windows to his soul reading me like I'm a puzzle he's trying to solve. And for a second, I wish he would kiss me again, as if his kiss would give me the comfort I so desperately need right now.

But kisses muddle my mind, and the last thing I need is to lose focus during our arrangement now. We have a deadline, an ending, and if I want this to be just a blip in the past, I need my brain to remain intact when it comes to this man.

"Thank you," I murmur as he continues to study me.

"You're welcome." He places two fingers under my chin, tilting my head up so our eyes lock. "And just so we're clear, Evelyn," he starts, his eyes darting down to my lips and back up again. "Our last name is Gibson, and you'd better start fucking using it."

CHAPTER NINE

Walker

It's taken me six hours to calm down. After leaving the mediation with John's parents, I dropped the girls off at home and then headed to the gym. Thanks to a good workout session that burned off the adrenaline and gave me some space to clear my head, I feel ready to slip back into our routine and head home to Evelyn.

This morning got my blood pumping. Staring across the table at two people I've known for years and watching them act so uncharacteristically—cruel, even—caused something in me to snap. I couldn't sit back and listen to their attorney attack Evelyn like that, especially when that woman has been doing nothing but the best at raising Kaydence on her own. Now she has me, but she doesn't *need* me, a fact that she's reminded me of several times by now. And I know it's true. She's always been fiercely independent.

But I want her to *want* me—that's the problem now, and solving it is taking a lot of patience on my part.

Plus, the mention of her former employer and the scandal surrounding that has me itching to know more about the woman I married on a whim.

All I remember when she moved to Newberry Springs was Kelsea introducing us, explaining that Evelyn moved here from Dallas and was opening up a store to sell clothes. It never dawned on me to ask why an eighteen-year-old girl would leave the big city on her own for small-town life. But now I realize there's a lot more to her story than she's shared, and I need to know every detail.

More importantly, I *want* to know. I want to know this woman inside and out while I have the chance.

As her husband, these are details I *should* know, correct? And what if the social worker mentions something that I can't answer? Or a judge wants to dig deeper into our relationship to prove its validity?

It's the perfect reason to give Evelyn if she decides to push back, too.

I need to have all of the relevant information at my disposal, and part of me wonders if whatever happened plays a much larger role in why Evelyn is so reluctant to let people in—more specifically, me.

"Hey, you're home," Evelyn says as I round the corner of the kitchen.

"Yeah. Sorry, I got caught up at the gym and had to stop by the bank." I find Kaydence playing on the kitchen floor with all of the Tupperware lids. "This is new."

"Well, I was washing dishes, and she crawled over to the drawer and started whipping them out, and I just decided not to fight it because it was entertaining her." She shrugs.

"Makes sense." I reach for Kaydence, tossing her up in the air before she lands back in my arms. "You like to fly, don't you, little owl?"

Her giggle is contagious, so I do it again just so I can hear the sound. How anyone would want to take this little girl from her mother is beyond me—grandparents or not.

"How are you doing?" I ask Evelyn as I place Kaydence back down on the floor. She reaches for the lids again and slams them on the ground, creating her own music.

Evelyn blows out a breath. "I'm okay, I guess."

"This morning was a lot."

"It was." That's all she says, and instead of pressing her to talk about it more right now, I decide to change the subject and ease into that conversation later.

"I'm gonna go take a shower, and then I'll start making dinner."

"Oh, that's okay. I can cook today," she offers.

"Nope. I have something in mind, but I don't want to cook dirty."

Evelyn bites her bottom lip. "Probably not a good idea." She turns away from me, focusing back on the dishes in the sink, and I take her reaction as a good thing before I head down the hall toward the bathroom.

Even though it's killing me, I know that pursuing this woman slowly is working. Hell, that kiss during our photo-shoot was enough to tell me that the attraction between us isn't one-sided like I thought.

But I feel like I'm getting whiplash daily right now. She has moments where she lets her guard down and relaxes with me, and then we have events like today that bring the reality back into our arrangement, and I can feel her pull away. I feel like I'm making progress in proving to her that I'm in this by moving at a snail's pace, but I'm determined to recover from this morning by getting Evelyn to understand that she can open up to me a little bit tonight.

I strip off my workout clothes and start the shower. As I wait for it to heat up, I glance at my physique in the mirror. Then I think about the image of Evelyn biting her lip in the kitchen just now, and my cock starts to rise at the thought —what would it be like to bite that lip myself? Would she moan again when I did it? Could I lift her onto the counter, bite the pulse in her neck, and then stick my face between her legs to make her come on my tongue?

Entertaining these fantasies of mine while I'm in close proximity to her feels like putting a bottle of Jack Daniels in front of an alcoholic and telling them they can take a sip if they want to—but it comes with a price.

If I push her too soon, it could backfire. But fuck do I want this woman more than ever with each passing day.

I reach down to stroke myself right before I hop in the shower, knowing the only way this erection is going to go away is if I relieve the pressure under the water. But right before I step inside, a scream carries down the hallway from the kitchen.

In a panic, I grab my towel, wrap it around my waist, and race toward the other side of the house. I find Evelyn holding her hand over the sink as blood trickles down her arm.

"What happened?" I shout as I crowd her at the sink, still holding the towel around my waist because the corners of it barely meet.

"I broke a glass while I was washing it, and when I reached into the water to fish it out, I sliced my hand on it." She glances over at me, and when our eyes meet, hers drop, taking in my bare chest—and my raging fucking hard-on.

"Shit." I thrust my hips away from her as I debate what I should do. But the damage has been done. Evelyn continues to stare at my groin, which isn't helping my cock go down in the slightest, and a part of me likes that she's so entranced by the sight. But then again, she could find this situation awkward as hell and pull away from me even more.

Wanting to avoid the latter while still gripping the

towel at my waist, I turn around, grab a clean kitchen towel from the drawer, and then turn back to her. I take her injured hand and wrap the towel around it one-handed as I try to push past the awkwardness. "We need to keep pressure on it and elevate it," I say, leading her over to one of the stools at the kitchen island. She follows my lead, sitting down while peering around me, checking on Kaydence.

That sweet baby girl is making her owl sound, still banging Tupperware lids together, oblivious to the chaos around her.

"I'm sorry," Evelyn says, studying my chest again before looking away. Thankfully, my cock is starting to register that now is not the time to be ready to play and is finally going down as fast as a sinking ship.

"No need to be sorry. I just hope you don't need stitches."

"Yeah, me, too." She sighs and looks up toward the ceiling. "As if this day couldn't get any worse."

"Hey. The day isn't over yet. I say we try to end it on a good note."

She looks up at me with hope in her eyes. "As long as I don't have to go to the hospital, I think that might be possible."

Smiling, I bring her hand to my face, slowly opening the towel to check her cut. It's not too deep, which is a good sign. But she definitely needs to bandage it to keep pressure on it. "I don't think you'll need surgery, so that's good."

She chuckles. “But I need to wrap it up until the bleeding stops.”

“I have a first aid kit under the bathroom sink.”

“Perfect. I’ll be right back.”

I hustle down the hall, chuck the towel, pull my dirty shorts back on again so I have use of both my hands, and then grab the kit and march right back out to the kitchen.

“Here, let me see.” Evelyn is staring at my chest again, gnawing on her bottom lip now.

And fuck if that doesn’t do something for my ego.

Kaydence crawls over to us at that moment, clawing at my legs. So I lift her up, and she reaches for Evelyn. Evelyn takes her in her good arm and sets her daughter on her lap.

“Of course she wants to be held now.”

“She’s just curious.” I get to work cleaning the wound and dressing it.

“You know what you’re doing, don’t you?”

I lift my eyes to meet hers, smirking. “Firefighter-paramedic, remember?”

She huffs out a laugh. “Right.”

After about ten minutes, I declare her good as new and then step away, knowing I must still stink. But Evelyn sure as fuck doesn’t, and inhaling her vanilla scent for the last ten minutes is making my dick happy again.

“Thank you, Walker.”

“Of course, Ev. What are husbands for?” She rolls her eyes, but referring to myself as her husband is starting to taste pretty fucking sweet. “I’m gonna try to finish my shower now, so stay out of the kitchen. I'll finish the dishes."

"Okay . . ."

"I'm serious, Evelyn. Don't fucking go in there."

"No need to curse," she fires back.

"Just want you to know that I'm serious."

She drops her eyes mockingly down my body but walks into the living room, following my orders. And once I watch her sit on the couch with Kaydence in her lap, I feel confident returning to the bathroom.

I hop in the shower and scrub the filth off of me, letting my mind retreat back to my fantasy. But this time, I imagine Evelyn thanking me for wrapping up her hand in a way that makes me come in a matter of minutes—one in which she's on her knees and wrapping her lips around my cock.

~

After dinner is done and Kaydence is in bed, I come out of my room, expecting to find Evelyn on the couch. But the living room and the rest of the house are silent. That's when the light on the porch catches my eye, so I grab a beer from the fridge and slide open the back door, discovering the most gorgeous creature curled up in a cushioned chair with a glass of wine in her hand, staring off into space.

Her long blonde hair drapes over her shoulders and

down her chest, wafting slightly in the cool breeze. She's wearing a navy-blue tank top and pajama shorts, and her long tan legs, tucked up underneath her, peek out from under the fabric. Her lips wrap over the edge of her glass as she takes a sip of her white wine.

She's so fucking beautiful I can't help but stare at her for a moment before breaking the silence.

I want her so badly. I want her lips on mine again. I want her breasts pressed into my chest and her legs wrapped around my waist. I want to see her nipples, suck and bite on them until she's begging for my cock. And I want to hear the noises that she makes when she comes and the change in the color of her eyes when she's turned on. Do they darken? Lighten? Dilate or roll in the back of her head?

"You found me," she says softly, breaking me from my trance. I just jerked off almost two hours ago, and suddenly I'm fighting the need for release again.

"I did." Walking over to the other tan, cushioned chair, I take a seat and survey the backyard as I pop open my beer. There's plenty of space back here for a playground for Kaydence as she gets older as well as room for more plants. Evelyn has one tree planted in the back corner, but it definitely hasn't matured yet.

"This is my happy place," she says, drawing my eyes over to her. She takes another drink from her glass of wine, smacking her lips in approval as she stares down at it. "My grandmother said if you can't find joy in something simple like a cup of coffee, you certainly won't find it in a yacht."

I hum in approval. "Smart woman."

"She was." She smiles fondly. "Tonight, I'm trading the coffee for a glass of wine, but I think the message is still the same."

"It's the small things, right?"

"Yup."

"How's your hand?" I ask, noticing that she's holding her wine glass in the one that's not bandaged.

"Still throbbing a bit, but I'll live. Thank you again for taking care of me."

Yeah, I too have some throbbing in my body that I think I'll have to live with for a while longer.

"You're welcome." I take a long drink from my beer. "Do you mind if I ask you something?" I venture, knowing there's no better time than the present to follow through with my intentions for this evening.

Evelyn twists her head to look at me. "Depends on what it is . . ."

"Would my question deter you from answering?"

"Again, it depends on what you're going to ask me."

"I just want to know you better, Ev." Her face softens. "I think it's important that we know each other better, especially to keep up the farce of this marriage," I say, knowing my reasons are far beyond just that. But to Evelyn, that reason makes sense, and she sighs reluctantly, so I know

I've appealed to her logical side. "This morning showed us how important this is, don't you think?"

"Fine. But there are certain things I don't discuss, Walker, and I need you to respect that."

"Okay. You let me know if we broach those topics." *Hey. Progress is progress, right?*

She lifts her glass to her mouth again. "Oh, don't worry. I will."

Chuckling, I say, "I didn't doubt it for a second. Now, humor me. Why is your shop called Luna?"

The corner of her mouth tips up. "That was not the question I anticipated coming out of your mouth just now."

Shrugging my shoulder, I say, "I want to know."

Evelyn clears her throat and then turns to look at me better. The soft porch lights allow me to see her more clearly now, and before I fall down a rabbit hole of pining after this woman some more, I tell my brain to focus on what she's saying. "Luna is the goddess of the moon in Roman mythology."

"That's a very specific answer."

"Well, that was a very specific question."

"Okay . . . so you're into mythology."

Evelyn shakes her head. "Nope. But on my drive to Newberry Springs from Dallas, I stopped by a gas station to load up on snacks, a requirement of any road trip." I nod. "There was a section of greeting cards in one of the back aisles. That people would buy something like that at a gas station boggled my mind, but I started reading them, and one said something that stuck with me."

"Oh, this has to be good." I lift my beer to my lips, taking a sip as I wait for her reply.

"It was life-changing for *me*, Walker. You don't have to understand it, but you asked, so I'm being honest."

I grow more serious in an instant. "I'm all ears, Ev. Tell me. I honestly want to know."

She shakes her head at me, blinking as the memory registers on her face. "The card said, 'Like the moon, we must go through phases of emptiness to feel full again. So remember, you do not have to be whole in order to shine.'"

A rush of goosebumps pebble on my arm. "Damn. That's deep. And that explains all of the pictures of the moon around your house now."

She bobs her chin. "It was exactly what I needed to hear at that moment, like a reminder that I made the right decision to leave Dallas."

Here it is, Walker. Here's your opening to dig deeper. "So why did you leave, Ev? Does it have anything to do with your employment at Ferguson & Associates that they brought up today?"

Her spine instantly stiffens. "I don't want to talk about that, Walker."

"Evelyn . . . I need to know these things. Shouldn't your husband know what they're referencing so I'm not caught off guard and don't lose face in front of them or, more importantly, the social worker?"

She avoids my eyes, staring out over the backyard again. I can see the glass of wine in her hand shaking, the liquid threatening to spill over the rim as the time between us speaking grows longer by the second.

"Evelyn . . ."

"I'll just say this, and then this topic is closed, Walker. Okay?" She finally turns to me, gauging my reaction.

"Okay," I reply, knowing that I have to take whatever she's going to offer to me at this point and just accept it for the time being.

"I worked for that company through high school. My father was best friends with the owner, and my parents insisted that I delve into the world of investment management so that I could be filthy rich like them. They weren't pushing me to get married but to be able to stand on my own two feet. I was lucky, or so I thought. So I started there at sixteen, learning the ropes, basically interning for a job that I would start doing for real as soon as I graduated from high school. Seth Ferguson told me he wouldn't even require me to have a college degree since I would have so much hands-on experience. But when I graduated, things didn't turn out the way I thought they would, so I quit and moved away."

Something about that story leaves me yearning for more, like there are details she's purposely leaving out. But I can't push at this moment. I'm already riding the line of pissing her off again, so I hum and stare out at the backyard as the wheels in my brain keep spinning.

"No comment?" Her voice cuts through the silence.

"Well, I have more questions, but I know you won't answer them, so I'm keeping them to myself."

She snorts. "You're not a foolish man after all."

"I'm sorry that whatever happened to you made you feel the need to run from your home, though, Evelyn." She meets my eyes as we turn to face each other again. "I truly am."

"I'm not," she replies, bluntly. "Where I lived before wasn't a home, Walker. I didn't have a childhood like you: two parents who cared about me, who taught me how to take care of myself or supported me. Thank God I had a passion for fashion and an inheritance from my grandmother that I could access at eighteen. That's how I opened Luna and ventured out on my own." I tilt my head at her, soaking up every piece of information she's giving me right now without having to ask for it. "I had a fashion blog I started at sixteen, and as I gained a following, I started working with designers who wanted me to feature their stuff. When I wasn't working at Ferguson & Associates, I was working on my blog. I still post on social media now, and the online portion of my business does far better than the store does. But I love that shop. It represents something tangible that I've done all on my own. It reminds me that I didn't have to be full to shine, that feeling empty for a while led to something better. And that was Newberry Springs . . . and Kelsea. I wouldn't have survived the past nine years without her."

"Thank you for sharing that with me."

"You're welcome," she says, taking another sip from her wine glass.

"Can I ask you one more thing?"

"Maybe . . ."

"Where are your parents? Don't they want to help? Be the doting grandma and grandpa?"

"Ha. No. And they never will get the chance to."

"Why not?"

"Well, it's kind of hard to be grandparents when they don't even know they have a granddaughter."

I sit up in my seat now. "Holy shit. Why, Evelyn?"

"Because my parents aren't good people, and I'll be damned if they ever make my daughter feel the way they've made me feel."

"What did they do?"

"And that's the end of this conversation," she says.

I want to reply with, *Don't. Don't fucking shut me out. I'm in this, Evelyn. I'm here, aren't I? If I'm your husband and we're as in love as we're trying to convince everyone that we are, isn't this something I should know? And secondly, I want you to let me in, dammit. Let me know you, the woman who captured my attention over a year ago, the one I wish I could have loved from the beginning.*

But that won't get me anywhere I want to be at this moment. So instead, I say, "Okay. My wife has spoken."

Luckily, she chuckles at that and takes another sip of her wine. I mimic her, drinking from my beer, and then she breaks the silence this time. "Can I ask *you* a question?"

"Absolutely. It's only fair."

Her lips lift in a mischievous grin as she rests her chin on her shoulder, leaning on the arm of her chair, directing her gaze to me again. "Why did you want to be a fire-fighter? It was the hose, right? Every boy's fantasy is to be able to play with a hose for a living, even if it's not their own."

I toss my head back, barking out a laugh. "Oh, fuck. I needed that laugh, thank you." She shrugs like what she said was no big deal. I already knew that Evelyn had a sense of humor, but getting a front-row seat to it and having it directed at me only deepens this attraction I have toward her.

Her witty personality is such a fucking turn-on.

"Answer the question."

After I compose myself, I say, "Well, I didn't want to go to college like my brothers did. I knew that early on, so I thought of what I could do that would be physically demanding, keep me busy and focused, but also help people. I always had too much energy to burn—ask my mother, she'll tell you. I was the one getting into trouble the most out of the three of us boys."

"So you became a firefighter."

"I did. The hose was just an added bonus." She laughs this time before taking another drink of her wine. "Little did I know that most days, the job is pretty boring. It used to bother me, but now I welcome those days." It means no one is dying or trapped in a car or experiencing a life-changing health scare that could alter their entire existence.

"The job has to have hard days, doesn't it?"

"None more tough than the night John died," I say. The lightness of our conversation before instantly disappears, and I find my mind flashing back through that night like it always does when I let myself think about it.

"I couldn't carry guilt like that, knowing I couldn't save everyone."

"It's a burden I wasn't aware of when I went into this career, Evelyn, if I'm being honest. I thought I'd be able to save everyone that needed help. But when I can't . . ." I don't finish the sentence, I just drain the rest of my beer and wipe my mouth with the back of my hand.

My mother found me the day after I lost my first victim in a car accident. I was staring at the wall, letting the image of the woman who collided with a big rig greet me every time I closed my eyelids. So I wouldn't go to sleep. I couldn't, because I didn't want to be haunted by the wreckage I saw that day.

Momma asked me if this was what I really wanted to do with my life, and I told her yes. But in that moment, I honestly wasn't so sure.

"If you're going to do this job, you have to remember that for every person you don't save, there will be three that you do," I say out loud.

"What?"

Finding Evelyn's eyes, I explain, "That's what Momma told me the first time I lost someone on duty. And I keep that saying in the back of my mind for those hard days." I clear my throat as my eyes begin to sting. "I just didn't know how hard it would be to remind myself of that when the person I lost was someone close to me."

Evelyn stands from her chair and walks over to me, holding her wine. "It wasn't your fault, Walker."

"I'm trying to make myself believe that, Ev, I am."

She brushes my hair back from my face as I stare up at her. And fuck, her touch lights my skin on fire, sending a flame all the way down to my cock. "We're quite the pair, aren't we?"

A pair of souls who could find solace in each other—yes.

"I think we're pretty strong people, Evelyn . . . especially you."

"Funny. I was thinking the same thing about *you*."

Crickets chirp in the background, the breeze flows around us under the patio, but all I see is this woman who opened up to me tonight like I wanted. If this were a reciprocal relationship, one where we were both aware that I was pursuing her, I'd yank her down onto my lap and kiss the shit out of her, drown in her body to remind me that I'm still alive.

"Any other questions you want to ask me?" she teases with a playful grin on her lips.

"I think I'll save them for another night. Keep you wondering what it is that I want to know."

"Trust me, Walker. I'm not that interesting."

Oh, that's where you're wrong, Evelyn. That's where you are so fucking wrong.

CHAPTER TEN

Evelyn

"I wore the top I purchased from you last week on a date, and he couldn't stop complimenting me on it." A girl I recognize from the farmers market last week returned today to give me an update on the success of her purchase.

"I'm so glad to hear that!"

"It's so hard for me to find shirts that flatter my shape. Having small boobs sucks sometimes."

"Girl, you're preaching to the choir," I say, referencing my modest chest. My boobs swelled a little after I had

Kaydence, but nursing did not go well for me, so my milk dried up fast, leaving me with slightly deflated boobs now.

"Your boobs are not small," Kelsea chastises me from the Gibson Ranch booth beside me.

"I second that, sweetheart," Walker says, winking at me when I turn to face him. His comment warms my entire body from the top of my head to the tips of my toes.

I know he said that because we're in public and that's something a loving husband would say to his wife, especially if she's speaking negatively about herself. But something about the tone of his voice tells me that it wasn't just for show—that perhaps he truly feels that way.

Yeah, I'm not ready to unpack that just yet.

"Well, I just wanted to say thank you again. I will be stopping by the store this weekend to spend more of my money," the girl says through a laugh.

"I look forward to seeing you. Here's a twenty-percent-off coupon you can use when you pop in." I hand the paper to her, watching her eyes light up.

"Oh my God. Thank you so much!"

"No problem. Take care."

The girl walks off, shoving the coupon in her purse and heading in the direction of the food vendors just as Kelsea comes up beside me. "Well, that sounded like a happy customer."

"Right? I love that. That's the part of this job I enjoy the most, making any woman feel comfortable in her clothes and therefore her own skin."

It's true. Every woman deserves to feel beautiful, and I take pride in helping women see that. I make sure I carry clothes that fit every type of body and never shy away from experimenting with new styles and fabrics that I think customers will love. My shop carries a lot of western-style fare—very country-chic, if you will. But even someone *not* from Texas can find clothing that will suit their style in my store.

Unfortunately, the high I was just feeling deflates as a group of women I've seen around town numerous times walks past my booth, casting me a side-eye glance and then whispering among themselves.

"What's their problem?" Kelsea asks. And when I turn to face her, I see Walker holding Kaydence behind her, pretending that he's eating her hands as she giggles.

Jesus. I should be thrilled at watching the two of them together, but in that moment, I know that those women weren't looking at the clothes I sell—they were looking at my husband doting on my daughter, my husband and the best friend of her dead father.

"It's nothing," I say, shifting my attention to organizing the jewelry on the table in front of me, even though nothing is out of place.

"What's going on?" Kelsea prods as I avoid looking at her.

"It's fine. Just drop it."

"Seems she found a man to replace her baby daddy." Mumbles from next door catch my ears as I look up and see the group of girls talking to the owner of the stand two booths down from us.

"Are they talking about you?" Kelsea places her hands on her hips.

"Seems they might be." Turning my back to them, I try to ignore them, but then I hear what they say next.

"I mean, if I could have that man instead of the one she had before, I'd trade up, too."

"Are you fucking kidding me?" Walker shouts as he comes out from under his booth, still holding my daughter, prepared to defend my honor. And as much as I appreciate him wanting to, I know it would only make matters worse.

This isn't the first time I've heard people talking like this. When Kelsea and I went to lunch at Rose's Diner just after Walker and I got married, I swore I caught people staring and whispering. But since then, it's happened more and more—at the grocery store, at Walmart, even at my own shop as people stroll around the boutique, pretending they're shopping. But really, they're just there for themselves—to see the woman who had a baby by one man and then married his best friend.

I press my hand against Walker's chest, stopping him from going any further. "Walker. Don't. *Please.*"

His eyes stay trained on the women behind me, but I can't turn around. I'm too busy admiring the harshness of Walker's jaw as he clenches his teeth together while carrying my child like she's the most precious cargo and he's afraid to break her.

He's both strong and soft in this moment, confusing me about my growing feelings for him even more.

Walker reaches for my waist and pulls me into him, making me almost trip as I struggle to stay upright. He tips my chin up with two fingers and then presses a soft kiss to my lips, catching me completely off guard—especially because I want more when his lips leave mine all too soon.

But when I look behind us, the girls snicker and then finally walk away, flipping their hair over their shoulders as they do.

"You didn't need to do that," I say, pushing myself off of him.

"Fuck them, Evelyn. You can't worry about their opinions. They're not the ones living your life."

"I'm aware."

"And you need to remember why we're doing this."

"Why don't you remind me?" I ask, planting my hands on my hips as Kelsea slowly retreats behind me.

But right now, the question seems valid. It's been almost a week since the mediation, and the reason for this marriage is growing fuzzier the more my attraction to Walker grows. And after that display of affection, I need a reminder of why we're doing this again. I need him to put my feelings in their place so that they know not to come out at the most inopportune times.

When we sat on my porch last week and talked, something in me shifted. Suddenly, I wasn't just battling a physical attraction—I was fighting against Walker pushing me to open up, not judging me for what I shared with him, and making me feel like I could tell him anything.

That shit is what's messing with my brain right now.

"For Kaydence," he finally says, adjusting her in his arms.

No other words are spoken between us. And they don't need to be. His reminder was perfectly clear and exactly what I needed to hear.

I go back to my booth, trying to brush off the incident that just occurred and focus on each and every customer who comes by. In a lull between people, Kelsea comes up to me, rubbing my shoulder. "You okay?"

"Yeah, I'm fine."

"As a woman myself, I know for a fact that the word *fine* is a dangerous one for us."

Huffing out a laugh, I reply, "What do you want me to say?"

"How about the truth?"

I lift my head to argue with her some more, but the sight I see out of the corner of my eye catches my attention and stops me from speaking.

Walker is holding Kaydence again, walking down the street lined with booths. The sun is beating down on them, casting them in a yellow haze that makes the sight even more breathtaking. He has a red balloon in one of his hands, showing it to my daughter as she shrieks with excitement. The vision of them instantly makes me smile, but then it fades as Kelsea pulls me out of my moment just as I feel my eyes start to well.

"Evelyn . . . what's wrong?"

"I just . . . I never thought she'd have this."

"Have what?"

Gesturing toward them, I answer, "A man in her life. A father figure."

"Oh, honey." She pulls me into her arms as I close my eyes and fight off the tears threatening to spill. I think that's one of my worst fears in all of this—her losing Walker, too.

Are you just afraid of your daughter losing Walker, or are you afraid of losing him for yourself, too, Evelyn?

I'm growing attached to him. I think that's what's got me so emotional this morning. Or maybe I'm about to start my period.

Either way, every day that passes with Walker around serves as a reminder of how alone I've been for so long. With the exception of Kelsea, I've created a life of independence, and I've thrived that way. But since Kaydence entered the picture, that solitary world I craved before becomes less and less enticing, and a new yearning has taken its place—one that is being exacerbated by the handsome, caring, selfless man walking right toward me.

God, I don't deserve him. And he has no idea what he's doing to me, either.

"What's going on?" Walker asks as he returns to the booth. My baby girl is tugging on the string in his hands, trying to get the balloon for herself, probably to slobber all over it.

"I'm fine," I say, swiping under my eyes.

"You and Kaydence were just too cute together," Kelsea explains. "And you know us girls . . . always crying." She shrugs nonchalantly, trying to convince him I wasn't just having a breakdown.

"Oh, okay . . ." His brow furrows as he studies me, but then he says, "I think she needs a diaper change or she just let out one hell of a fart just now."

Laughing, I grab her from his arms. "I can do it."

"I was going to do it, I just needed someone to hold onto this while I did," he says, lifting his eyes to the balloon he's still holding.

"No, it's okay. I've got it. Thanks for entertaining her."

"Of course. We have fun together, don't we, little owl?" Kaydence lets out her owllike sound, and Walker gives it right back to her.

Kelsea has hearts in her eyes as she watches them, and if I looked in a mirror, I bet I look the same way.

Don't get attached, Evelyn.

Walker stands tall again, peering down at me. And as he cups my face in his palm, his words fight like hell to break through the barrier I am trying to erect higher and stronger as time progresses. "I haven't had this much fun at the farmers market since before I can remember. I'm kind of getting used to spending my days with you two. Thanks for letting me."

Yeah, I'm kind of getting used to spending my days with you, too.

~

"Thank you. Hope to see you again soon." I hand the bag containing a few dresses and tops to the customer, smiling at her as she walks away happy. Yesterday was a roller-coaster day, one where my emotions were so up and down, I felt like I was going crazy. But this morning, I woke up determined to focus on my store and my daughter and remind myself that I'm in control of my life and my feelings.

"Today is a good day," I mumble to myself, nodding as Kaydence yells from her playpen behind me, blatantly asking for my attention.

"What's up, baby girl?" I reach in and pull her out, kissing her cheek. "You hungry? It's almost lunchtime."

One of the perks of being my own boss is that I'm able to keep my baby with me while I work. I don't come into the shop every day anymore or stay all day long like I used to—I hired a few employees while I was pregnant because I knew I'd need the help once my daughter arrived. But when I'm here, I can have her with me, and that gives me a sense of peace, knowing I won't miss out on all of these stages of hers. Her most recent one is grabbing my hair every second she can.

"Ouch, baby."

"Ugh. Kids." I spin around to find Janise Brown standing on the opposite side of the register counter, her lips curled up as she stares at my daughter. I didn't even hear the chime above the door, so she must have slipped in when my previous customer left.

"Excuse me?"

She visibly shudders. "I don't understand why people think babies are so cute. They're grabby, covered in drool, and smell half the time," she continues as Kaydence blows spit bubbles at that very moment.

That's right, baby girl. Show her just how gross you can be.

"Well, the door is right behind you if she's bothering you that much." Hoisting my daughter on my hip, I glare at the woman standing before me.

Janise is Wyatt's ex from high school, and her father is now the mayor of Newberry Springs. She was a self-absorbed person while Wyatt, Walker, and Kelsea were growing up—so they've told me—and apparently, nothing much has changed.

When Kelsea and Wyatt were figuring out their feelings for one another last year, Janise tried to capture Wyatt's attention again with no luck whatsoever. But since then, she likes to stick herself into the Gibson brothers' business any chance she can get. Maybe she's trying to convince Wyatt or herself that he missed out on something, but it just makes her seem desperate.

And I assume that's why she's here right now.

"Can I help you?" I ask since she just stands there, continuing to stare at my child.

"Not really. I just wanted to come in and see what all the fuss was about."

"Care to explain?"

"Well, I mean, if Walker married *you,* there had to be a reason. I know it isn't this store," she says, circling her eyes around the room. "And it certainly can't be because of your baby." She grimaces again.

"Funny. I don't give a rat's ass about your opinion of my life. In fact, I think you've just reminded me to exercise my right as a business owner to refuse service to anyone I want. Congratulations, you've just made that list."

She rolls her eyes. "Please. It's not like I was going to buy anything, anyway."

"Then leave before I call the cops and give you a legal reason to stay the hell away from me and my daughter."

Janise smirks as she takes a step toward the door. "How did you do it, then? Did you and Walker sneak around while Schmitty was still alive? Do you even know if that's Schmitty's kid or Walker's, Evelyn?"

"Go to hell, Janise, and get the fuck out of my store!" I raise my voice, even though doing so lets her know that her words got to me. But at this moment, I don't care. It's better than punching her in the face and dragging her out by her hair like I really want to.

"Good luck keeping him, Evelyn. Walker will get tired

of playing baby daddy sooner or later, and then what will you do?"

"Fuck you, Janise. Now leave."

She doesn't say another word, and she doesn't have to. The slimy smile on her face as she exits my shop lets us both know that she won that round.

My entire body is shaking as I stand there fuming, wondering how someone gets the nerve to go into a place of business and verbally attack the owner like that.

Part of me wants to call Walker and let him know what happened. But what would he do? And more importantly, I don't need him to fight my battles. I can do that on my own —even though it does feel nice when he defends me. He's done it several times already, but I can't depend on him to do that forever.

This is just a consequence of agreeing to marry him. It may be helping my daughter, which is really what matters at the end of the day, but it's wearing on me.

I'm not someone who generally cares about what people think. I've lived my life too long in that kind of world to know that no good can come of it. And as soon as my life fell apart back in Dallas, I knew I would never put myself in a position again that would alter how I feel about myself and who I am as a person.

How I think about me is the only opinion that matters in this world. But right now, I feel pretty shitty and could really use a stiff drink.

As if the universe knows to rub salt in my wounds, and

not the kind that rims a margarita glass, my phone starts vibrating on the counter beside me. When I see my mother's name on the screen, my blood pressure rises even more.

I haven't heard from her in so long that just wondering about her reason for reaching out makes me anxious. She'll call every once in a while, just to make sure I'm not doing anything to sully the family name. But as I think about it, it's probably been almost a year since I've heard from her.

Knowing I can either face this right now and just take all the shit the universe wants to give me all at once or ignore her and risk causing yet another day full of emotional turmoil down the road, I settle on the former choice and swipe across the screen as Kaydence shoves my hair in her mouth.

"Hello?"

"Evelyn." It's not even a warm greeting. It slides off her tongue with a hint of annoyance.

"What can I do for you, Mom?"

"Well, I need to verify some recent information with you."

"Okay . . ."

"Records indicate that you had a child—is that correct?"

My mouth gapes. Records? Did they run a background check on me or something? Did my hospital records come up?

Knowing there's no point in asking *how* they found out, I just answer. "Yes, it's true."

"Goodness, Evelyn." There's that disappointment I've been waiting to hear. "You couldn't let us know?"

"Why do you care? It's not like you're going to rush down here and be the grandparents she needs."

"No, but we have a reputation to uphold. You know this. And something like a child being raised out of wedlock is a disgrace to the Sumner name."

That's what it always comes down to—protecting their precious reputation.

"Well, I'm actually married, too, now, so no need to worry about that." If she hasn't mentioned that, perhaps her "records" are a few weeks old.

"At least there's that."

"Heaven forbid I be a single mom, right?"

Her scoff comes through the line before a rustle of papers. "Well, I got the information I needed from you, so I best be going."

"Nice to speak with you, Mom. Hope you and Dad are enjoying your child-free life with no responsibilities to me and my well-being," I spit out.

"Don't be dramatic, Evelyn. And try to stay out of trouble so we don't have more messes to bury," she says before ending the call.

I toss my phone on the counter and blink away the tears filling my eyes. I'm not sad. I'm angry. Furious. Have you ever been so mad that you start to cry?

My past is haunting me just as much as my future today, and I'm not sure I can take much more. Knowing that staying in the shop will make me feel better, I reach for Kaydence's diaper bag, settle her into her highchair, and serve us both lunch, counting down the minutes until I can go home and drown my frustrations in wine—lots and lots of wine.

~

By the time I make it home, I'm more angry than I was earlier, but at least the tears have stopped. The comforting reality of today is that I won't have to expect a phone call from my mother for a good while now, and if Janise knows what's good for her, she'll stay the hell out of my store, too.

When I step through the door, I anticipate Walker being in the kitchen. He said he had a new recipe that he wanted to try making tonight. But the sight before me stops me in my tracks and blows all of my preconceived notions out of the water.

Walker is hanging up a photo on the wall—a canvas, more specifically. And on it is a picture from Kaydence's six-month photo session, one of the three of us together.

It's a shot even Kelsea couldn't pose if she tried. Kaydence is smiling at the camera, her toothless grin impeccably perfect and adorable. Walker is looking down at me with a crinkle at the corners of his eyes that speaks of admiration and devotion.

I don't know that a man has ever looked at me like that.

Then there's me, glancing up at him, a small smile on

my lips that looks as though I was trying not to laugh at something he said. But the easiness between the three of us is what has my heart beating wildly.

We look like a family.

"What are you doing?" I ask as I set the diaper bag and Kaydence's car seat on the floor. She's still strapped in, but she's content for the time being, and at this moment, I'm too distracted by the man in front of me to reach for her just yet.

"I wanted to surprise you before you got home, but you're a tad early." He steps back, surveying his work proudly, propping his hands on his hips. "What do you think?"

"I didn't realize the pictures were done." This means that Kelsea showed them to Walker, and either she sought him out or he asked for them, bypassing me entirely. I might just need to have a conversation with my best friend about why that was.

"They aren't entirely, but I thought it would be a good idea to have something like this up on the wall in case the social worker stops by, you know?"

Ah. There's the reasoning behind this gesture. *This is a transactional relationship, remember, Evelyn?*

But the more I tell myself that, the more I wonder exactly what Walker is getting out of this? Especially after days like today where I can't help but question if he's faced the same scrutiny I have.

"I see." I reach down, take my baby girl out of the car seat, and walk her over to her bouncer, one of those that has toys all around that she can spin in. She's been obsessed with this thing lately. And when I stand up, I come face-to-face with a photo from our wedding at the courthouse on the mantel.

Seems my husband has been busy today concocting a plan to wreak havoc on my emotions. Maybe he, my mom, and Janise decided to team up.

"What's wrong?" Walker's brow furrows when I meet his gaze.

"Nothing. You just didn't need to do that." I turn my back to him and head for the kitchen, seeking out the wine I've been thinking about all day.

Gestures like this make me even more confused. And after the day I've had, I need some space. But by the sound of Walker's footsteps behind me, it seems like I'm not going to get it.

"I know I didn't *need* to. I fucking *wanted* to, Evelyn." The sharpness of his voice makes me retract a bit. "Did something happen today? You're clearly pissed, but I don't think it has to do with the picture I hung up."

Slamming the fridge shut, I take the bottle of wine over to the counter and dig in the drawer for my wine opener. "Oh, I had a *lovely* day. In fact, it just felt like the shit from yesterday carried over right into today."

"Tell me about it."

I shake my head, not wanting to relive it. I've already

been stewing about it for the past five hours. But Walker doesn't accept that.

"I need you to talk to me, Evelyn."

"Why?" I pop my head up and meet his eyes.

"Because we're fucking married, and I'm not a goddamn mind reader," he says, planting his hands on his hips again.

"We're only married in title, Walker. I don't have to tell you shit." I know I'm acting childish right now, but the inquisitions I faced from Janise and my mother today are making me want to push back against anyone who tries to tell me what to do at the moment. How dare either of those women express their opinions about my life? And how dare Walker push me to talk when I don't have to do anything I don't want to?

He rounds the kitchen island, crowding me against the cabinets. "We may not be in love, but I still fucking care about you, Ev. I hope to God you realize that." His eyes dance back and forth between mine. And then he reaches up and tucks a strand of my hair behind my ear, trailing his finger down my neck. "We're friends. You can talk to me. Let me in. Whatever it is, you don't have to handle it alone."

But that's the only way I know how to operate . . . and the way that you're touching me right now doesn't feel like we're only friends.

"Janise came into the store today," I admit, not going into detail.

Walker's jaw hardens. "Fuck her. I can only imagine what she said."

"Basically what those girls at the farmers market did yesterday."

Walker breathes out a harsh breath. "Did you kick her ass?"

"Almost." The corner of his mouth tips up in approval. "And then my mother called."

His jaw slackens now. After our conversation the other night, Walker knows that I don't have the best relationship with my parents. And for some reason, it feels good to know that he knows that. "What did she say?"

"She was just calling to confirm that I had a child. Apparently, they've been keeping tabs on me, checking hospital records and all that."

"Jesus."

"Yeah. It was a truly memorable conversation," I say sarcastically. "And I told them that I'm married now, too. That actually made her happier since having a child out of wedlock is a sin, apparently."

"Fuck, Ev. I'm sorry." He leans forward and kisses my forehead. And like a balm soothing a sting, that move makes my entire body relax. "Thank you for telling me those things. See? Was that so hard?" Walker cups the side of my face now, and suddenly, I find it hard to breathe. "You can talk to me about anything. I'll always listen and help however I can."

This is what he does to me, as if his voice and touch soothe my demons and insecurities. I feel like I can face anything when he's standing this close, like I have someone on my team that isn't Kelsea.

And it must be the endorphins running through me paired with the mental exhaustion from today that propels me to demand, "Kiss me, Walker."

His eyes bounce back and forth between mine. In a second, I instantly regret saying the words. That's not what I wanted to say, but my brain didn't get the memo from my heart fast enough, I guess.

Jesus, what was I thinking? I haven't even had any wine yet, so I can't even blame my outburst on that.

But before I can move away, Walker grips my jaw, holding me in place, and slams his mouth to mine, making all of my self-doubt fly right out the window.

Walker stumbles back for a second as I push against him before his arms encase me and hold me to his chest as his lips work mine over. With each pass of his tongue, I let the anger of today flit away. With each groan from him, I'm reminded of what it feels like to be wanted by someone. And with every second he holds me to him like I might run away if he doesn't hold on that tight, I feel myself give in to that support.

This wasn't supposed to happen. This marriage was about my daughter being able to stay with me where she belongs. But somewhere along the way, my heart started telling me that maybe something else could come out of this, too.

I just don't want to admit that yet, because then it

means I have something to lose—something *more* to lose than I already have.

The way this man makes me feel is unlike anything I've experienced. I can do the physical stuff in a relationship. But feelings?

Yeah, I don't have much experience with those.

What I *do* have experience with is sex, and every time this man touches me, he makes my entire body come alive. I can admit that. But it's different, too.

Walker's kiss doesn't feel like a means to an end. It's full of passion, possession, and reverence. His mouth commands mine as he pushes me up against the counter again, pressing his hips into me, showing me how much his body wants me.

But is that all this is?

Could we enjoy the physical benefits of being married without the muddled feelings? The answer in my brain is a resounding *no*.

Walker breaks our kiss, leaving us both breathless without releasing me from his arms yet. His eyes are so dark, they're almost black, and the rise and fall of our chests is practically in sync.

I don't know why I wanted him to kiss me in that moment. Maybe I just needed to feel wanted, desired by someone or something instead of the person who is always cast aside.

And then I let out the question I didn't even realize I've been stewing on all day.

"What happens when this is all over, Walker?" I ask, peering up at him. I can feel how hard he is between us, and knowing that makes me want to push for more. But I don't know if I can handle that until I understand exactly what I'm feeling at this moment. "What happens when I'm no longer your wife?"

"I . . . I don't have the answer to that yet, Evelyn." He clears his throat and stands up taller. "But I do know this. As long as we're together, everyone will know that you're mine. And no matter what happens between *us,* Evelyn, I will always be there for Kaydence in any way she needs. *That* you shouldn't question one bit. Okay?"

"Okay."

He lets out a sigh and then reluctantly pulls away from me, running a hand through his hair. "The fire station fundraiser is this coming weekend."

Dread fills my gut. "Oh, yeah."

"I want you there," he says as he faces me. "I know this past week has been rough. People have opinions that we can't change, Ev. But you being there with me will send a message loud and clear. This is *real,* and people just need to accept it."

Is this real? After that kiss, my brain is telling me that *something* between us is.

"I'll be there, Walker. You might have to drag me kicking and screaming, but I'll be there."

His body visibly relaxes. "Great. My mom agreed to

watch Kaydence, too, so there's one less excuse you can use."

Oh, God. Momma G is going to babysit? I've barely spoken to the woman since I married her son without her knowing. Great. Now there are even more reasons for the mounting anxiety in my chest to grow. Not only do I have to face the entire station full of men who knew John, knew that we were sleeping together, and know that I married Walker now—but I also have to face the two people who were hurt by our actions more than anyone: Mr. and Mrs. Gibson.

Yet another reason this arrangement we've entered into is growing more complicated by the day.

"Well, I don't know about you, but I'm hungry." Walker tosses his thumb over his shoulder, not waiting for me to argue with him about the information he just spewed. "Gonna get dinner started."

"Okay."

And just like that, we slip into our normal routine again, never once bringing up that kiss. And I'm not sure if that's a good thing for me or not.

CHAPTER ELEVEN

Walker

"Kiss me, Walker." Evelyn's lust-filled voice is music to my ears.

I've been waiting for this for so long that I give myself just a few more seconds before my fantasy becomes reality. And then I slam my lips down on hers and drown in her mouth, showing her another way, besides alcohol, to forget the bullshit of life.

She's had a rough day. I could see it on her face the second she walked through the door. Pushing her to open up is becoming a little easier with each passing day that we spend together, but when her walls go up—fuck, does she build them high.

"Walker." Her voice hums against my lips as I press my cock into her stomach. I'm wearing fairly thin gym shorts, so I know she can feel what she's doing to me.

"Fuck, Evelyn. God, I want you so fucking much."

"Then take me, Walker. Own me. Make me forget about today."

I lean back and stare down into her eyes, and then I notice she's biting her bottom lip again. And shit, when she does that, my dick fucking twitches.

I lift her up on the counter and slide her shorts down her legs, tossing them to the side. And then I stare down at her pussy, admiring the wet spot on the front of the navy lace thong.

I fucking did that to her.

"I'm gonna lick your pussy so fucking good, Evelyn, because honestly? I feel like I was put on this earth to do exactly that at this moment."

"Prove it," she taunts me, planting her heels on the counter beside her.

But when I begin to lower myself to the sweet heaven between her legs, smoke fills the air around us. "What the fuck?" Flames grow from the ground, and I spin to see them encircling us in orange and yellow.

"Evelyn!" I shout, but when I turn back around to look at her, she's gone. "Evelyn! Where the fuck did you go?"

"Walker!" she calls out, but I can't tell where her voice is coming from. The flames grow ten feet tall, and the smoke gets so bad I can barely see.

But then a figure comes out of the chaos, and suddenly, I'm face-to-face with my best friend.

He's here. What the fuck is he doing here?

"You've got to save them, Walker," John says to me, standing stoically still. The fire doesn't even touch him, but I can still see it all around us.

"Where did they go, man?"

"You have to save them, Walker. I couldn't do it. But you can."

"John!" He disappears right in front of me, and then I hear a loud crash, the same one that happened the night he died.

And then I wake up.

I stare in the mirror by the front door, adjusting my tie while waiting for Evelyn to come downstairs. Kaydence is playing with her toys in her playpen, and her overnight bag is packed. The only thing I am waiting on is my wife.

Tonight's the fundraiser at the fire station. I doubt Evelyn slept much last night because of it—I know I was tossing and turning all night.

Part of that was due to my dream, which has rattled me all day. It felt so fucking real that I woke up in a panic, sweating and searching the house for anything out of the ordinary that could spark a blaze. But after going into Evelyn's room to check on her and looking in on Kaydence, too, I felt like I could finally breathe. Something happening to those girls is one of my worst fears, and I find it ironic that my mind decided to remind me of that the night before Evelyn and I face practically the entire town for the first time as a married couple.

Sure, we've been spotted around town here and there. Obviously, people know that we're married now. But tonight, almost the entire population of Newberry Springs will gather to help raise funds for a new engine for the station. Federal funding isn't enough, so this silent auction should help bring in the rest of the funds required to update our equipment. After the fire that stole my best friend's life, more updates and precautions have been made in the name of safety, and that takes money. But it's a small price to pay to keep everyone safe.

So the good people of Newberry Springs, Texas, will gather to support a worthy cause, and I'm sure they're going to bring their opinions—that nobody asked for—with them as well.

But my nerves aren't because I give a shit about what people think. No, I'm anxious because, for the first time since we got married, I intend to push some boundaries with this woman tonight, some physical ones. I'm worried that Evelyn will pull away if she starts to feel uneasy.

We've had four kisses between us now—*yes, I've been fucking counting*—but tonight, there will be many more. I plan on doting on my wife in front of every single person I can, leaving no question in anyone's mind as to how crazy I am about her. I only hope she starts to see it, too.

As soon as Evelyn comes downstairs, we're headed to my parents' house so they can watch Kaydence for the evening. My mom insisted on keeping her overnight so we could enjoy ourselves and not feel rushed to leave, but Evelyn has been twitchy about it for days. This is the first time she's going to come face-to-face with my parents since the wedding.

I know she's been avoiding it. But this is also the first time she'll be away from the baby overnight, so I want to try to distract her as much as possible.

I know of a few very particular ways I could do that, but how far I take it is all up to her. The last thing I want is for anything physical to happen between us and to have her regret it. That would be worse than never having her at all.

After that dream last night and every touch, stolen glance, and kiss before that, I know we would be explosive together. My mind and body are ready to show her just how crazy she makes me. But again, crossing that boundary is up to her, and I'd wait forever for her if that's what she needs.

So tonight, I'm following her lead, but I'm also going to lay claim to her in every way I can while making sure we have a good time.

We both fucking deserve that.

"Okay, I'm ready."

I spin to face the staircase, and all the oxygen leaves my lungs as I take her in.

That is my fucking wife.

Jesus Christ, I'm the luckiest man on the goddamn earth.

"Fuck, Evelyn." My eyes trail her legs as she descends the stairs, her feet encased in black heels that look sexy as fuck on her. They instantly make me want to see them in the air as I make her scream my name with my mouth between her legs. Her dress is red—*great fucking color*—and satin, which hits just above her knees and is held up by thin straps on her shoulders. It flows flawlessly from her hips as she shimmies closer to me.

Her hair is pulled off her neck in an updo of some sort, but she has a few tendrils hanging down around her face, framing her cheeks, and her lips are painted red. God, I want those lips to leave marks all over me.

I'm gonna have such a hard time keeping my hands off her tonight. Good thing the goal is to do the opposite.

"You look incredible." I'm sure there's a more elaborate word I could use to describe her appearance, but my brain isn't fully functional right now.

"Thank you." Her cheeks flush as she looks away from me when she reaches the bottom stair and stands right in front of me.

"I'm serious." I shake my head as she glances my way, and I drop my eyes down her entire body again. "You took my fucking breath away just now."

"You don't have to lay it on that thick, Walker," she says, diverting her eyes again.

I reach out, grip her chin slightly, and force her to look

at me. "I'm not laying on anything, Evelyn. You are the most gorgeous fucking woman I've ever seen. You're stunning. Breathtaking. Showstopping. You give me goddamn heart palpitations. Seeing you just now made me feel like the luckiest man on the planet. And I mean every fucking word, okay?"

I can see her swallow, her eyes wide. "I think you made your point."

"Believe me, there are other ways I could make that perfectly clear if you still don't believe me." But instead of acting on that promise, I release her chin and take a step back, afraid that if I stand too close to her, my restraint will snap, and this night will have been for nothing. So I gather my wits, readjust my jacket, and then ask, "You ready?"

I can tell she's shocked by my declaration, but then she grimaces. "No." And then her eyes drift over to Kaydence.

I gather her from her playpen, fasten her in her car seat, and lead Evelyn to the door. "She'll be fine. And so will you."

We settle into my truck, making sure the car seat is secure, and then start heading for the ranch.

"I just feel so weird asking your mother to watch her when we've barely spoken in months," Evelyn says once we're underway.

"You didn't ask, I did. And she agreed eagerly."

"Still. I think I'm more nervous about coming face-to-face with her than going to this stupid fundraiser."

"Once you see how great she is with Kaydence, you'll be

able to relax. And if not, tonight is an open bar, courtesy of Gibson Brewing."

That makes her finally crack a smile. "Okay. You got me there. Free booze? I think I can handle that."

When we arrive at the ranch, I help Evelyn down from my truck so she doesn't fall in her dress and heels. Then I grab Kaydence and her bag from the backseat and lead them up the front porch steps.

"We're here," I announce as we walk inside. And in one second flat, my mother comes flying around the corner from the hallway, excitement in her eyes.

She stops in her tracks, clasps her hands over her chest, and gawks at us. *Jesus, Mom. This isn't senior prom.*

"You two look so lovely," she coos, taking a step closer.

"Thank you, Mrs. Gibson," Evelyn timidly replies.

"Evelyn, dear. Now, you know better. You know to call me Momma G."

She smiles and nods. "Yes. Sorry. I just wasn't sure . . ."

My mother reaches out for Evelyn's hand, yanking her into her chest. "You are family now. No matter how this started, you will always have a home here, and so will that little girl, do you hear me?" My mother locks eyes with Evelyn, and if I didn't know any better, I'd say that Evelyn is about to cry.

I can't imagine not having my parents in my life or not having their support, even when I make decisions they may not agree with or understand—like getting married without telling them, for instance. But Evelyn hasn't had that for the past nine years, and I'm not sure that she really had it before then. So I can only imagine what my mother's reaction is doing to her right now.

Before Evelyn loses it, I gently pull her from my mother's arms. "Momma, you're going to wrinkle Evelyn's dress."

The glare my mother shoots me makes my balls shrivel up a bit. "You don't get to tell me I can't hug my daughter-in-law, Walker Bradley. You know better than to try to dictate something like that, young man."

I hide my smile. "I know, Momma. But aren't you ready to meet Kaydence?"

My mother's shriek echoes off the walls. It's so loud, it draws my father from the back of the house. "Oh my goodness, yes! Give me that baby girl." She rushes over to the car seat and unbuckles Kaydence, wrapping her in her arms. Kaydence stares at my mother with wide eyes, assessing her like she does with all new people, but then she reaches up, tugs on a chunk of my mother's hair, and initiates her into her circle with her baby seal of approval.

"I haven't stopped hearing about our babysitting duties all week." My father comes around her, reaching out to shake my hand while my mother gets Kaydence to release her hair.

"Well, we appreciate it."

"I really do," Evelyn echoes my sentiment, biting her lip. "She's obsessed with grabbing hair right now. Sorry about that. Also, she's crawling and moves really fast. She's not sleeping through the night yet, either, just so you know . . ."

"Oh, honey. I raised three boys, and two of them were twins, in case you forgot." My momma winks at Evelyn. "I know a thing or two about getting a baby to sleep and what to expect at this age. Don't worry your heart one little bit, okay? This baby is in good hands."

My father nods. "Best momma around."

"I can attest to that as well," I add, just in case Evelyn needs any more reassurance.

She takes a deep breath and blows it out. "Okay. I believe you."

"As you should. Now, you two have fun tonight. Stay out late, sleep in tomorrow. There is no rush to come pick her up, you hear?"

Evelyn's nerves are written all over her face as she nods. "Okay. If you're sure. And you can call if anything happens or if you have questions."

"Babe," I say, gaining her attention since I've never called her that before. It just came out naturally. I place my hand on the small of her back, drawing her into me. Might as well get a kickstart on the physical connection early in the evening—and in front of my parents, no less. "She's going to be fine. You deserve to have fun tonight. We both do. Now, let's say our goodbyes and get going." And to really hammer my words home, I place a chaste kiss on her lips.

That's kiss number five, in case you're keeping count.

Evelyn stares up at me, swallowing before saying, "You're right."

"Careful with those words. You're going to give me a complex," I tease her.

My parents chuckle, and then Evelyn kisses Kaydence to death before reluctantly pulling away. "I love you, baby girl."

"She knows, Ev. Let's go." I get one more kiss in on those chubby cheeks I've come to love, and then I lead my wife out the door, back out to my truck, and head into town, ready to face whatever the night throws at us. And ready to do whatever I can to show Evelyn what it's like to be mine.

The town hall conference room is filled to the brim with people as we walk inside, fashionably late. Everyone is decked out in suits and cocktail dresses, and murmurs of celebration and networking are taking place all around us. The space has been decorated with white linen tablecloths, cushioned chairs, vases of red roses as centerpieces, and décor in black and gold. It's by far one of the classiest events I've been to, and it's a testament to what a small town will do to help out their own.

Even though I feel ready to face whatever comes our way, Evelyn's hand grips mine tighter as we walk in, hand in hand. I know her well enough to know that she needs a drink to help her relax.

"Just breathe," I whisper in her ear, watching the skin on her neck pebble right before my eyes. I'd love nothing more than to run my tongue along those bumps right now, but that might be taking my task for the evening a little too far. Instead, I place a soft kiss right below her ear, loving how her breath hitches when I do, and say, "Let's get you a drink."

I lead her over to the bar—sponsored by my brother's brewery, of course—and grab us two beers.

"Thank you," she says as she takes her glass from me.

"Of course."

"So how does this work?" she asks, her eyes scanning the room and her lips pursed.

"Well, local businesses donated items for auction, and everyone can go around and place bids on things they like."

"I wish I would have known about this. I would have donated something in a heartbeat."

"Well, Janise had a hand in organizing the event, so that might be why you weren't approached."

Evelyn's jaw clenches. "I should have just gone over her head and donated something to spite her."

Laughing, I guide her further into the room. "Next time, babe. Next time." With my hand on the small of her back, we begin to walk along the tables, looking at all the items for auction. I donated free horseback riding lessons from the ranch, and I grin when I see a few people have already bid on it.

As we stroll, I search for my brother and Kelsea, knowing they're here somewhere. And if Evelyn has Kelsea near her, I know it will help her relax even more.

"Walker! Evelyn!" Sydney Matthews runs up to us, beaming. Sydney is a lawyer in town, specializing in estate planning, and her husband, Javi, works for my brother, Forrest, as one of his construction managers.

"Hey, Sydney. Long time, no see." I've crossed paths with her and her husband at the brewery numerous times, but it's been a while since we've held a conversation.

"I know. And when I heard you got married, I had to come over and congratulate you guys." Sydney's dark-brown locks sway as she visibly holds back her enthusiasm.

Evelyn draws in a breath next to me. "Thank you. It was a little sudden . . ."

". . . but we're happy," I finish for her, drawing her into my body, placing a kiss on her cheek.

"Hey, you don't have to explain anything to me. I know what it's like to be so in love you can't wait." She waves off Evelyn's comment. "But I've got to say, I think it's so great. I always kind of wondered why you two weren't together, you know? Given that Wyatt and Kelsea are your brother and sister-in-law and you guys have always hung out together." She chuckles. "Oh God, listen to me. I swear, I read too many romance novels. I see storylines everywhere I turn."

"Those novels do more good than harm though, Princess." Javi comes up behind his wife now, wrapping his arm around her possessively. It inspires me to do the same to Evelyn, pulling her into my chest now before I kiss her temple.

Sydney blushes. "Oh, yes. Javi reaps all the benefits of my reading hobby. Don't you, babe?"

He arches a brow at her. "Absolutely."

"I'm telling you, Evelyn. Read romance, and you won't be able to keep your hands off of Walker here."

Evelyn nearly chokes on her beer. "Oh, uh . . . thanks for the suggestion."

Fighting to cover up my smile and tell my dick not to get too excited at that idea, I say, "Have you two seen my brothers, by any chance?"

Sydney points in the far corner, up by the stage. "Wyatt got a table over there. I ran into Kelsea earlier and had to say hello, of course."

"Thank you." I clear my throat and then squeeze Evelyn's waist. "Well, we'd best be finding them ourselves. It was good to see you two."

"It was. And congrats again. You three make such a sweet family," she says before Javi nods his chin at me and the two of them walk away.

"I'm not gonna lie. I'm a little curious about what type of stuff she's reading," Evelyn whispers as I lead her toward the front of the room. "Some of those books are pretty kinky."

Laughing, I say, "How would you know, Ev?"

She casts me a side-eye glance, partnered with a smirk that makes her red lips look even more tempting. "Come on. You know me, Walker. Have I ever shied away from owning my sexuality?" she teases. But all it does is remind me that I want to own her sexuality, too.

I want to memorize every fucking inch of her body.

I want to know what she looks like, tastes like, and sounds like, what her curves feel like under my fingers.

And I want her to do the same to me.

"Walker!" A loud, boisterous voice I know by heart calls out from my left. And when I turn, I see the chief striding toward us, dressed to the nines, his round belly covered by a dress shirt and tie that I've only ever seen him wear a few times since I started working under his direction.

His bushy mustache and bald head complete his signature look, and the beer he's holding sloshes a bit as he closes the distance between us.

"Chief."

"Gibson. Nice to see you in something other than a sweaty t-shirt," he jokes before reaching out to shake my hand. And then he turns his attention to Evelyn. "Is this Miss Evelyn Sumner?"

"It's Gibson now," I correct him.

"Yes, sir, it is." Evelyn reaches out to shake his hand this time. "It's nice to see you, Chief."

"Please, call me Tom. And Gibson? I take it the rumors are true, then? You two got hitched?" The chief tends not to listen to town gossip, which I appreciate, but I didn't exactly approach him on the subject of my marriage, either, so I can understand his uncertainty.

"We did," I reply with a tilt of my head.

That makes him laugh. "What the hell are you doing here on the arm of this fool, then?" he asks Evelyn, jutting his thumb in my direction.

Evelyn looks over at me with an arch in her brow and a coy smile. "Oh, he's not all bad." She presses up on her toes and kisses my cheek this time.

"Not all bad"? And a kiss on the cheek? Hell, I'll fucking take it.

The chief raises his brows. "Oh boy. Well, when you're young and in love, what's the point in waiting, right?" He shakes his head. "I have to say, I was a little surprised to hear this, though, given . . . well, you know."

Evelyn stares at the ground, but I tilt her chin up and make her look at me when I say, "Well, my desire to play with fire is what got me into this job in the first place, Chief. And when you know something's right, the past shouldn't matter."

I've had many conversations with myself—and maybe a few with my best friend on the other side if he can hear me—asking for forgiveness. The thing is, John's not here, so it shouldn't matter. But it does on some level, and I know it matters to Evelyn.

The chief's face turns serious in a heartbeat. "You're right, Walker. Life is too short. Cherish each other. Make each day count. I married my Tammy after just one month of being together, and we've been married for thirty-five years now. People thought we were crazy, but I'd do it again in a heartbeat."

"When it's true love, you just know," I say to him, releasing Evelyn's chin but keeping my arm around her selfishly.

"Exactly."

"So do you think we'll make enough to cover the cost of the engine?" I ask, changing the subject to help Evelyn relax. She's practically chugging her beer at this point, and now is not the time to process everything I just said.

"I hope so. Your brother made a rather sizable donation this morning, so that definitely helped."

"Wyatt?"

"No, Forrest. Said he couldn't make it but still wanted to contribute."

"Well, that doesn't surprise me. Forrest isn't a very sociable guy, but I'll be sure to extend my thanks to him as well." My big brother will often commit to things and then throw money at it instead. Avoidance is his MO.

"Hank Baker also dropped off a check this morning," the chief says, turning his attention to Evelyn.

"Kelsea's dad is gone a lot, but I know he loves this town just as much as everyone else does," Evelyn replies. "In fact, I'm going to make a donation myself. It's the least I can do."

The chief smiles proudly, taking another drink of his beer. "You see? That's what makes a town like Newberry

Springs different from other places. We take care of our own. We spend our lives around the same people and know that no one gets through life without someone else's help at some point. This community is unique because of the people. Makes me proud to serve it."

"Couldn't have said it better myself, Chief," I reply. "Well, if you'll excuse us, I need to get this lovely lady a seat at our table."

"Understood. Well, it was wonderful to see you, Evelyn. My wife loves your shop, by the way," the chief says.

"I am so happy to hear that."

He tips his chin at us both. "You two have a good night, and Walker . . . try to stay out of trouble, you hear?"

"I'm always on my best behavior, Chief."

He throws his head back in laughter before sauntering off.

"How many more times do you think we'll be stopped before we make it to our table?" Evelyn asks as we power walk toward it.

"Are you doing okay?"

She blows out a breath but nods. "I'm okay. It hasn't been too bad so far. I feel like everyone is watching us, though." Her eyes dart around the room.

I lean over to whisper in her ear, "They're watching *you* because you look stunning in that dress, Evelyn. Any man staring in your direction is jealous of me because I'm the lucky bastard who gets to parade you around on my arm tonight."

Her breath hitches. "You're pretty good at this doting husband thing, Walker."

"Just practicing for when it's real."

And God, do I want it to be real. Every fiber of my being yearns for this woman in a way I didn't know was possible. I've never felt this way about any other girl I've dated or been with romantically.

Evelyn is the only one I want.

Her brow furrows as she glances at me, but she doesn't say anything else before we arrive at the table where my brother and Kelsea are sitting, talking to each other.

Evelyn finally relaxes once she's next to her best friend, even though I see her texting my mother on her phone here and there. But to keep her happy, I grab two more beers for us as we wait for dinner to be served and the speeches to be given.

So far, the night is going swimmingly.

But of course, I spoke too soon.

Scrubbing my hands, I look up in the mirror, checking my face for any remnants of food. I rushed to the bathroom after the chief's speech, having held my need to pee all evening so far.

Evelyn has finally started to loosen up, and any time her eyes start skittering around the crowd, I direct her attention back to me, reminding her to focus on us and ignore everyone else.

And then I plant a kiss on her lips.

So far, she's complied—and the kiss total is past ten—but now I want to dance with her before the evening is up. Every time we touch, my hunger grows more intense. Every time she bites her bottom lip, I want to yank on it with my own teeth. I'm desperate to put my hands on her some more, and dancing with her will give me the opportunity. I know it will draw attention, but if I keep hers instead, she won't even register the abundance of stares we'll accumulate.

As I shove open the bathroom door, ready to enter the ballroom again, a conversation to my right catches my attention. Spinning around, I find Drew, Tanner, and Brad talking amongst themselves, each with a beer in one hand and another in their pocket like they are fucking clones.

"She's making her way around the station, that's for sure. If this thing with Walker ends, I call dibs next," Drew says, laughing like the douche he is. "If I realized that sharing Evelyn was an option, I would have put my hat in the ring. The ass on that woman is reason enough to want a piece for myself." Brad and Tanner nod in agreement. "The worst part is, his best friend was there before him. I mean, that'd be like me climbing Mount Everest, putting my marker on top, and then the two of you following in my footsteps, acting like your climb was better. I don't know how he doesn't have a complex about it."

These guys are supposed to be my friends, my colleagues, men I should trust with my life. They know me, and they knew John, and for Drew to have the audacity to speak about Evelyn like that—and for the other two to agree—makes me go from zero to fucking fuming in an instant.

My restraint snaps. My body vibrates with anger. I see nothing but red and stalk toward them. Drew's eyes widen as he puts two and two together and realizes I just heard everything he said.

"Hey, Walker," he says timidly, backing up as I close the gap between us. He backs out of the hall into the ballroom full of people, but all I see right now is his face and my fist about to fly toward it.

"You son of a bitch!" I shout, pushing him backward as he stumbles, drops his beer, and scrambles to stay upright.

"Hey, take it easy."

"Fuck you, Drew. That's my fucking *wife* you're talking about!"

The crowd becomes eerily silent as all eyes descend on us. But again, I don't give a shit.

So much for being on your best behavior tonight, Walker.

This guy just spoke about Evelyn in a way that no man should ever speak about a woman, particularly a woman I care about—the woman I've wanted for far too long.

"Walker!" Evelyn shouts behind me, but I block her out.

"Look, dude. I didn't mean anything by it."

"Then why fucking say it?" I shove him against the

wall, gripping his shirt in my fists. "You have no fucking clue what that woman has been through . . . or what I have, for that matter. I don't understand what makes you think you, or any of you"—I seethe, glaring at the people who are watching us, people I know have said shit about Evelyn and me—"have the right to pass judgment on how any other person chooses to live their life." I slam him into the wall again, holding back my desire to beat him to a fucking pulp. "Evelyn and I are in love. We're fucking married, and everyone needs to shut the fuck up about it."

"Walker," the chief says from behind me, grabbing my shoulder as I tense up. "Walker, son. You need to step back."

Huffing out air through my nostrils like a bull that's about to be let out of his pen, I release Drew's shirt and take one step back. But I have one final thing to say.

"If I hear my wife's name come out of your mouth one more fucking time, you'll be waking up in a hospital bed. Do you hear me?"

I shrug the chief's hand off me and head for the door, hearing the clack of heels behind me. I don't have to look to know it's Evelyn trailing me—my body just senses her on instinct. That woman has been on my radar for over a year now, and that probably won't ever stop.

"Walker," she says as I reach my truck and unlock it.

"Get in the truck, Evelyn."

She doesn't argue as I open her door and help her inside. And after I shut her door and round the hood, I fire up the engine and peel out of the parking lot, headed back to our townhouse.

Neither of us says a word the whole drive home. Only what Evelyn says to me once we're home is enough to make this evening take another turn neither of us was anticipating.

CHAPTER TWELVE

Walker

"Walker." Evelyn tries to get me to speak once more after I shut us inside her house. But I'm so wired right now and my blood pressure is so high that I'm still not able to talk. Instead, I head for the kitchen and grab the only alcohol in the house—an already open bottle of wine from the fridge—to soothe my fury. I pull the cork from the bottle, lift it to my lips, and chug until I see Evelyn join me in the kitchen in my periphery.

"Talk to me, Walker." Her arms are wrapped around her body, every line on her face gives away her concern, and she nibbles on that bottom lip again as she waits for me to say something.

"I'm sorry," I finally say, dropping my head down, staring at the floor and blowing out the breath I've been holding since we left the fundraiser. "I'm sorry I made a scene. I know that probably made tonight even worse for you, and that was never my intention." Lifting my head back up, I meet her gaze.

"What did he say?" she asks nervously.

"Nothing you need to hear, Evelyn. I just hope to God he never repeats it again."

"Apparently, it was bad enough that it made you want to beat the shit out of him."

I huff out a laugh. "Yeah, it did."

"Why did you react like that, Walker? That's not you."

Standing tall, I lock eyes with her.

She's right. That rage I felt *was* uncharacteristic of me. I've always been wild, but anger like that has never been my go-to unless my brothers and I were intentionally riling each other up. We've come to blows a few times over stupid shit, but I've never felt *that* kind of rage before, the powerful desire to hurt another human and inflict harm. But listening to him speak like that about her made me realize that I *do* have that side of me—and she's the woman who brings it out.

What I feel for Evelyn is new to me, so I'm still trying to understand why everything is so different with her. But that's the thing—I think it's different for me *because* it's her.

Whenever anyone tries to mess with her, this instinct to protect her overcomes me, and I lose control anytime I feel she's being threatened. And our proximity in the last month has only exacerbated it.

"It kills me that I can't protect you from them, Evelyn—from their words, glances, and snickers," I finally say. "I fucking hate it, and tonight, I think it finally hit me that I would be willing to beat one of my friends' asses to defend you."

She takes a few steps toward me, crowding my space now. "Why is that, Walker?"

"What do you mean?"

"You know what I mean," she says, challenging me. And at that moment, I know this is my chance, my chance to tell her what I wish I could have told her over a year ago.

My palms grow sweaty as I stand there. I can hear my heart in my ears, my stomach feels like there's a rock inside, and my eyes flicker back and forth between hers so fast that it's making me dizzy.

But it's time to speak my truth.

"This isn't fake for me, Evelyn," I admit, trying to keep my voice steady. "I want you more than just temporarily. I always have."

Her mouth falls open. Silence rests between us. I can see her pulse thrumming in her neck, and I want to reach out to her, assure her that she doesn't need to be afraid.

Suddenly, she retreats a few steps, her eyes wide, and I can feel her pull away, like we're connected by a rope that is growing more taut by the second. "What?" she whispers. "Are you saying . . . ?"

". . . that I have feelings for you?" I finish for her. "That's exactly what I'm fucking saying, Evelyn."

Her hand comes up to cover her mouth. My heartbeat speeds up. "Oh my God." Then her hand drops, and a fire blazes in those blue irises as the wheels start turning in her brain. "All the time I was with John?"

Her question is warranted, but there's no going back now. The confession is out there. Time to lay out everything else.

I point a finger to my temple. "You think I don't know it's not right for me to feel this way? That the minute my best friend put his hands on you I wished it had been me? That it killed me to see him get to touch you and then find out that you were having his baby? And then to know that I couldn't save him? I fucking tried, Evelyn! And because of me, his daughter has to grow up without a dad."

"Why didn't you ever say anything?" she shouts back at me. "Why didn't you—"

"Because he was my best friend!" I cut her off. "Because I didn't know what I was feeling at first, and by the time I did, it was too late! You were seeing my *best friend,* Evelyn! What was I supposed to say? He's wrong for you? You should be dating me?"

"That would have been a start," she fires back, the tension between us palpable.

"How was I supposed to do that, Ev? And more importantly, I didn't realize what my problem was until it was too late. You were already too far down the Schmitty rabbit hole. I didn't want to interfere if you were happy, even though I knew he wouldn't be the man you deserve."

And fuck, I hate saying that about John now that he's gone, but that's the thing—*he's* not here, and *I* am. He had his faults, and I believe he would have done right by his daughter eventually, but he wasn't in love with Evelyn. He didn't care for her the way I would, the way I did—*the way I still do.*

"He may not have been my happily ever after, but he did give me Kaydence, and that's something I will always be grateful to him for, even if she wasn't planned," Evelyn explains.

"I understand."

"This is a lot to take in." She shakes her head. She turns her back to me as she paces along the tile, the click of her heels the only sound as I wait for her to speak again.

I know I caught her off guard. I didn't mean to lay this all on her tonight, but how else was I supposed to explain my reaction? It's not just about keeping up the façade of this marriage. My reaction came from somewhere deep inside that I've been locking in a cage, but the steel bars couldn't contain it any longer.

After a few minutes, she turns to face me. "So what's the point of you saying something now? Guilt? Curiosity?" She tosses her hands in the air. I'm not sure why she's angry, but I owe her honesty. I owe it to the both of us.

"No. It's—"

"What?" She stands there, waiting for my answer with wide eyes and a fiery gaze. But what do I say?

I couldn't save you from the pain you've been through then, but I want to save you now?

Every time I see you, my heart feels like it's bursting in my chest?

Your daughter has brought some joy back into my life for the first time in a year, and I don't want to let go of that?

"I want my chance." I take a step closer to her, settling on laying down those cards instead. "I want to know what it's like to kiss you every day, hold you, make love to you. I want to know what you look like right before you go to sleep and the second you wake up and wrap my body around yours in between. I want to be there for you because I don't know if you've ever had someone to do that for you—put *your* needs first, *your* desires, *your* heart. I just want a chance to know that what I feel isn't fleeting . . ." I stand right before her now, so close I can feel the rise and fall of her chest against mine, our short breaths mingling between our bodies. "Because if it were, I feel like I would be past it by now and no longer walking around feeling like there's a knife lodged in my chest and knowing no one can pull it out but you."

The woman looks like she's just seen a ghost, like my confession shocked her to her core. "Oh . . ."

"Oh?" My heart beats wildly. "That's all you have to say?"

Jesus, I overdid it. I played the wrong cards, and now I have to fold.

This could change our entire dynamic. This could make the next few weeks even more painful to go through if I know she doesn't feel the same.

So maybe I need to ask her that question.

"I-I . . ." she stutters.

"Do you feel it?" I take her hand and place it in the middle of my chest, right over my heart. "Do you feel like this around me, too? Please, Ev, please tell me I'm not the only one."

I can't be the only fucking one.

Her eyes bounce back and forth between mine before she finally whispers, "You're not the only one."

"Thank fuck." Relief rushes through me, but I don't waste one more second before slamming my mouth onto hers. Our bodies crash together like a meteor hitting the earth, leaving a dent so deep that we couldn't miss it if we tried.

I back Evelyn up to the island, lifting her onto the slab as I step between her legs, hiking up her dress along her thighs as I do. Our tongues tangle, our hands wander and grip, my cock grows painfully hard, and I press into her so she can feel what she does to me—what she's always done to me. And her body moves toward mine in the same way.

"Fuck, Evelyn."

"Walker," she moans, digging her hands in my hair as we continue to lick and suck and nibble on each other. I break our kiss and trail my mouth down her neck as she tips her head back, panting with every flick of my tongue against her skin.

"This is what you do to me, Ev." I grab one of her hands and bring it down to my cock so she can palm me through my slacks. "This is what I'm like every time you bite that fucking lip of yours, every time you sass off to me or anyone else, and every time you smile at me like I made your fucking day."

She pushes me off her, her eyes wild, her lipstick smeared all over her mouth. But I honestly think she's never looked more fucking beautiful. "Walker . . . I have never had anyone fight for me like you did tonight."

"That's a damn shame."

"But when you did?" She runs her nails down the back of my scalp. "It made me realize that I want you, too. It's been building for weeks, this attraction, this magnetic pull I feel to you. I've never had someone protect me." She licks her lips and brushes my hair from my face. "But you do. *You* protect me. You stand up for me. I don't *need* you to save me, Walker. But just knowing that you would, it's . . ."

"What?" This time, I frame her face in my hands.

"It makes me think you should fuck your wife."

Groaning, I tip my head back while Evelyn rubs me through my slacks another time. When I find her eyes again, I say, "You know there's nothing I'd love to do more than that."

My mouth is on hers again, and then my body temperature rises to a thousand degrees. As we kiss, I chuck my jacket across the kitchen, and then Evelyn's fingers loosen my tie before starting on the buttons of my dress shirt.

My hands push up the bottom of her red dress, revealing the black lace thong she has on underneath. When I remove my lips from hers to take in the sight, she grabs my hand before I can touch, pulling my attention back up to her.

"Walker . . . I . . ."

"Are you okay? Do you still want this?" *Please, still want this.*

"No, I do. It's just . . . I had a C-section with Kaydence," she explains, uncertainty in her eyes. "It left a scar, and I . . ."

I place my finger over her lips, shutting her up. When I'm sure she's done talking, I reach down to her thong, grab both strings at the sides, and rip the fabric from her body, shoving the flimsy remnants in my pocket. I drop to my knees, push her legs open wide, and lick her entire pussy from bottom to top while looking her dead in the eye. And then I kiss the scar she's so worried about, knowing nothing—not even a minuscule scar like this—could change how much I want this woman.

"This is where Kaydence came from, Evelyn. I could never hate this, and you shouldn't, either."

"Walker . . ."

"Every inch of you is fucking perfect. You have no idea how many times I have thought about everything I'm going to do to you tonight." She whimpers, still locking her eyes on mine. "Now, hold on tight, babe. I have a lot of fantasies to live out, and licking your pussy is at the top of the list."

Diving back in, I feast on the woman who has become a craving I don't think will ever be satisfied. Evelyn moans, gripping my hair like a handle, holding on for the ride.

My tongue finds her clit, flicking her, circling her, and sucking that sweet little nub between my lips, making her wetness flood my mouth.

And fuck is she addictive.

Eating her pussy is a religious experience. Not only does her taste drive me wild, but the way she's reacting to my touch is fueling my fucking ego and making me feel like I found the meaning of life.

"Oh, yes. Right there. Just like that." She moans as I figure out what she likes, changing my touch and listening for her cues.

I love that she's not afraid to talk, to tell me what she wants. Although, I wouldn't expect anything less from this woman.

And lucky for her, I like to talk during sex, too.

I circle her opening with one finger, slowly sliding in and out and stretching her in the process.

"More, Walker," she says, pulling my face closer to her body. I'm already nose deep in this woman's cunt. But if she needs more, I will gladly give it to her.

"So greedy," I tell her, lapping her up. "So fucking wet for me, Evelyn. This pussy is weeping for me."

"*You* make me wet, Walker."

"Fuck right, I do."

"Please, I need more," she says as I circle her clit again with my tongue. I shove two fingers inside her this time, curling them just right to hit the magical spot inside that will make her come apart for me.

As I work her up, I can't stop staring at her from between her legs. Her head is tossed back, her chest is rising and falling with each labored breath, her nipples pebble against the fabric of her dress, and her legs begin to squeeze my head as her pussy does the same to my fingers.

And then she fucking comes.

"Oh, fuck!" she shouts, riding my face, letting me know how good I'm making her feel. "Yes, yes, yes!" Her wetness floods my hand, but I don't stop using my fingers and mouth on her until she unclenches and starts to relax.

Standing from the floor, I find her lying back on the counter, heaving and utterly spent, her arm covering her eyes. "Holy shit."

I bring my fingers to my mouth, making sure she watches me lick her juices from my hand. And then I undo the final two buttons on my shirt, pull it down my arms, and toss it into the living room. "We're not even close to being done yet, Evelyn."

She props herself up on her elbows and licks her lips as she stares at my chest. "God, your body."

"It's yours, baby."

"The amount of times I've thought about licking your abs, Walker . . ." She shakes her head. "It's embarrassing."

I grab her hand and press it right against where my cock is tenting my pants. "Definitely doesn't sound that way to me." Cupping her face, I say, "In fact, I'm pretty sure I'd let you do whatever the fuck you want to me, woman."

She licks her lips, hops down from the counter, and drops to her knees in front of me. "I wanna taste you," she says, undoing my belt.

"Fuck, yes."

I watch her unbutton my pants, drag the zipper down, and then pull on the band of my briefs, baring my cock to her.

"Jesus." She wraps her hand around me, stroking my length while watching pre-cum bead at the tip. "This is going to feel so good."

After tasting her—and just this simple act of her jerking me off accompanied by the words coming out of her mouth—I'm so fucking close to coming that this might end with me embarrassing myself at this point. But I'm going to keep it together as best I can because I want those lips wrapped around me more than I want my next breath.

"Evelyn . . ." I warn, and she stops to stare at me with every ounce of her attention. "Put my cock in that perfect little mouth of yours. Suck me hard, beautiful."

Her eyes sparkle from my words, and if I didn't know any better, I'd think this woman likes to be ordered around. No matter how she might pretend otherwise.

She sticks her tongue out and licks from the base to the tip of my dick. My cock turns to steel as I do everything in my power to memorize the sight of her before me, on her knees, lipstick smeared, eyes bold and open, looking up at me as she takes me into her mouth.

She swirls her tongue around the head and then takes me deep, reaching the back of her throat before pulling away and then doing it all over again.

"Shit, Evelyn. Fucking suck me, baby."

I bury my hand in her hair, messing it up, but I don't give a shit—and I'm pretty sure she doesn't, either, right now. We're both fucking in this, this messy, carnal, lust-filled attack on one another.

I can't look away. Everything about her sucking me off is perfect, a memory I'll never forget. But I know there are so many other things I want to do to her tonight, so, painfully, I pull back.

Evelyn pops me out of her mouth, wiping her lips with the back of her hand. "Are you gonna fuck me now, Walker?"

I bend down, lift her off the floor so her legs wrap around my waist, and then head toward the stairs. "You bet your ass I'm going to fuck you, Evelyn. You have no idea how long I've wanted this."

"Give it to me, Walker. Show me. Please." She drags her dress up over her head, dropping it to the floor at the base of the stairs, and then unclips her bra and tosses it away from her body.

Her breasts are right in front of my face, goddamn perfect handfuls with rosy pink nipples. My mouth finds one in a flash, and I suck and nibble on the bud as I climb the stairs.

"Your room or mine?" I ask when I hit the landing, still licking and sucking on her breasts.

She tugs on my hair again. "I don't care. Just hurry, please."

Thinking she might feel more comfortable in her own space, I head for her room, kicking the door open with my foot. I kiss her roughly, clutching her hair with one hand to keep her head where I want it. I lick her jaw, bite her neck, and then suck on her nipple one more time before tossing her on the bed, making her squeal.

God, she's so fucking perfect.

Her round ass, thick hips, soft stomach, supple breasts, that coy smile—the one she's directing at me right now . . . This reality is so impossibly perfect, it could be a dream.

But I know it's fucking real because I'm feeling all of it.

"I'm gonna fuck you until you can't walk tomorrow, Evelyn," I say as I shove my pants and briefs down, stepping out of my shoes and my pants completely now. Stroking my cock, I stare down at her, feeling this possessive urge to come all over her silky skin, to claim her in the most carnal way.

But tonight, the only thing I care about is *her* coming again and again.

"Do you have condoms?" she asks, and at that moment

I'm grateful I bought some a few weeks ago. I wanted to be prepared in case we got to this moment. Optimism was driving that choice, obviously.

"Yeah. Be right back." I practically run across the hall, grab a strip so we'll have plenty for later, and then rush back, ripping one open and covering myself as Evelyn watches.

"How do you want me, Walker? How do you want your wife?"

In the forever kind of way, Evelyn, I want to say. I want to keep this woman as my own. I want to protect her, honor her, show her everything she makes me feel.

But instead I settle for, "Every way I can have you."

Right now, the focus is making this woman feel like a fucking goddess. And what do I get out of it? Knowing me and my dick made her feel that way.

"Lay right there, baby. Let me fuck you for a while before I watch you ride me."

She smirks at me from where she's lying on her back. "I definitely want to ride you, cowboy."

Placing my knees on the bed, I crawl over her, parting her legs, and lap at her pussy a few more times to make sure she's ready for me. I'm thick, and I want her to be comfortable.

When I line my cock up to her entrance, we both watch as I slide in slowly so I don't hurt her. The sight is one of the most perfect fucking things I've ever seen.

"Jesus. Look at you, Evelyn. Look at you take my cock."

I can't stop watching. Her pussy is sucking me in, and it has me fighting the urge to come already.

"You're so big, Walker," she moans as she thrusts her hips toward me, trying to take more of me. But it's too fast.

"Relax, Ev. Go slow, baby. Open up that pussy, and feel every inch of me."

The fire in her eyes melts me. "God, your mouth."

"You like that, don't you?" I ask as I lean over and thrust forward a little more. She nods. "You like me talking about your pussy, don't you? You like hearing filthy words come out of my mouth?"

"God yes," she says on a gasp as I slide in a bit more. I'm almost all the way in, but part of me is loving this, watching her open up to me, be comfortable with me, be in this with me.

It's so fucking hot.

We've barely even started, and I already know this is going to be the best sex of my life.

I slide all the way in, making us both groan when I bottom out, and then Evelyn sighs, moans, and starts to wiggle her hips. "Oh God, Walker. Please move."

I pull back then thrust forward as we both watch me slide in and out of her again. This time, she reaches down, scissors two of her fingers around me, and keeps her hand there as she feels me move.

"Jesus, that's so fucking hot. Touch your clit, Ev. Show me how you touch yourself as you feel me claim your greedy little pussy."

She leans back and puts her other hand to work, circling her nub the way she likes.

"Did you ever touch yourself to the thought of me?" She nods, biting her bottom lip. I lean down and take it between my own teeth this time. "Every time you bite this lip, I just want to do it for you."

"Walker. Please . . ."

"Please, what?"

"Keep going. Keep fucking me."

"I never planned on stopping." Little does she know, I don't ever plan to.

I lick her lips, tangle my tongue with hers, and then lean back, gripping her thighs so I can thrust even harder.

Evelyn is soaked. Her hand is moving at hyper speed, and I can feel her tighten around me as we keep moving.

"I'm gonna come, Walker," she breathes.

"Fucking do it, Ev. Soak my cock."

She cries out as her release slams into her, and I keep fucking her through it, each thrust making her orgasm build higher and higher until she reaches the end. I almost come myself, but I'm not done. I want more.

Sex with this woman is better than every fantasy I've ever had put together.

Falling forward, I latch onto her nipple, sucking on her as she comes down from her cliff. I'm slowly sliding in and out of her because I can't stop, even though I know she must be sensitive.

"Walker . . ." she mumbles, running her nails up and down my back, making my skin break out in goosebumps.

"Fuck, Ev. Dig your nails in. Claim me."

She does as I say, digging in deep. The pain sparks a fire within me, giving me another burst of energy as I pick up my pace again and hammer into her. Listening to her shrieks as I fuck her hard, the way I know she needs—the way I know she wants it now—is pure bliss.

Sweat drips from my forehead, but it doesn't even phase me as Evelyn's body wraps around mine, taking every thrust I give her.

When I feel my energy deplete, I flip us over, placing her on top, my dick still inside of her. Tucking my hands behind my head as I get my breathing under control, I stare up at this beautiful creature—*my fucking wife*—and tell her, "Ride me, Ev. Ride this cock like it's yours."

"I thought it *was* mine," she says as she circles her hips and pivots up and down my length.

"It is." I sit up, grip her chin in my hand, and tell her, "I want you to ruin me, Evelyn. Fucking break me, use me, and take everything I have—because I've already given all of me to you. Now I just want you to accept it."

She freezes, locks her eyes with mine, and then leans down to kiss me deeply. Our kiss is sloppy and desperate, and then, as if someone whipped her ass into gear, Evelyn gets to work swiveling her hips, pumping her body up and down, and sliding me in and out of her like a fucking professional.

I reach up and play with her nipples, gently tugging on them as she grinds on me.

"Yes. Keep doing that."

"You like that?"

She nods, biting her lip again. "Uh-huh."

I leave one hand on her nipple and bring my other between her legs, gently applying pressure in the form of small circles on her clit. "How about this?"

"God, yes, Walker. Touch me."

"Whatever you need. Just tell me, Ev. I'll fucking give you everything you want." *And that's not a fucking lie.*

"Just more of that." She closes her eyes and rocks back and forth, moaning as I hit a spot deep inside her that makes her grow even wetter than before. And then her shallow breaths tell me she's about to come again.

"Come for me, baby. Squeeze my dick, Ev. Fucking use me."

"Fuck, Walker." She flicks her hips a few more times, and then she's detonating, shaking wildly as another orgasm wracks her body. "Oh my God." She falls to my chest, so I plant my feet on the mattress under her and keep thrusting up, harder and faster, as she screams, drawing out every last tremor. And as I do, my dick lets me know he's ready to blow, too.

"I'm gonna come, Ev."

"Come inside me," she whispers in my ear as she bites my earlobe, and I explode. Hot spurts of cum shoot from me and into the condom, and they just keep going.

I haven't had sex in over a year, so I'm surprised that I've lasted this long, anyway. But as Evelyn milks me for every drop of my release, my entire body melts into the bed. I'm on the verge of passing out from how hard I just came.

"Fuck, Evelyn." I hold her to me, wrapping her in my arms, kissing her temple as we stick together with sweat.

"Walker. That was . . ."

"I know."

That was the last of all my firsts.

Evelyn is mine. Evelyn will be my ending.

She just doesn't know it yet.

CHAPTER THIRTEEN

Evelyn

I want you to ruin me, Evelyn. Fucking break me, use me, and take everything I have—because I've already given all of me to you. Now I just want you to accept it.

Light cracks through the blinds in my room, stirring me awake as memories from last night swirl through my mind.

Walker and I had sex. Mind-blowing, bruising, dirty, and emotional sex.

As I stretch out my limbs, I revel in how deliciously sore I am, how used my body feels and how much I'm craving that physical release again even after we had sex three times last night.

I think we finally fell asleep around three in the morning after Walker bent me over the bed and pounded into me from behind, bringing my final orgasm count for the evening to seven.

That man is an animal. God, he wrecked me last night, but in the best way. I didn't have to ask him to be rough, control me, or touch me where I needed it. It was as if he already knew.

He knew what I needed, which is more than I can say for myself right now.

And his confession.

This isn't fake for me, Evelyn. I want you more than just temporarily. I always have.

It took me by surprise, to say the least. But at the same time, it was a relief because it meant that my feelings were justified as well.

I can't believe that all this time he's had feelings for me. But now that I think about it—in the afterglow of my sex-induced haze—his reaction to John's death and how he avoided me since makes so much more sense.

And his reasoning for marrying me a little more complicated.

He wants this to be real. He wants to stay married.

But is that what I want?

After last night, my body feels sated, but my mind feels

the opposite. Walker is the type of man you keep forever—and forever is a word I don't have much experience with.

I never dated boys exclusively in high school. Hell, I didn't even lose my virginity until I moved to Newberry Springs. Casual sex is all I've ever known because it's the best way to stay unattached. And after what happened back in Dallas, the last thing I wanted was to let anyone in again. I've learned I can never be too sure about someone's intentions, even someone I thought only wants what's best for me.

Do I think that Walker's intentions aren't pure? Absolutely not. That man was *very* adamant about his desire to help me.

But was there an underlying pretense to the marriage, too? Was he hoping this would all happen once we were legally tied together? Did he let his feelings drive this decision more than rational thought?

"You're thinking too loudly over there." Walker's raspy voice has me turning over to face him. His hair is standing up on all ends, he has lines on his face from the pillow cover, and his jaw is covered with stubble that I'm itching to run my fingernails through.

God, he's so hot—so strong, so noble, so freaking addictive.

"I have a lot to think about," I say, running my hand over his shoulder and down his arm as he grips my waist and pulls me flush to his body. His cock is hard as a rock between us, lining up perfectly with my slit as he holds me.

And even though I had more sex last night than I have in over a year, my body is ready and eager for more already.

Show me how you touch yourself as you feel me claim your greedy little pussy.

"Are you thinking about how I fucked you last night?" He rocks his hips, sliding his length along the juncture between my legs.

Yes. "No."

The corner of his mouth tips up. "Liar."

"Fine. I was. It's kind of hard not to be reminded of that when your dick is talking to my belly button."

He thrusts his hips into me again. "If I had my way, we'd never leave this bed, Evelyn." He squeezes the flesh at my hip before reaching down and running his fingers through me. "Jesus, you're fucking soaked already." Groaning, he closes his eyes, removes his hand, and sucks on his fingers. "God, I could eat you every day. But . . ."

Disappointment rushes through me because I was ready for him to make good on his promise. "But what?"

"I think we should talk."

Anxiety rushes in to replace the disappointment. I hate talking. It's terrifying to voice my thoughts, my fears, and my feelings. But I know I can do that with Walker.

And after last night, he deserves that.

"Can we fuck after?"

He laughs and thrusts his erection into me again. "Abso-fucking-lutely." Then he sighs, puts the sheets between us, and cradles my jaw in his palm as we lie there on our sides, facing one another.

"How are you feeling?" he asks.

"A little sore. But very happy about that." He flashes me a shit-eating grin, and it makes me want to lean over and kiss it off. But I refrain.

"Last night was the best night of my life, Evelyn. Besides almost beating Drew to a pulp, that is."

We share a laugh.

"It *was* pretty amazing."

"But I also said a lot of things last night. And if I know you as well as I think I do, I know you're internalizing them right now."

Sighing, I say, "Well, you did admit some pretty strong feelings, Walker. And I guess I'm just wondering . . . what happens now?"

He brushes my hair from my face. "Like I said, I want my chance, Ev. I want my chance to make this real. We're already married, but I want to date you, dote on you, prove to you that you mean so fucking much to me—you *and* Kaydence."

"I . . . I don't date. I never really have." As a twenty-seven-year-old woman, I feel silly admitting that. But I've lived my life protecting myself from pain, and my love life was where I most insisted on maintaining control.

"I'm aware. But there's a first time for everything. Don't think about it so formally." His hand finds my hip, pulling me even closer to him so I can feel his cock between us again. "Think about it as the two of us both being aware that feelings are here now and acknowledging that we're able to act on them." His eyes search every inch of my face. "I can't tell you how many times I've wanted to kiss you just because, smack your ass as you walked by me, or promise to do filthy things to you once Kaydence went to sleep."

God, tell me more, please. "That sounds nice," I say instead, which makes him smile.

"But it's more than just the physical. I want to take you out, spoil you, do things for you that will assure you of how much I want you in my life. And I want you to know that I'm doing them not just because I'm your husband and someone is watching, but because you deserve them, and it makes *me* happy to make *you* happy."

How does he make me feel like the center of his universe? I've always wondered what it would feel like to have someone so infatuated with me that I can't breathe without them. Like the way Wyatt and Kelsea feel about each other.

Can I have that with Walker?

"You're comfortable telling me exactly how you feel, aren't you?"

"Now, yes. But Evelyn, I've been holding this in for a long time. I know it might sound insane, but if this past year has taught me anything, it's that life is too fucking short not to say what we mean and mean what we say. No one has time for that bullshit. I'm done being afraid to voice what I'm feeling, especially when it comes to you."

"Wow," I breathe out, in awe of his honesty. "Walker . . . I don't want to disappoint you. I feel like there's this pressure on me to be the person you've put up on a pedestal." I hate saying that, but that's how I feel in the afterglow. His confession was eye-opening. If he's had these feelings for over a year, then what if the fantasy of me doesn't live up to the reality?

Gripping my chin, he says, "You could never disappoint me. I don't want you to be perfect, even though I already think you are. I want you to be *you*, Evelyn Gibson." He winks at me. "The woman who was my friend first and now is my wife. I just want you, Evelyn—any way you'll let me have you."

I don't have anything to say. How on earth can he be so resolute in how he feels? My emotions toward him are new. I feel like I'm running a race that I started late, and because of that, I can never catch up.

Do I think I could fall in love with Walker? Yes. How can I *not* fall in love with a man like him?

But what happens if he leaves after I've fallen? What happens if he realizes that I'm not the woman he's built me up to be in his mind? Can I survive this if it ends in tragedy again or we realize that the farce of marriage was much more blissful than the reality?

"I want you, too," I say, because it's the truth. I've been

dying to act on these desires for him for over a month. "But I need you to be patient with me."

"Have I been anything *but* that with you from the start?"

"No," I answer honestly. "But this is different now, too."

He nods. "Okay. We go slow, then. Take this one day at a time, and just enjoy each other in the process."

My smile takes on a life of its own as optimism rushes through my chest. "Okay."

Walker's face mimics my own. "Good girl. It's settled, then. Now, if you're ready, I'd like to fuck you into this mattress so hard that we leave a dent." He winks. "Again."

Giggling, I rip the sheet from between us and spread my legs. "Please."

Walker reaches over, grabs a condom, and lays it on the bed between us as he strokes my cheek with his thumb. "Jesus, Ev. You're so fucking sexy. I've never been this hard in my life."

"I love your cock, Walker." It's the truth. He's the biggest man I've been with, but he knows how to use it, too.

"Can't hear that enough."

I reach between us, grab him, and start to stroke his length. "Then let me tell you." I push up on my elbow and line my lips up to his ear. "You're so big it hurts, but within seconds, you make me feel so incredibly full. Your cock is like steel velvet—hard yet smooth, long and perfectly curved so your head can hit me where I need you to. The way you feel moving inside me is so fucking addictive that I don't think I'll ever stop wanting you."

And that's part of what scares me—becoming so addicted to this man but then losing him. Because I think losing him would alter my entire being.

"Fuck." He closes his eyes and reaches between my legs. Then he strokes me, rubbing his thumb softly over my clit. "Tell me more."

"I love how you controlled me last night, how you knew what I needed without me asking. I like your rough touch, but I also know that you would never hurt me. I love how you circled your hips from behind me, stretching my pussy out and giving me one of the most intense orgasms of my life. I love how—" My words are cut off by the sound of my doorbell ringing.

Walker's hand stops, and we both freeze. "Are you expecting someone?" he asks, searching my eyes.

"No. You?"

"Nope." We disconnect, and Walker marches over to the window of my bedroom, peering down to the front door since we're on the second floor. Then he spins to face me, his eyes wide. "I think that's the social worker."

"Oh my God! What?" I launch out of bed, grabbing the first clothes I can find and tossing them on. I forget a bra, but the last thing I want to do is make this person wait any longer. "What are they doing here on a Sunday?"

Walker stumbles as he runs to his room to grab a pair of shorts. "I don't know! But they could come at any time, right?" he calls out from his room.

"I guess." Flying down the stairs, I stop to look at myself

in the mirror by the front door. "Oh my God. I look like death."

Walker nearly slams into me as he rounds the corner from the base of the stairs as well.

"You were about to fuck me looking like this?" I whisper, rubbing away the mascara that is all over my cheeks and the red lipstick smeared around my mouth. I look like I dressed up as the Joker for Halloween and then fell asleep with the makeup still on and my face planted into the pillow.

"Hey. I did that to you, so to me, it was hot." He shrugs.

Rolling my eyes, I run down the hallway. "I have to wash my face. They can't see me like this."

After I scrub at my face and brush my teeth with my finger and some toothpaste I found in the downstairs bathroom, I rush back out to the living room, finding that Walker already let the woman into my house.

Our house.

"Good morning," I say, grabbing her and Walker's attention.

"Hello. I'm Samantha Brown." She steps forward with her hand outstretched. I shake her hand then pull mine away, smoothing down my hair since I just now realized I forgot to brush it. "I hope I didn't wake you." She peers around the house, and at that moment, I do the same.

The house isn't extremely messy, we just have a few things out of place. But the most glaringly obvious items that don't belong are the clothes we stripped off last night in a rush to get each other naked.

I flash my eyes at Walker, silently asking him why he didn't pick up the clothes. He shrugs and turns back to Ms. Brown. "We were already awake, we just hadn't rolled out of bed yet."

"I see."

"Would you like some coffee?" I ask as I duck around her and grab my dress and bra from the floor. I'm pretty sure she's already noticed them, but they don't have to stay on the ground. Does this encounter fall into the walk of shame category, even if it is in my own house?

"Coffee would be great."

"I'll start a pot," Walker announces as he hustles toward the kitchen.

"Please, have a seat. I'm just going to throw these clothes in the laundry room." With a placating smile on my face, I find Walker's shirt and jacket as well and then run toward the laundry room, tossing all of the clothes inside and then slamming the door shut before returning to the main part of the house.

"Coffee should only be a few minutes." Walker joins me in the living room now with the social worker.

"Perfect." She takes the loveseat as Walker and I sit on the couch, and she then places her bag on the floor, reaching inside for a folder full of paperwork. "Do you mind if I ask you some questions while we wait, then?"

"Not at all." Walker pulls me closer to him, practically

yanking me onto his lap. But I gently shove him away so there's an appropriate amount of space between us. I don't need to be straddling him to convince this woman that we're a happily married couple—one that hadn't slept together until last night, that is.

"Um, I just realized," the woman says as she glances around the house. "Where's the child?"

I can feel my face go white.

"She's with her grandparents," Walker answers for me as I try to recover. "My parents."

"Do they live locally?" Ms. Brown clarifies.

"Yes. We had an event last night for the fire station where I work, so my parents offered to watch her overnight. They love babies, and my mother was adamant about us having an adults-only evening so we could enjoy ourselves."

I elbow him in the ribs. "We were about to get ready to pick her up," I say as Walker pinches my hip.

"I see. Well, parents deserve nights off every now and again. Do your parents watch her often?" She directs her question to Walker.

"No," I answer for him. "Most days, she's with me. I take her to work with me."

"And what is it that you do?" she asks me this time.

"I own a clothing store in town. Perks of being your own boss. I don't have to rely on daycare or anyone else to watch her."

"Are you opposed to that?"

Her question makes me tense. "No. I'm just grateful to be able to keep her with me, even when I need to be in the store to oversee things."

"And Mr. Gibson is a firefighter, correct?"

"Yes."

"Does the danger of your job ever concern you about your ability to provide for Mrs. Gibson and the child in question?"

Walker stiffens this time, and his reply makes my chest ache. "Every day. Kaydence's biological father was a firefighter as well, and he died in the line of duty."

Ms. Brown's face remains stoic, but my heart is thrashing in my chest.

"But you can't live in fear, Ms. Brown. And I think that's what John's death taught us." Walker grasps my chin and speaks directly to me as if there isn't another person in the room. "Fear cannot stop death, but it can stop life. I can't live like I'm afraid I'm going to die because then I won't be able to appreciate this woman and her daughter and the fact that they chose me." He leans forward and presses his lips to mine, his words blanketing my body in both warmth and fear.

He knows I'm afraid. I don't even have to say it. He just knows.

But I don't want to live in fear, either.

"I'm pretty sure you chose us first," I whisper as his lips spread into the signature grin that makes my panties melt. Too bad I don't have any on under these shorts.

Then I kiss him back before resting my head on his shoulder.

Samantha breaks through our moment by clearing her throat. "Well, if you don't mind, I need to do a walk-through."

Walker rises from the couch. "No problem. We have nothing to hide. But there is some dirty laundry on the bedroom floor I need to pick up so it's not in your way." He kisses my temple and then leaves me alone with the woman who's going to report on the environment in which I'm raising my child.

"The coffee should be ready," I say as I head for the kitchen. "How do you like yours?"

"Just a spoonful of sugar, please."

I pour her a cup and set it on the island, watching her assess the living room. She makes a few notes on her paper, stopping to admire our wedding photo and the canvas that Walker hung by the door that leads to the garage. "You're very lucky to have found a man who looks at you like that."

"Yeah, I am." Funny how I welcome that reality now, knowing it's Walker who's doing the staring.

"Believe me. The dating world sucks." As if she just realized what she said, her eyes widen, and then she shakes her head. "Sorry. That was very unprofessional of me."

"Don't worry. I get it. I never realized there were men like Walker until he pursued me." *Not a lie*.

"Well, hang on to him. Trust me. It pays to wait for someone who knows your worth. That's what I keep telling myself, anyway." I smile but don't say anything in return because I can't speak from my own experience to how she feels.

She walks over to the island, takes a sip of her coffee, and says, "Do you mind if I go upstairs now?"

"All clear," Walker announces as he rounds the corner and joins us in the kitchen.

"Thank you. I'll be back." We watch her disappear up the stairs, and then Walker grabs my hips, lifts me onto the counter, and steals my breath with a kiss.

I give in for a moment before I shove him away. "Walker!" I hiss. "What are you doing?"

"She's all the way upstairs. Don't worry. I settled for the kiss instead of eating you out. I'm behaving."

I swat his chest, and he captures my hand and kisses the inside of my wrist. "You're ridiculous."

"No, I'm just crazy about you."

"I'm crazy about you, too," I whisper before kissing him again.

When we part, he says, "By the way, I made the bed and put away the condoms that were out."

I cover my mouth with my hands. "Oh my God. Good thing you went up there, then."

"Yeah. And I realized, all of my stuff is still in my room. What should we say?"

"That you sleep in there after long shifts so we don't wake you. And it's easier if you have some clothes and things in there, too, I guess?"

"Sounds good. I did move my bathroom stuff into yours, though. I thought that would make more sense."

"Thank you." I touch my forehead to his.

"There's no need to thank me, Evelyn. This is exactly where I want to be."

I think this is where I want him to be, too. But will I always feel this way?

Here's hoping I do.

"God, I can't wait to see her." Staring out the passenger window of Walker's truck, I see grassy fields line both sides of the road that leads out to the Gibson Ranch. It's another warm, humid July day complete with a bright blue sky and barely any clouds. This is the same town I've lived in for nine years, and yet somehow, it feels very different today.

"Me, too, babe." Walker lifts my hand to his mouth, pressing his lips to the back of it. He hasn't let go of my hand since we got in the truck. And at this moment, I'm not complaining.

The atmosphere between us has changed, like an imaginary boundary we built has vanished. After Ms. Brown left our house, Walker and I showered and then rushed to get dressed so we could pick up Kaydence, even though he made good on his promise to eat me for breakfast before we left.

So much has changed in the last twenty-four hours, but

I'm grateful that I at least get to squeeze my baby girl soon. I need that to ground me again.

"I hope she slept well for them."

"Even if she didn't, I know Momma didn't mind the baby cuddles."

"I sure did miss mine."

"Yeah, but you got to cuddle with me instead. Was it that bad?" he teases me from the driver's seat.

"If I recall, there wasn't a whole lot of cuddling going on, sir. More like fucking, licking, sucking, and biting."

"Are you complaining?"

I turn away from him, fighting my smile. "Absolutely not."

"That's what I thought."

"Last night was incredible, Walker. I just miss my girl." I can feel myself grow emotional at the thought of holding her soon.

"We're almost there, Evelyn. I promise, she's fine."

When we finally pull up to the ranch, I don't even wait for Walker to get out of the truck to walk with me. My feet carry me at full speed up the front porch and right through the front door. "Hello?" I call out.

"In the kitchen," Momma G replies, and I rush there to find Momma stirring something on the stove with a baby on her hip. *My baby.*

"Baby girl," I croon as I walk over and pull her from Momma G's arms, cradling her to my chest. She melts against me as I bounce her around the room, letting a few tears build as the relief of holding her again rushes through me. I inhale her magical baby scent, willing it to calm my racing heart that's already slowing just by feeling her in my arms again.

"You did good, Momma," Walker's mom comes up behind me, rubbing my shoulder.

"I feel like I barely held it together."

"You only texted about five times," Momma G teases.

"Sorry." I tried really hard not to bother her, but I did text a few times at the fundraiser before everything went south.

"Don't be sorry. The first night away is rough. I hope you were able to find something to distract you, though."

Uh, yeah. Your son.

"We kept ourselves busy," Walker says as he joins us in the kitchen, reaching for one of Momma G's famous biscuits before he walks over to us and kisses the top of Kaydence's head.

I glare over my baby's head at him, but he just smiles back at me as he chews. "How did she sleep?"

"Only woke up once, actually." Momma grabs the pot from the stove and takes it over to the sink to drain the liquid from the potatoes. "I think I scared her a bit when I picked her up because I wasn't you, but we sat in the rocker, she told me a few stories, and then she drifted off to sleep in less than thirty minutes." Releasing the pot on the counter and discarding her pot holders, she comes over and rubs her hand over the top of Kaydence's head, smoothing down her wild baby hair. "We're friends now, aren't we?"

Kaydence smiles at Momma G, and something about it makes tears well up in my eyes again.

"Well, I'm gonna head outside. I have a lesson today." Walker rounds the island and places a kiss on my lips then takes Kaydence from my arms. "But I need some baby love before I go. I missed my little owl, too." He tosses her up in the air, and her squeals echo off the walls. Momma G and I watch the two of them together, only now that I know how Walker truly feels, these moments are even more real to me.

He wants to be in her life forever. With me.

Smothering her cheeks with kisses, he gives her one final peck and then hands her back to me. "Come outside and see me later, babe." He plants a kiss on my lips, and then he exits the house, leaving me and his mother alone.

"Do you need any help?" I ask as I spin around, needing something to distract me from the whirlwind of emotions running through me.

"I think you've done enough, Evelyn." She casts me a knowing look.

"What do you mean?"

Placing the potatoes in the pot, she takes it back to the stove and then turns to look at me. "You've given my son his light back."

"What?"

She shakes her head, staring up at the ceiling as if she's

fighting tears. When she drops her head, she pins me in place with her eyes. "When I found out that you two got married, I was shocked. Hurt. Angry. Sad." She places a palm over her heart. "My baby boy got married, and I wasn't there."

"I know," I say, taking a step closer to her. "And I'm so sorry. It was so sudden—"

She holds a hand up to stop me from talking. "I've made my peace with it. I don't know what had been going on with you two, but my son was clearly so overcome with love that he had to make you his wife, as unexpected as it was. But regardless of how it happened, I have to be thankful. Because that man"—she points to the door that Walker just walked out of—"is the boy I raised again. When John died, I wasn't sure if he'd ever be the same. I worry about a similar thing happening to him every day, Evelyn. I've seen firsthand what that job can do to a person's mind; he's seen things that no human should ever have to see. The only antidote to combat the evil and tragedy in this world is love. I'm a firm believer in that."

One lonely tear streaks down my cheek.

"You two are good for each other. And I just want you to know that no matter how this started, Randy and I will be here for you. Okay?"

My bottom lip trembles as I absorb her words. This woman has so much love for her children it's overwhelming.

I never had that. Even when I was a child, my parents

didn't devote time and attention to me. I was more of a bargaining chip, a checklist item, a pawn who could be used later to get ahead.

But Momma G just showed me forgiveness and gratitude, compassion and understanding, acceptance—things I don't feel I deserve but can't help but cherish nonetheless.

She closes the distance between us and wraps me in her arms. "You are a part of this family now, Evelyn. You and this little girl. And we take care of our own. So anything you need, you know where to find me." When she stands back, she smiles down at my daughter. "And this little bug—she is absolutely precious. You've done a great job so far, Momma. Raising kids is the hardest thing you'll ever do. You'll doubt everything you've ever done at one point or another, but I promise you, the effort is worth it. One day, they hopefully turn into adults who are good people. That's all you can really ask for, anyway."

"Thank you," I whisper as I reach out and grasp her hand.

"We're huggers in this family, Evelyn." Her free arm wraps around me and my daughter. "And Gibsons give the best hugs."

"Hey there, sis." Wyatt takes a position at the fence line next to me, resting one of his boots on the bottom rung as the giggles of children fill the air. After I gathered myself from the talk with my mother-in-law—which sounds so surreal to say—I grabbed a hat for Kaydence and decided to get some fresh air while Walker taught a few kids the basics of riding a horse.

We didn't get very far, though, since the sight of him speaking with the kids and guiding the animals around with a commanding presence mixed with love has kept me frozen here, unable to see anything else.

"Hi," I breathe out through a laugh. "Is Kelsea here?" I glance around him, searching for her.

"No. She had a photography session this morning. I'm surprised you didn't know that."

Kelsea texted me numerous times after Walker and I left the fundraiser last night, but the last thing on my mind in the last twenty-four hours was texting her back. I was too busy having mind-blowing sex, putting on a smile for the social worker who will help decide if I get to keep custody of my child, and battling a mental breakdown from the conversation I just had with my mother-in-law.

Sorry, Kelsea. Life's been a little crazy.

"We haven't spoken since last night."

He nods. "Yeah. Makes sense. Last night was . . ."

"Intense?" I finish for him.

Wyatt grins and tips his head toward Walker as the latter leads a child on the back of one of the horses striding around the pen. "I have never seen my brother act like that before, Evelyn." He clears his throat. "How were things after you left?" He flicks his eyes over to me, and I'm sure he can see how rosy my cheeks turn.

"Um . . . they were eye-opening."

Wyatt chuckles. "I'm sure they were. I guess I don't really need to tell you that my brother cares deeply about you, now do I?"

"No. He told me himself, actually."

Sighing, Wyatt says, "Fucking finally." He squares his shoulders as he faces me head-on. "Evelyn, don't take him for granted, please. He's been through a lot, and I know you have, too, but if you think you might break his heart . . ."

"I don't want to hurt him, Wyatt. But—"

He rushes to cut me off. "I'm not saying that you'd do it intentionally. But under my brother's tough exterior is a man who dedicates his life to other people. He needs someone who will do the same is all I'm saying." And then his brow pinches together. "If you don't think you can do that, you have to let him know."

My throat suddenly feels like it's closing up. I think that's my worst fear in this, that I won't be able to be who Walker wants and needs me to be, mostly because I don't know how to put someone else first in my life. The only person I've ever had to do that for is me—until Kaydence, that is.

But loving my daughter and taking care of her is different than being romantically involved with someone.

And this conversation with Wyatt is putting all of those insecurities on display for me right now.

"He's so good with the kids," I mention instead, trying to steer the conversation in another direction.

"He is. He's going to make a great father someday. Of that, I have no doubt. See ya 'round soon." With a wink, he pushes off the railing, tips the bill of his ball cap toward me, and then walks away, leaving me to stew in my restlessness a little bit more.

After watching for a few more minutes, Kaydence gets fidgety and hungry. I take her inside, feed her a bottle, and then put her to sleep in one of the spare rooms that Momma G directs me to. Seeing as how I got to the ranch in Walker's truck, I need to wait until he's finished in order to leave. Luckily, Momma G has no problem listening for Kaydence in case she wakes up, so I use the time to my advantage and explore the property a bit more.

Last year, when Mr. Gibson had his surgery, I volunteered to help Kelsea and Momma G with anything I could in my spare time. I grew attached to this land and farm—the scenery, the smells, the feeling of serenity that hits me as I stroll across the grassy fields and take in the wildflowers, gardens, and beautiful structures designed as event spaces. And the wide-open areas are utterly magnificent, especially in the evenings when the sun sets and highlights the sky in shades of pink and orange.

The wind whips at my dress as I stroll along, and I'm

grateful I brought my sunglasses to shade my eyes from the strong rays beating down on me. As I walk around, my eyes keep drifting back to the man who has flipped my entire world upside down in a way I didn't think I'd ever want.

Walker laughs and praises the children for their work today, a brother and sister duo who have been nothing but eager to learn everything he shared with them while also being extremely respectful and polite. I watch them leave with their parents before striding up to where Walker's standing, admiring just how sexy he looks in his jeans, boots, plain gray t-shirt, and that cowboy hat.

God, it isn't fair how attractive he is and how I never let myself see it before.

"Nice work today, cowboy," I tease him as he twists around to face me while washing his hands at an outdoor sink. Dirt is smeared on his cheek, but the way his eyes eat me up as I walk toward him makes me want him to dirty me up, too.

"It felt good to do that again." Once he finishes drying his hands with a paper towel, he pulls me into him by my waist, shading me under the rim of his hat because he holds me so close. "I haven't given a lesson since . . ." He doesn't have to finish that sentence for me to know what he's not saying.

I lock my hands around his neck. "You were so good with those kids. It was hard not to get turned on watching you move around like it was second nature. And this hat," I say, pinching the rim between my fingers and tugging on it. "I never realized how sexy it is."

His eyes darken from my words, and then he lifts the Stetson from his head and places it gently on mine. "Funny. I think it looks a hell of a lot sexier on you."

"I'd have to look in a mirror to verify."

He thrusts his pelvis into me. "Here's your verification." And then without blinking, he says, "Where's Kaydence?"

"Napping. Why?"

"Because I have to have you right now while you're wearing my hat." Before I can argue, he yanks me by the hand, leading me to the barn where the horses are kept. The shaded structure shields us from the sun.

"Walker . . ." He ignores me, pulling me further into the barn, so I try again. "We can't. Someone could see." I struggle to keep up with his pace, taking two steps for each one of his.

"Don't worry, I don't share. I don't want anyone to see what I'm about to do to you, either." Spinning me into his chest, he backs us into an alcove that I didn't even see. And since he knows his way around this barn better than anyone else, I'm sure he's confident that this little corner will keep us hidden away for the pleasure he's about to give me.

My body is vibrating with anticipation.

"You wore a fucking dress today," he says as he reaches down, unbuckles his belt, and then pops the button on his jeans.

"I did."

"Did you do that on purpose?"

"No." Our breaths are short, practically frantic as his words work up my body.

"I think you did," he says as he takes his cock out of his pants and starts to stroke it. "I think you wanted me to have easy access to you, to watch you sway your hips as you walked around, teasing me with what's underneath here." With his other hand, he reaches under the fabric and strokes me over my underwear. "Yup. I think your pussy wanted this just as much as I do."

"Well, she sure as hell does now."

He pushes my thong to the side, stroking his fingers through me. "I had you all night long, and I think I want you more now that I know what you taste like, how you sound when you come, and what your pussy looks like as it sucks me in."

"Then show me." I press up to tug on his bottom lip with my teeth.

"I don't have a condom, Ev," he mutters as his eyes bounce between mine.

"I'm on the pill." And even if I weren't, I don't think I would deny us this.

"Then hold on, babe. I'm about to pound this pussy and make sure you remember who it belongs to."

A shiver runs down my spine as he lifts my left leg off the floor, hooking it around his hip. Keeping my thong pushed to the side, he drags the head of his cock through my wetness and then pushes inside me, filling me up with one deep stroke.

I'm sore from last night, but as soon as he starts to move, that pain morphs into pleasure.

Sex is easy. Putting all of my energy into grasping onto that physical release is something I've always been good at.

But sex with feelings? This is an entirely new domain.

I mean, hell, we're fucking in a barn surrounded by animals, but all I can focus on is surrendering to Walker's voice, his body, and his eyes that keep me pinned in place, waiting for what he'll do next.

Walker wraps his hand gently around the front of my neck while his other hand keeps me steady against the wall. "Look at me, Evelyn. Look right at me as I fuck you."

"Walker," I gasp as every stroke of him inside me builds my release. The pressure on my throat doesn't scare me but rather makes me feel alive and heightens my pleasure.

"You are so fucking addicting. You are more perfect than I ever could have imagined. And you wearing my hat right now," he says as the rim of said hat hits the wall behind me. "Goddamn. I don't think I've ever seen anything so sexy." He releases his grip on my throat, lifts my other leg so both are wrapped around his waist now, and buries his head in my neck as he continues to pound into me.

My body is shaking, not only from relying on him to keep me off the ground but also because his dick is so fucking magical and it's hitting me so deep inside that I know when I come, the earth will shatter.

"I can feel you clench around me, Ev. You're enjoying this, aren't you?"

"God, yes, Walker. More. Keep fucking me," I say as the hat falls off my head, but it doesn't deter either of us. I nibble on his neck, kissing and licking my way up to his ear. "Your cock is so perfect. You fill me up so fucking good."

"Fuck. Keep talking like that."

"I want you to come so hard that you can't breathe. I want you to take us both there."

"Jesus. You need to get there soon."

I reach down between us and circle my clit, willing my orgasm to come out as quickly as possible. And luckily it does, making itself known in less than a minute. "I'm there, Walker. Fuck, I'm gonna come."

"Soak me, Ev. Give it to me."

When I cry out, Walker reaches up and places a palm over my mouth, muffling my cries. He fucks me through my orgasm, making sure I ride every last wave before he sets me down on my feet and pulls out of me, stroking his cock with intensity. And when he pushes up my dress and shoots his cum all over my stomach, it's so fucking hot I swear I could come again just from the sight.

"Fuck. Fuck!" he whisper-shouts, painting me, branding me, and claiming me with his release.

Our breaths are frantic as we come down from our

high, staring at each other across the space between us now.

Through an unsteady breath, he finally says, "Hold this. I'll be right back." He hands me the bottom of my dress, tucks himself into his pants, and then walks off, returning a few seconds later with a handful of paper towels. "Let me clean you." Gently, he rids me of his cum and then falls to his knees, licking every drop of my arousal from my pussy. Once he puts my thong back in place, he lowers my dress. "There. All clean."

As Uncle Jesse from Full House *would say, "Have mercy."*

"Are you okay?" Pressing our bodies together again, he cups the side of my face.

"More than okay. That was—"

"—fucking amazing." He leans down and kisses me deeply, making me wonder if he's about to initiate round two. But something about the kiss doesn't make me yearn for more sex. This kiss makes me want to just crawl back in bed with him, wrap my body around him, and never leave.

"Yes, it was," I whisper when we part.

"I don't think I'll ever get over the fact that I can fuck you now, Ev. God, it makes me hard again just knowing I don't have to hide that desire anymore."

Smiling, I reply, "You won't hear me complaining about that anytime soon."

The corner of his lips lifts as he leans down to pick his Stetson up off the ground and places it back on his head.

Then he takes me by the hand, leading me out of the alcove and toward the main house. "Are you ready to go home?"

"Sure. I just need to make sure Kaydence is awake."

He stops us in the middle of the yard. "Well, I have a few things I need to put back in order before I can leave, anyway. So go inside, relax a bit, and I'll be there in less than thirty minutes."

"Sounds like a plan." I push up on my toes to kiss him once more, but then he smacks my ass as I start to walk away. "Walker!"

"I told you I've been dying to do that. Don't think I wasn't being serious, Ev. You should know by now that when I say something, I fucking mean it." With a wink, he walks away from me.

His words make my heart pound. He means what he says and says what he means. It's refreshing and terrifying all at the same time.

The question is: Can I learn to accept it and be happy with him? Or will I constantly be waiting for the other shoe to drop?

"I find it absolutely absurd that I had to wait three days after the fundraiser to get brought up to speed on your life, Evelyn Sumner." Kelsea pops her hip out as she stands in my kitchen, watching me pour us each a glass of wine.

"It's Gibson now, Kelsea." If Walker could have heard

me just now, he probably would have given me three orgasms with his mouth to praise me for correcting her. Too bad he's working tonight.

But that is why Kelsea is over at my house, so I can bring her up to date on my relationship with Walker. Lord knows I need my best friend to help me process what's going through my mind and my heart at the moment.

"Oh, lord. If you're changing your last name already, then this has to be serious."

I slide her glass toward her before picking up my own. "Um, well . . . things have definitely changed since last weekend."

We both find a seat on the couch, and I tuck my legs underneath me as I settle into the cushions. Kaydence is asleep, so I can focus all of my energy on spending time with my best friend.

Kelsea smacks her lips after taking a large drink and then pins me in place with her eyes. "All right. Spill."

"Walker and I had sex," I blurt out.

Kelsea's eyes bug out of her head. "Oh. My. God," she says in her best Janice-from-*Friends* impression.

"Yeah. After Walker almost beat Drew's ass at the fundraiser, we came home, and I pushed him to talk to me about why he acted that way. I knew he was intent on standing up for me if people were saying things about us, which I know they were. I could feel eyes on me all night. But that thing with Drew? That was different."

"God, part of me wants to know what he said, but part of me doesn't."

"Yeah, Walker wouldn't tell me." And honestly, I think it's better that I don't know so I don't internalize it. I already let other people's opinions get to me.

"So, what did he say after you guys got here?"

"He admitted that he has feelings for me, Kelsea," I say as Kelsea sucks in her lips. When I narrow my gaze at her, she looks away. "Wait. Did you know he felt this way?"

"Maybe . . ." she draws out.

I nearly launch myself across the couch at her. "Oh my God, Kelsea! Why didn't you say anything?"

"It wasn't my place!" she fires back. "Walker hadn't even admitted it to himself when Wyatt and I both noticed it."

"When did you know?"

"Back when you first started seeing Schmitty."

My shoulders fall. "That's what he said when I asked him why he never said anything." I take a long sip of my wine. "It's just so wild. Part of me keeps wondering what if . . ."

"No, don't do that." She cuts me off. "You can't play that game, Ev. Life worked out the way it was supposed to. If Walker had stepped in, you wouldn't have Kaydence."

"Yeah, I know." Silence rests between us for a minute as I try not to fixate on the past.

"So once he admitted his feelings, you decided to have sex with him?" she asks through a laugh.

"Kind of. But honestly, Kels . . . it was more about how

he stood up for me. He was about to beat Drew to a pulp to defend me. I've . . . I've never experienced that from a man before. And I felt so safe with him in that moment."

Kelsea tilts her head to the side. "That's the kind of person Walker is—fiercely loyal. Granted, I've never seen him in that state of rage before, but that boy has always protected people he cares about. And I think, based on his reaction, it's obvious he cares about you."

"I care about him, too."

"So what does this mean? Did you guys talk after all the sex?" She giggles. "Sorry."

"Kelsea . . . I have never been fucked like that in my life." She cackles this time. "The man is an animal, and you know sex has never been an issue for me. I don't know if it was because it had been so long for me or if it was just him, but I'm dickmatized."

"Well, I am married to his brother, so please refrain from telling me all of the details, but I can relate." She bounces her eyebrows up and down as we share a laugh. I'm so glad that she's not as timid while talking about sex anymore, and I think Wyatt's to thank for making her feel more comfortable and confident about it.

"We did talk, but . . ."

"But what?"

This is the first time I've been away from Walker since that night, and every day between then and now has been filled with orgasms that were clouding my mind from seeing reason. Now that I have some space, I can assess the situation with a clearer mind. And what I've realized is that I'm terrified because the stakes in this relationship are really fucking high.

"I don't know. I'm attracted to my fake husband. I'm developing feelings for him, too. I don't know what the hell to do about any of that."

Kelsea scoffs. "First of all, he's your *real* husband. And second, how about you just keep doing what you're doing and see where it takes you? Stop overthinking it."

I point a finger at her. "This coming from my friend, the queen of overthinking?"

Kelsea laughs. "I know, but look at where all of that overthinking got me. Wyatt and I tiptoed around each other for years, wasting time we could have been together. Schmitty's death should be a wake-up call for all of us, Evelyn. Time is never guaranteed, so we've got to make each day count. And sometimes, that means turning off the rational part of our brain, the part designed to keep us away from danger and harm, and just live."

"I don't know how to do that."

"Yes, you do. You did it when you left Dallas and moved here."

"That was different, though, Kelsea. The only person I had to worry about then was me. Now there's Kaydence, and Walker's feelings are a factor in this as well. I just don't want to be blindsided again or hurt him—or end up hurt myself."

Kelsea takes a drink from her glass. "Have you told him

why you're so afraid? What happened that has you so cautious?"

"Not everything. Bits and pieces." Kelsea is the only person who knows everything that forced me to leave my home and start over in a new place. I vowed to keep that information to myself because the rumors and speculation that surrounded me back then brought up feelings I never wanted to feel again. Unfortunately, because of the mediation, that time of my life is being brought into the present. Perhaps that's why I'm even more uneasy.

"That might help him understand, Evelyn."

"John's parents know something about it, Kels. They have to. During the mediation, their lawyer mentioned something about the firm."

"Yikes." She bites her bottom lip. "Did Walker ask you about it?"

"Yes, and I gave him the CliffsNotes version. But . . ."

"Don't you think it would be better if he heard it from you, got your side of the story instead of risking him finding out from someone else?"

"But what if John's parents don't know the entire story and are just pretending to have information they actually don't? I would have told Walker for nothing."

"Not for nothing, Evelyn," she corrects me, but it makes my stomach clench. "You will have told him because confiding in him is what relationships are all about. Do you trust him with the information?"

"I think so," I reply, even though I know, deep down, the answer is yes.

"Then maybe you need to push yourself to open up to him like you've done with me."

"Kelsea . . ."

She stands and moves closer to me on the couch, reaching for my hand as her knee knocks against mine. "I promise you, Evelyn, Walker is one person you can count on. You obviously have feelings for him, and if you're willing to give this thing a shot between the two of you, then he needs to know you—the messy parts, too. It's time to grow up a bit."

"But I don't want to," I whine, making us both laugh.

"I'm pretty sure we don't have any say in getting older, Evelyn. In fact, you're about to be twenty-eight next week, right?"

"Ugh, don't remind me."

"Oh, I will, because you're older than me and I like to remember that."

I playfully shove her away. "Punk."

"We can't control getting older, Ev. But we *can* control getting wiser if we're willing to put in the work. You've been through a lot in the past year, and when I was having my own crisis, when I was trying to figure out my life and feelings for Wyatt, you were there for me, pushing me to go after what I wanted. It was terrifying, but I don't regret it for a second. And now, I'm gonna do the same for you.

Because you're definitely at the same type of crossroads. Ease into this, but don't push him away. Instead, push yourself to be vulnerable with him the way you are with me. You both deserve that type of relationship, and I know you can have it if you rely on him to catch you when you're afraid."

"I'm so proud of the woman you've become, Kelsea Anne Gibson."

"I wouldn't be her without you, Evelyn Grace Sumner."

"It's Gibson now," I correct her.

"It can be, Ev. You just have to let yourself claim it wholeheartedly."

CHAPTER FOURTEEN

Walker

"Gibson!" The chief comes around the corner, locking eyes with me.

"Yes, Chief?"

"My office. Now." He spins on his heel, and I follow his lead, noticing that Drew is approaching the same door from the opposite end of the hallway.

This is my first shift on duty since the fundraiser, and it's time to face the reality of my actions from last weekend.

Honestly, I forgot about coming so close to wrecking my friend's face because I've been immersed in Evelyn and her body for the past forty-eight hours—which, believe me, is the best fucking distraction and way to live *ever*.

"Take a seat, gentlemen." The chief moves behind his desk as I close the door behind Drew and we sit in the chairs facing him. "I don't think I have to tell you why I called you two in here."

"No, sir," I reply.

"Good. But for the sake of the station and everyone's safety, we need to discuss what happened." He turns to me first.

"I think I made myself perfectly clear at the fundraiser, Chief," I declare, glaring over at the man sitting beside me. "It sucks that I had to overhear his opinions about Evelyn, but I can't pretend I didn't."

"I'm sorry, man," Drew breathes out, running a hand through his freshly cut brown hair. "I fucked up. What I said—"

"—was fucking atrocious," I finish for him.

"It was. I guess . . ." He stares off into space. "I guess part of me was jealous. First Schmitty finding a girl like that, and then you marrying her? Evelyn is a catch, and watching your happiness with her just reminds me that I'm all alone."

"And you'll continue to be if you keep talking about women the way you do," the chief interjects. "I didn't hear everything you said, but I heard the tail end of it before Walker got his hands on you. And boy . . . no woman deserves that kind of verbal degradation."

Drew hangs his head. "I know, sir."

The chief turns his eyes to me. "Now, that doesn't excuse your behavior in a public place, Gibson. You caused a scene. The entire town witnessed you threatening him. That doesn't paint you or the station in a good light."

"I understand, sir. And I'm sorry. But—"

He holds his hand up, silencing me. "I get it. If someone said something like that about my wife, I probably would have responded the same way. But we can't have animosity amongst the crew. We have to have a safe environment for when we need to band together to face a fire or a tragedy. So both of you are on housework duty until further notice."

Fuck. Cleaning up after everyone—scrubbing the toilets, washing all the sheets, mopping the floors—it's the worst fucking job here. But if that's how I can get back in the chief's good graces, I suppose there are worse things to have to do.

"Yes, sir," Drew and I echo.

"Good." The chief stands from his chair, pulling up his pants and straightening his belt under his belly. "Now, get out of here and try to prove that everything is okay between you so everyone else around here will unclench their butt cheeks. There's too much fucking tension going around, and I refuse to deal with it."

Drew and I exit his office. I head for the bunk space I share with him and a few of the other guys, but he follows me in. "Walker . . ."

"Drew, let's just move past this," I say when I turn around to face him.

"I really am sorry, man."

I shake my head slightly. "I'm not the one you need to apologize to. Evelyn deserves the apology more."

"You're right."

"I know."

We fall silent for a few awkward moments.

"So we're good?" he eventually asks, stretching out his hand.

I drop my eyes to his waiting palm, debating if it's worth holding a grudge. Fuck, do I want to. But I also know that if push comes to shove, I need this man to have my back and vice versa. So for the sake of both our lives and our jobs, I meet him halfway. "We're good."

"Where are you taking me?" Evelyn sits blindfolded in the passenger seat of my truck. It's her birthday, and even though she said she didn't want to do anything, I wasn't going to take that for an answer. I don't know that the woman has ever had someone make a big deal out of her birthday. But if she's my wife, I sure as hell am going to celebrate the day she entered this world.

But more importantly, I'll show her what it's like to be mine.

"It's a surprise. Hence the blindfold, woman."

"Don't get snarky, Walker. That attitude of yours isn't going to help you get lucky later."

"I don't need luck. By the time I'm done worshipping you tonight, you'll be begging for my cock, Evelyn."

I catch the smirk on her lips before focusing back on the road.

When I was thinking about how I wanted to spoil her tonight, I knew that privacy would probably make her feel the most comfortable. With all the murmurs still going around town since the fundraiser, taking her out to eat didn't seem as thoughtful as cooking her a meal and showing her a part of Newberry Springs that's important to me.

I have a basket in the back full of food and wine and one more little surprise up my sleeve that I hope she loves. I had to run up to my old room at the ranch when we dropped off Kaydence to grab it.

The sun is setting in the distance and thank God, because between the heat and humidity, the end of a Texas July is brutal. But I'm going to make the most of our time tonight and lay my heart on the line a little bit more.

I can feel Evelyn's walls are still up, but each time we touch and laugh and find that comfortable silence together, the more I can see a real future with her.

I just need her to see it, too.

When I pull to a stop on the dirt road I've been driving on for a while now, I put the truck in park and then turn to

Evelyn. The sight of her in that blindfold gives me ideas for later if she's up for it.

"Are we here?" she asks, turning her head in my direction.

"We are." I step down from my side, round the hood of my truck, and open her door, helping her onto the dirt road beneath our feet. She's wearing a white sundress that reminds me of what she looked like on our wedding day with her cowboy boots. Her hair is down in waves of curls, and her lips are painted a blush color that I can't wait to kiss off or have all over my body.

Reaching around her head, I untie the blindfold and watch her eyes flutter open as she takes in our surroundings.

"Where are we?"

"The middle of nowhere," I reply.

Her head swivels around us before her eyes land back on mine. "Really?"

"Yup. Just us. No one around to stare, no one to bother us—just peace, quiet, food, and silence if you want it."

Her smile builds slowly until she throws herself at me, slamming her mouth to mine. I lick the seam of her lips, thrashing my tongue against hers the second she allows me to, and I hold her in my arms while the passion of our kiss ignites a spark between us that I hope never goes away.

"This is perfect, Walker."

"I'm glad you think so. Now I have to set up a few things, but feel free to explore a bit."

Evelyn strolls away from me, striding through the grass field, and I take a moment to appreciate the sight of her before I get back to work.

This empty field used to be the perfect place for us to throw parties in high school. It wasn't as overgrown back then, so we would build a bonfire, get our older siblings to buy us beer, and send out a mass text to our high school about when to meet. Unfortunately, that didn't last long because law enforcement quickly caught on, but now the property belongs to Old Man Higgins. Last year, I helped keep his wife alive when she got in a car accident and had a life-threatening bleed in her leg, so he told me if I ever needed anything from him to just ask.

This week, I called in that favor.

Once everything is in place, I search around for Evelyn, only to find her in front of the truck, staring at the sunset in the distance. The sky is a shade of purple tonight, sprinkled with a twinge of pink and blue. Rays from the sun fan out across the horizon, but the sight of her with that sky in the background is the real view I'll never forget.

"I swear, the sunsets here are nothing like anywhere else," she murmurs as I come up beside her.

"I mean, I don't have anything else to compare it to, but I think I'd have to agree." Reaching down, I take her hand in mine and bring it to my lips, kissing her wrist delicately, nibbling on her skin. She looks up at me, watching my lips move across her arm, and I can tell she's as dialed in to my thoughts as I am. "Are you hungry?"

"Starved."

"Then let me feed you before I have you for dessert."

As she giggles, I pull her around to the back of the truck and to the side of the road where I've set up a picnic on a blanket.

"Walker," she gasps as I help her sit and then plop down on the blanket next to her. "You did all this?"

"Of course." I reach into the picnic basket and bring out the chicken parmesan casserole I made. I actually tweaked a recipe I found online from some billionaire in California. His video went viral, and with good reason—his version of this dish was fucking fantastic.

Evelyn helps me dish out the chicken, pasta, and salad, and after I light a citronella candle to keep the bugs away, we dig in.

"This is so good, Walker." She finishes chewing. "I could get used to you cooking for me every night. I don't think I've ever eaten this well in my life."

"I'll cook for you every night if you let me," I reply as she swallows but doesn't respond.

Every time I mention anything along the lines of forever, Evelyn freezes. I try to remind myself that I have to be patient. My feelings have been developing far longer than hers have. But now that I have her, I'm going to fight like hell to keep her—and that means not shying away from my intentions and desires.

"So how was your shift?" she asks as we eat.

I just got home from work last night, and we didn't

really talk much once I arrived at the house, if you know what I mean.

"Not too bad. Just a few calls for chest pain. Pretty normal."

She stares down at her plate when she asks, "What about with Drew?"

"Oh. Well, the chief pulled us into his office and gave us both a little bit of an ass-chewing. But it was warranted. We're on housekeeping duty until further notice, which is the worst duty to have at the fire station, but it's fine." I shrug as I pick up another piece of chicken and deposit it into my mouth.

"So you two are okay?" She lifts her head, and I can see so many questions in her eyes.

"We are."

Shaking her head, she says, "I don't understand men. If Kelsea and I got into a fight like that, we wouldn't be friends after. But men can literally come to blows and be friends again two seconds later."

I let out a laugh that echoes around us. "Listen, Ev. Am I still furious about what he said? Yes. But I also have to work with the guy. I need to know that he's going to have my back in a blaze if need be. In this instance, I had to remind myself that Drew is human and made a poor choice. He actually admitted that most of his words came from a place of jealousy."

"Jealousy? Of what?"

I reach out and stroke the side of her face with my finger. "Us."

"Oh."

"Yeah, seems Drew's lonely and wonders how John and I both got so lucky to call you ours."

"I didn't belong to John," she counters.

"Yeah, I kind of feel that way, too." *Because you belong to me. You were always meant to be mine.*

"I mean, my last name is Gibson now, right? I think it speaks for itself."

"Fuck, Ev. Hearing you say that just made me hard."

She pushes her plate to the side and then crawls to me, giving me a soft kiss that has me fighting my restraint to get through the rest of the evening. But I have to make sure we do everything I have planned. I can wait to have this woman again.

At least, I think I can.

Once we've finished eating, I put all the dishes and food away and place the basket back in my truck. While I'm in the cab, I hook my phone up to the stereo and start the playlist I prepared for act two. "Slow Dance in a Parking Lot" by Jordan Davis filters out of the speakers, catching Evelyn's attention as I make my way back over to her.

"I love this song."

"I do, too." Reaching for her hand, I pull her into my chest, holding her by the waist as I lead us around in the dirt, dancing to the beat of the music. "And since I didn't get to dance with you at the fundraiser like I wanted, and we've been doing a lot of horizontal dancing in your bed since then, I figured tonight was the perfect time to make sure I got a dance in with my girl for real."

The blush that graces her cheeks is exactly the reaction I wanted. "Walker . . ."

"Shhh . . ." I say. "Just follow my lead."

Evelyn rests her head against mine as we twirl and spin around, her occasional laughter like music to my ears that is only made for me. When that song ends, "My Wish" by Rascal Flatts comes on. I hum the tune in Evelyn's ear as I keep her close to my chest.

"It's so very sexy that you can dance," she mumbles.

"Did you think it was when we were taking pictures?" I ask, thinking back to Kaydence's six-month photo shoot when I danced with her the first time. But that was different. She didn't know how I felt back then.

"Yes. It took me by surprise and made you even more attractive."

"Oh, yes." I waggle my eyebrows. "Tell me more about how you think I'm sexy." She playfully shoves at my chest, but I cage her in. No way am I letting go of her until I'm good and ready.

"God, you're full of yourself."

"You can be full of me later, if you want."

She tilts her head at me and purses her lips. "Walker . . ."

"Fine. I'll behave. But honestly . . . when did things change for you, Ev? When did you realize that I was irresistible?"

She rolls her eyes. "Honestly, I think it was the wedding. When you kissed me, this weird sensation came over my body. It felt like an electric current ran through you and into me. I was so nervous that I chalked it up to that. And then I saw you shirtless." *Kelsea already told me that bit.* "But then every time I saw you with Kaydence, and each time you stood up for me and tried to protect me, this attraction started to grow." She runs her hand through my hair and down the back of my neck. "And now it feels uncontrollable."

"You have no idea how hard it was to bury my feelings for you, Ev. And now that I don't have to? I feel fucking free, like a brick has been lifted from the center of my chest." I reach down and palm her ass before placing my lips on hers. "I can't get enough of you. Or that little girl." I remove my hands from her butt and then break our connection, helping her into the bed of the truck.

"You're so good with her, Walker," she says as we settle onto the mat I placed back here to make us more comfortable.

"I've never been around babies, Ev. But I'll learn it all to help take care of her. Her happiness is priority number one."

"And what's number two?"

"Showing you that you can trust me."

Her eyes bounce back and forth between mine before she leans forward and kisses me again. It's a soft meeting of our lips, but it doesn't lack passion at all. And because she initiated it, I know it's her feelings coming out, which tells me that she might just be catching up to me sooner rather than later.

When we separate, I reach behind me for the other part of my surprise. "Now, I have something else planned." The sun has completely set now, painting the sky in a midnight blue that will morph to black very quickly. "So ever since you told me about your gas station greeting cards, I've been looking for them around town. And I found some."

Her entire body perks up. "You did?"

"Yeah, at the Quick Trip on the edge of town before you cross over into Newberry." I pull a card from the bag behind me and hand it to her.

"You got me a card?"

"I did."

With shaky hands, she opens the envelope to reveal a plain card with a picture of the moon on the front. The background is black, and the moon stands out against the dark color, especially the craters in the surface of it.

She opens it and reads the inside. "'Everyone wants to be someone's sun, to light up someone's life. But you are more like my moon, brightening up my life in the darkest hour.'" She stares at the card for so long, I wonder what's going through her mind.

But then she lifts her eyes full of unshed tears and looks at me. Her bottom lip trembles as she chokes down her emotion. "Walker . . ."

I cup the side of her face. "It's true, Evelyn. I was in a

dark fucking place before we got married. And now, the world is still a little dark, but you have put light back into mine. You and Kaydence."

"I . . . I don't know what to say."

Huffing out a laugh, I reach behind me and pull out the other part of my surprise. "Well, how about we look at the moon instead and see it for ourselves?" I hold my old telescope in my hands, the same one that I've had since I was a kid and used to take out on the ranch to look up at the stars. I went through a phase where I was obsessed with everything in outer space. My parents bought me this telescope for Christmas when I was eight, but as I got older, my interests changed. Luckily, I never got rid of it.

Evelyn giggles. "Oh my God! How old is that thing?"

I stare up at the sky as I do the math. "Almost twenty years?"

"Does it still work?"

"We're about to find out."

I tinker with the knobs, adjusting the settings and trying out different views until the moon appears crisp and clean through the lens. "There you go, babe. Check it out."

Evelyn moves to the eye piece and gasps as she stares up at the moon. "Luna," she whispers, lighting my chest on fire.

This is what I wanted for her—to show her that I listen, that I care about what makes her unique; to show her that if she loves the moon, I can give it to her in any way I can.

When she lifts her head, her smile is brighter than the rock we're staring at through a lens. "Want to see?"

"Yes." I take my turn, admiring how simple yet breathtaking the moon is. And because Evelyn has an attachment to it, it suddenly becomes meaningful for me, too.

We look for a few constellations that I can recall and then lay down in the bed of the truck as I hold her in my arms.

"This is the best birthday I've ever had, Walker."

Rubbing her shoulder as she rests her head on my chest, I say, "I'm glad."

"Seriously. This was so thoughtful. And beautiful. And I . . ."

I tilt her head so she's looking right at me. "And you deserve every bit of it."

"Thank you," she whispers before kissing me chastely.

"You're welcome. But it's not over. I still need to give you a few orgasms. You up for it?"

Her lips spread so fast, I almost miss the transformation in her smile. "More than ready."

"Good girl. I just need to clean everything up, and then we'll head home."

I hop down from the bed of the truck and then help Evelyn down next. "Walker?" she asks before walking away from me.

"Yeah, babe?"

"Can you call me a good girl later while you spank my ass from behind?" she asks with an arch of her brow.

My dick hardens in a flash. “Fuck yeah, I can.”

“Good. Because I think that would be the cherry on top of this perfect birthday.” She opens her door to the truck, settling inside.

“The birthday girl gets what she wants,” I mutter to myself and then head home to make all her wishes come true.

CHAPTER FIFTEEN

Evelyn

"I love the new display," I tell Melissa, one of my employees, as we both admire the hard work she put in today. She has been busy all morning moving some items around the store, and the way she put together the window display for the new arrivals looks so freaking good.

"Thank you. I love all the colors you chose to lead us into fall." The entire line I ordered is full of sage green, burnt orange, dark brown, and creams. It's a melty fall masterpiece of color, but it still includes lightweight summer pieces because the Texas heat won't leave us completely until almost November.

"I'm obsessed. I hope customers will be, too."

"Same."

"Okay. Well, I have somewhere I need to be, so you're okay with closing down the shop, right?"

"Absolutely." She reaches out and grabs Kaydence's hand, kissing it. "I'm gonna miss this little bug, though."

Kaydence smiles at her, and I'm grateful to have employees who accept that she will always be by my side when I'm here. "She's in a good mood today. Hopefully that means she'll sleep well tonight."

Melissa laughs. "I'll pray that she does."

As I buckle Kaydence in her car seat in the back, my phone rings from the front. "I'm busy. Gonna have to call you back," I mumble to myself before blowing raspberries on Kaydence's cheek. I hustle to finish securing her, and then as I start the car, I reach for my phone to see who called me.

My mother.

Dread fills me as I stare down at the screen, debating whether I should return her call or not. I can anticipate how the conversation will go, and I already have enough anxiety about what I'm about to do that I don't need her to add to it.

So I close my phone, ignore her request for my attention since she's rarely shown me any in my life, and head for the fire station to visit my husband.

After Walker told me about his reconciliation with Drew, I had a come-to-Jesus moment with myself. I can't let people's opinions—Drew's included—prevent me from living my life. Walker and Kelsea have both told me this lately, but I think I'm finally reminding myself that the old Evelyn sure as hell wouldn't have cared what they think.

That woman isn't around anymore, though, not after having a child and losing the child's father. But parts of her are still deep inside of me, and I refuse to let those parts drift away.

Last night, as I sat on my porch and enjoyed a glass of wine by myself since Walker had already started his next shift, I realized that I'm in the process of discovering a new version of me—Evelyn, the mom, a woman who has lived her life with boundaries in place to protect her from disappointment but now has a little girl of her own to raise. And even though I don't regret her, I created a life and gave birth to a daughter who deserves a mother unlike my own—someone who isn't afraid to be vulnerable but is still strong in the ways that count.

I owe it to the girl I was before not to jeopardize the strength I fought for already, but I also owe it to the woman I want to be to desire a life where I'm not alone—and that means opening myself up to the possibility of more with Walker.

When I pull up to the station, nerves race through my veins. The steel doors on the bays are open, showcasing the engines, and I see a few of the guys walking around inside.

Walker told me the new engine hasn't arrived yet. But he also said the fundraiser was successful in securing it, so everyone is very excited about it.

As excited as a little boy getting a new toy to play with, I guess.

Three guys are playing a game of basketball to the left of the building as I exit my car. Walker has told me that most shifts consist of a lot of downtime between calls, so the guys try to find things to keep themselves busy and not sit around on their asses. The bounce of the ball echoes against the walls of the station as I grab Kaydence from her car seat, sling her diaper bag over my shoulder, lock my car, and stride up to face a few of my biggest critics.

One of the guys on duty sees me heading toward him, so he comes out from under the shade, shielding his eyes from the sun. "Evelyn?"

"Hey, there." I honestly don't remember this guy's name. Schmitty and I hung out with a few guys from the station here and there when we were sleeping together, but I think this guy might be new. Obviously, though, he knows who I am. "Is Walker around?"

"Yeah. I'm pretty sure he's inside cooking." *Sounds about right*. "Follow me."

"Thanks."

I trail behind him, feeling sets of eyes on me as he opens the door that leads from the garage to the living quarters of the building. We walk down a narrow hallway before I enter a room full of commotion. All of that stops when I enter behind the guy in front of me.

"Uh, Walker? You have visitors," the man announces as Walker spins around from his position at the stove, his entire face lighting up when he sees us.

"Hey," I say, feeling silly now that I chose to surprise him like this. My eyes dart around the room and land on Drew in the corner, who locks eyes with me and then drops his gaze to his plate in front of him.

In a flash, Walker stands before me, commanding my attention. "Hey, babe." He smooths his palm over my cheek before leaning down and kissing me in front of everyone. And if anyone needed any more confirmation about the validity of our relationship, Walker gave it to them in spades. He makes it perfectly clear that we're together as he swipes his tongue inside my mouth.

Kaydence decides that she wants Walker's attention, so she palms Walker's cheek, forcing us apart.

Chuckling, Walker pulls away from me and grabs her from my arms, tossing her in the air until she squeals. "Hey, little owl. Did you miss me?"

She grabs his cheeks and lets out a shriek that might just shatter glass.

"I take that as a yes."

"Is that a baby in my kitchen?" The chief asks as he enters the room and makes eye contact with me.

"Oh. Sorry." I go to take her from Walker, but the chief waves me off.

"Nonsense. You're fine. I was just making sure my eyes still work."

"Say hello to Kaydence, Chief," Walker says as he carries my daughter over to him while I watch the two of them dote on her. A few of the other guys walk over to meet her, too, and I realize in that moment, they probably all see John in her.

Suddenly, the room feels two inches big, but I fight to keep it together.

Maybe this wasn't such a good idea.

No, you've got this. You're not only doing this for you, but you're also doing it for Walker, too.

"Brad? You mind finishing up dinner? All you've got to do is stir in the sauce," Walker says over his shoulder.

Brad stands from his stool. "No problem."

Walker turns to me, pulling me into his chest as he still holds Kaydence. "This is a surprise."

"I know. I just figured we could come say hi before I went home from the store." *And I kind of missed you.*

"Well, I'm glad you did. Would you like a tour?" He waves his hand around.

"Sure."

When he spins us, I can see that the kitchen we're standing in also opens up to a living room filled with recliners that all face a massive flat-screen TV. There are two long tables to the right lined with chairs where several guys are now eating the dinner that Walker made, and the wall on the far left of the room is floor-to-ceiling windows, offering a view outside.

"This is the kitchen and living room, obviously."

"Do you think that TV is big enough?" Sarcasm laces my words.

"Believe me, if there were a bigger one, we'd have it."

"Men," I joke as I roll my eyes.

"Come on." He takes me by the hand and leads me further down the hallway I just came from.

"This is one of the sleeping quarters," he says as we enter a room on the left. The walls are lined with bunk beds that have very thin mattresses.

"Oh my God. Those beds look horrible!"

Walker chuckles as he bounces Kaydence in his arms. "Yeah, your bed is definitely preferred to this. But when you're exhausted, your mind doesn't really care what you're sleeping on by that point."

"Until the next morning when you wake up in pain, right?"

"Precisely."

He shows me two more rooms like that one, and I count twelve beds for the guys to use.

When we move back down the hallway and turn a corner leading to a staircase, a picture on the wall to my right stops me.

John's headshot is framed, his face stoic, the complete opposite of who I knew when he was alive. He's in his uniform against a blue background, but it's the gold plaque engraved underneath his picture that makes my eyes begin to well.

"They hung this up shortly after he died," Walker says as we both stare at the photo and the dates that mark the beginning and ending of his life. And then he points to the others that are hung in a line along the wall. "All of these guys died in the line of duty."

I reach out and trail a finger down the glass. Maybe this wasn't a good idea. Maybe coming here to prove that I could handle the feelings the last few months have thrown at me was all for nothing. Maybe I was wrong and I can't outrun the past.

When I turn to look at Walker, he's staring at Kaydence, smoothing her hair from her face. And then he walks her closer to the picture, points at John's face, and says, "That's your daddy, little owl."

Kaydence smacks the glass. "Da!"

The first wave of tears roll down my cheeks.

"That's right, baby girl. Dadda."

"Da!" she repeats and then looks at Walker when she says it again. "Da! Da!" Then she leans forward and kisses him with her open-mouthed kisses that everyone can't help but love—every slobbery drop.

Walker looks over at me, moisture filling his eyes now. We stare at each other, letting our eyes say what our mouths can't. And then he pulls me into his chest as I cry against his arm.

"He'll always be her father, Evelyn."

"I know."

"Even if he's not here. I have to believe that when he saw her, he would have been the man she needed in her life."

"I'd hoped he would."

The rise of his chest as he takes a deep breath prompts me to do the same. "I may not be her dad, but I sure as hell will always love her as if she were my own. I promise." I lift my head and find him staring down at me.

So many things are going through my mind, but the only thing that comes to the front is a moment I know I don't ever want to forget.

"Can I take a picture of you with her? Next to the photo of John?"

"Are you sure?"

"Yes." I wipe the tears from under my eyes as Walker releases me. "I think she'll want that one day."

I watch him swallow and then move to the side of the photo so she can see John's face. "Good?"

"Yes." I pull my phone from the diaper bag, open the camera, and snap a picture of Kaydence and her dads—the one who will watch over her from heaven, and the one who will love her here on earth.

And in that moment, I realize that maybe I could let him love me, too.

CHAPTER SIXTEEN

Evelyn

"Come on, boys!" Kelsea shouts from beside me, clapping her hands so hard that I know her palms will be red later. They always are after these games.

The season's first game of the men's football league that Newberry Springs started a few years ago is underway, and even though this isn't the first game I've ever attended, it's the first one I've been to since I married Walker. It's all the more nerve-wracking now.

Two years ago, I was here supporting Kelsea while she cheered on Wyatt and celebrating wins for the team with Schmitty afterward. Last year, I was pregnant, fighting with my baby daddy day in and day out and preparing for my life to change.

But this year, I'm in the stands with my daughter, cheering on my husband—who happens to be my daughter's dead father's best friend—eager to celebrate their inevitable win with him later in bed.

Jesus, my life sounds like a goddamn soap opera. But it's also kind of amazing, too, that time and change can bring tragedy, growing pains, and optimism as well.

"What kind of call was that, ref?" Kelsea screams beside me, planting her hands on her hips.

"I missed it. What happened?" I straighten after picking up the toy Kaydence tossed to the ground. That's her new favorite game this week.

"They said Walker was out of bounds when he caught the ball, but he had both feet in. Stupid," she grumbles. "I wish this was the NFL and they could review the video footage to challenge the damn refs."

Laughing, I glance up at my best friend. "You're too much sometimes, Kels."

She snaps her neck to meet my eyes. "Your husband was the one who made that catch. Why aren't you more angry?"

"Because if Walker's mad about the game, I get to reap the benefits later." I bounce my eyebrows, which makes her cackle.

"Touché. Wyatt always has plenty of adrenaline left after these games, which makes for a pleasant evening."

"Well, I will find out tonight just how wired Walker will be. And I won't lie and say I'm not looking forward to it."

Kelsea sighs, taking her seat on the bench beside me. We're up in the bleachers of the Newberry Springs High School football field. Friday nights are reserved for the high school games, but Saturdays belong to the men's league every two weeks for the next few months.

I readjust Kaydence in my lap as the game continues on the grass below. "Is it weird that I keep thinking back to last year when I was sitting here pregnant with Kaydence and remembering how differently I felt?"

"Absolutely not. If it makes you feel any better, I was thinking about that, too." She reaches over and grabs my hand.

"Really?"

"Yeah. I mean, I think it really hit me how much your life has changed when I gave you that shirt to wear today."

The wives and girlfriends of all the players get together at the beginning of each season to make shirts with the men's last names on them, pom-poms they use during their cheers, and even signs to hold in the stands.

I wasn't able to attend the meeting last night, so Kelsea made mine for me and gave it to me this morning after she and Wyatt had breakfast at Rose's Diner.

"There's actually something else I made, but I'm kind of afraid to give it to you," she says out of the corner of her mouth.

"What is it?"

Kelsea reaches into her bag on the bleachers and pulls out a tiny navy-blue shirt that matches mine. Holding it up, she turns it around and says, "It's for Kaydence."

I reach out and trace the name on the back that matches mine—Gibson—and my chest constricts as I internalize the gesture. I'm wearing a shirt with his last name on it, though I haven't legally changed mine to Gibson because I didn't think I needed to worry about it. But having Kaydence wearing his name sends a big message to him and everyone else.

When Kaydence was born, I gave her my last name because John had died and I didn't want my daughter to have a different last name from mine. But if I let her wear Walker's, what does that say?

Am I dishonoring her dad?

Does that mean Walker would want me to change her name to his at some point?

If I change mine, then I'd need to change hers, too, which would make this very real . . .

"Evelyn? Your mind is spinning. I can tell."

Nodding, I stare at the tiny t-shirt for a few more seconds and then flick my eyes away.

"You don't have to put it on her. Walker doesn't even know about it. I just thought maybe you'd want to feel like a family is all."

"No. It's just . . ."

Why am I questioning this so much?

Walker has done nothing but love my daughter

from the moment he stepped back into our lives. Why can't she wear his name proudly? That's how I felt when I put this shirt on today with his name on the back.

And we *are* a family after all, legally and in reality, the more time passes.

"Can you help me change her?" I ask Kelsea, watching her brows rise in shock.

"Are you sure?" I can see the hope in her eyes, and I know her intentions were pure. But part of me also knows my best friend, and I'm sure she's testing me right now, too.

"Yes."

Before I can talk myself out of it, I strip Kaydence's shirt off her—it already had stains on it, anyway—and place the navy shirt over her head, pulling it down to cover her little belly.

She coos, squeals, and then begins to make her owl noise as a bird flies by us.

"I think she approves," Kelsea jokes as a whistle rings out from the field.

"Yeah, I think so, too."

"This is going to mean a lot to him, Evelyn," Kelsea says as she bumps her shoulder against mine.

"Well, maybe I'm beginning to realize that he means a lot to us, too."

And I think I just sent myself a huge message about where my feelings really are.

Kelsea's eyes light up. "Things are still going well? Still taking it day by day, then?"

"Yes. My birthday was amazing, and even though the final mediation is in two weeks, I don't feel as undecided anymore about what I want."

"Holy shit," she breathes out. "Really?"

"I think so."

"Have you told him how you're feeling?"

"No. I'm just now coming to grips with it, so I don't know if bringing it up right now is the best idea."

"You have to talk to him about what you want eventually, Evelyn."

"I know. But everything is easy right now, almost effortless. I don't want to ruin it."

Kelsea raises a brow at me. "You realize that being in a relationship doesn't mean that everything is wonderful all the time, right?"

"I know."

"So thinking that a real conversation about your feelings is going to ruin things just sounds silly."

"Well, sorry, Kels. But I don't have much experience with this, okay?"

Sighing, she rubs my shoulder. "I know. I'm sorry. I just don't want you to have this skewed perception of what being in love looks like."

"I'm not in love with Walker."

She raises her brow at me again. "You sure?"

Am I in love with him? Isn't it too soon for me to know?

"Has that man shown you nothing but loyalty, honesty, and support since he offered to marry you?" Kelsea asks me, lowering her voice.

"Yes," I reply instantly.

"Has he proved how much he wants you?"

"Yes."

"Do you want this marriage to end when the mediation is over?"

"No," I answer so suddenly that I shock both Kelsea and myself. "Oh my God," I whisper as another whistle pierces the air.

Kelsea grabs my hand again, turning fully in my direction. "I think you just answered your own question, friend." But before we can discuss this any further, her eyes flick past me, and she mumbles under her breath, "What the hell?"

"What?" I spin to find what she's talking about, but she squeezes my hand, commanding my attention again.

"Don't look now, but you should probably know that John's parents are behind us in the bleachers."

"What?" I whisper. "Why?"

She spins around to face the field again. "I don't know. But just ignore them."

"I never would have known they were there if you hadn't said anything, Kelsea." My heart is racing for two reasons now.

She rubs the top of my hand while we stare out at the field. "I know. I'm sorry. But I didn't want you to be blindsided later. I didn't see them before, or I would have mentioned it earlier."

"Do you think they came to spy on me? Or Walker?"

"It's a possibility. But you're out in a public place. What could you do that is considered inappropriate? It's not like you're going to mount him in the middle of the football field in front of everyone . . ."

"Before I had Kaydence, I probably would have."

Kelsea snorts, which causes me to huff out a laugh. "Well, let's not give them any more ammunition to use against you."

"Probably a good idea."

I spend the rest of the game feeling like someone is watching me, and I know that they are. But I refuse to look behind me and play whatever game they're playing.

On top of that, my confession from earlier has me feeling antsy and eager to get out of here so I can process it in peace.

When the game is over, though, Kelsea and I both realize why Mr. and Mrs. Schmitt are here.

Both teams gather in the center of the field to present John's parents with his jersey. Since he died after the season ended last year, they wanted to honor him at the start of this one.

Silence descends on the crowd as the chief and a few of the guys say kind words about John. I expect Walker to hand them John's jersey, but Walker remains rooted in place, off to the side, as Wyatt hands it to John's parents.

Wyatt is one of the team captains, so it doesn't seem too suspicious, but I wonder if other people in the crowd are questioning the gesture coming from Wyatt and not Walker like I am, since John and Walker were best friends.

However, the way Walker practically glares at John's parents tells me that he's still angry about the custody battle, which brings the reality of our marriage and the impending decisions I need to make back into stark focus.

Once the ceremony ends, the crowd in the stands rushes the field, as per usual. Kelsea runs up to Wyatt to jump in his arms, smothering him with kisses. She told me the first time she was able to do that felt like giving her teenage self the permission to give in to all her fantasies from back then.

I remember being so ecstatic for her in that moment, that she finally got to experience the feeling of showing Wyatt how she felt. And as I reminisce on that, I use it to fuel my own desires.

I walk up to Walker with Kaydence on my hip. He's talking to one of the other players, but when he sees us, his eyes lock on mine and stay there until I'm standing right in front of him.

"Hey there," he says in greeting.

But I don't respond. I just reach behind his head, grab the back of it, and pull his lips down to mine.

Walker doesn't miss a beat, pulling me into his chest, slipping his tongue between my lips, and showing me how much he enjoyed my little display of ownership. And that's the thing—he's claimed me so many times now, it honestly feels good to do it back.

Forget John's parents being here. Forget everyone else in town.

In this moment, it's just the three of us—and I don't think I've ever been this happy.

Yes, I'm almost certain that this is what I want.

When Walker slows down the kiss, I whimper because my body is ready for more, but I know there'll be time for that later.

"Babe," he breathes out as he lines his lips up to my ear. "You can't move away yet. I'm hard as a fucking rock."

I giggle. "Sorry—you were just so good out there. So sexy. Apparently, there was a bullshit call by one of the refs. I missed it, but don't worry. Kelsea was extremely irritated on your behalf."

"Yeah. It wasn't the best call, but that's bound to happen in these games." He leans back and brushes away the stray hairs the wind is whipping around my face. "Having you up there cheering for me, though . . . that was the best fucking part of today. And this little owl?" he says as he grabs Kaydence from me, tossing her up in the air. When he brings her back down, he assesses her attire, turning to look at the back of her shirt before telling her, "I love your shirt, baby girl."

"Well, we had to match, you know?" I spin around so he can see my back as well.

A fire lights up his eyes as he pulls me into his chest

again. "My girls," he growls, kissing me deeply, working up my body once more. And then he closes his eyes, rests his forehead on mine, and whispers, "Thank you."

"How about we show each other just how appreciative we are of one another later once Kaydence goes to sleep?"

His lips lift in that sexy grin I've come to love. "Sounds like a fucking plan."

Still holding Kaydence, he wraps his other arm around my back, and we head for the parking lot. I drove separately since he came early to warm up, so I'll probably follow Walker home or vice versa. But as we approach my car, we catch Mr. and Mrs. Schmitt staring at us from a distance.

I freeze. Walker freezes. And for a good thirty seconds, no one moves.

Walker and I are showing a united front. I think our affection toward each other speaks for itself. And Kaydence is happy as a clam in Walker's arms right now. So if they're looking for something to use against us, they're not going to find it here.

But they can still find something, *can't they, Evelyn?*

I hate that my subconscious is right.

CHAPTER SEVENTEEN

Walker

I reach forward, wrap her hair around my fist, and pull her head back so I can see her face. "Squeeze my cock, Ev. Tighten that fucking pussy and milk me."

I feel her clench while I continue to thrust into her from behind. And as I stare down and see my last name on her shirt—the shirt I insisted she keep on while I fucked her tonight—I know my restraint is going to snap anytime now.

"Harder, Walker. Fuck me harder."

I give her what she wants, slamming my hips into her

ass over and over, harder each time. My mouth covers hers as I keep my grip on her hair, muffling her cries.

"Oh, God," she breathes out when I release her lips.

"Jesus, Evelyn. You've fucking ruined me. You know that, right?" I growl in her ear.

"You've ruined me, too, Walker." Her breaths are shallow, and I feel her clench around me again. "Fuck, I'm gonna come."

"Do it. Come with me." I hold her in place, staring into her eyes as our bodies slap together, and then she shatters, screaming as she falls apart. I follow along right behind her.

When we're both spent, we fall to the bed, and I pull her into my arms.

"I need to use the bathroom," she announces after a few minutes, so I reluctantly release her to do her business. On her way back, she rips the shirt over her head, unhooks her bra and tosses it aside as well, and then struts back over to the bed, climbing right back where she was moments ago: in my arms with her head on my chest. "That's better."

"I don't know what's sexier—you wearing my last name on your back, or you completely naked."

She laughs. "Why choose when you can have both?"

I spin us until I'm on top of her, holding her hands over her head. Her eyes light up from my move, and I want to take her again so badly. When I nudge her opening with my cock, she nods, giving me permission, allowing me to slide inside.

Fucking heaven.

I don't think I'll ever get enough of this woman—her body, her eyes, her smile, her light. I meant what I told her on her birthday: She's put light back into my world.

She's my moon. She and Kaydence are my family. And I love them so fucking much that I don't know what to do about it. Because telling her how I truly feel reminds me of the bunny rabbit analogy Kelsea told me. I'm terrified of scaring her.

It's only been a month—a month of fucking bliss, of course, but also a month of living out every fantasy I've ever had featuring this woman.

We have a little less than two weeks left until the final mediation, and I want to know, walking into that meeting, that Evelyn is mine completely. But every day, I battle with pushing her to make a decision or letting things happen naturally. So in the meantime, I just keep trying to show her what she means to me. I want her to know how much I want her in every way without speaking the actual words.

"Walker," she moans, our eyes locking. I slowly glide in and out of her, her feet hooked behind my back as I circle my hips. I'm in no rush. I just got done fucking her, but now? I want to worship her, fall apart together, show her just how much she means to me.

"Fuck, Ev. God, it's so good." *It couldn't feel this good if it weren't real, right?*

"I know." She lifts up to kiss me, and we say nothing else until we come together once again.

This can't be fake. This can't be a mistake. And in this moment, I trust that everything happened for a reason, leading us to now.

Still inside her, I push up on my elbows so I can look into her eyes. Hers are closed at the moment. Her head is turned to the side, and her chest rises against mine with labored breaths.

God, I love her. I can't live without her.

"Evelyn . . ."

"Hmm?"

"Look at me, baby."

Slowly, she turns her head and meets my eyes. "What is it, Walker?"

Swallowing down the lump in my throat, I battle with whether to say what's on my heart, what I know down in the marrow of my bones, or hold off until later this week when I show her just how committed I am to her.

My gut tells me to wait, so I go with, "You're so fucking beautiful."

Her smile is contagious. "Thank you."

"I'm so addicted to you," I continue as I trail a finger down the curve of her jawline.

"Ditto."

I trace my hand over the swell of her breast and down her rib cage, landing on her hip and smoothing around to her ass. "I'm still in denial that I get to touch you like this."

She reaches behind me and grabs my ass cheeks, pulling me deeper inside her. "Don't be. I think I've stared at your ass more in the past six weeks than I've ever looked at my own."

Her candidness is just another reason I've fallen in love with her. God, she makes me laugh.

"It's late, Walker. Kaydence will be up early."

Nuzzling her neck, I inhale the smell of vanilla that she always wears, implanting it in my veins so it never goes away. "I know. I just . . ."

"What?" She stares up at me, tilting her head.

The words are on the tip of my tongue, but I settle for, "Sleeping means I don't get to stare at you."

She rolls her eyes and pushes me off her. "You can stare all you want, honey. But I'm going to bed."

As I watch her walk back into the bathroom while I lie on the bed, I know that what I have planned for later this week will be the true test of my feelings—and hers. I just hope I don't freak her out.

"Are you sure about this?" Wyatt stares down at me, his arms crossed over his chest. The buzz of the tattoo gun creates background noise for our conversation.

"It's a little late for that question, don't you think?" I flick my eyes down to Gage, the tattoo artist who is already in the process of inking my skin.

When I first had the idea for this tattoo, I knew it needed to be perfect. Gage has done work on all of us

Gibson boys, but etching this image into my skin is taking a huge leap of faith.

"Evelyn has no idea?"

"No. Did Kelsea know when you got that camera tattooed on you back in the day?"

"Touché. But . . . I knew that Kelsea and I had a friendship beyond our feelings. That tattoo was before we became a couple and crossed that line. You're putting ink on your skin for a woman and her daughter without really knowing if you'll be staying married to her. Isn't that a little crazy?"

"Do you regret getting that tattoo for Kelsea? Even before you were together?"

"Absolutely not. But that was different, too."

Shaking my head, I look down at the needle buzzing across my skin. "Thanks for your support."

"Fuck, Walker. It's not that I don't support you." He pulls a chair up to the table I'm lying on, spins it around before he straddles it, drapes his hands over the back of it, and leans in closer to me as people move around the tattoo shop. "I just don't understand why you haven't settled the feelings between you two before you do something permanent like this."

"I know she's in this, Wyatt," I say, more confidently than I probably should. But after the other night, and every night since I told her how I've felt about her all along, I just can't believe she doesn't reciprocate my feelings.

I'm in love with her. I know this. I think I've always known this.

And even though she hasn't said the words, I know she feels strongly for me, too. This marriage became real very quickly, and I need it to stay that way.

I can't go back to living my life without the two of them in it.

And even if, heaven forbid, things don't work out between Evelyn and me, I will always be there for those girls. They will always have a place in my life and my heart, just like this tattoo.

So that's why I don't feel nervous about the ink I'm putting on my skin for them. Tattoos can represent something important in the present or in the past, even though the thought of this time with Evelyn and Kaydence being just a memory makes me nauseous. I keep trying to convince myself it just won't happen.

"I think you're right. I've seen you two together. Hell, Kelsea is over the moon that Evelyn has even opened herself up to you at all."

"She has, but I also know that she's still a bit guarded, too. She's keeping something close to the vest, Wyatt."

"Like what?"

"I don't know exactly, but it has to do with whatever sent her running from her life in Dallas. She worked for an investment firm owned by a friend of her parents, and things didn't work out. But that's all I know."

When Mr. and Mrs. Schmitt showed up to the football

game last week, I was reminded of what's yet to come. Evelyn and I have been living in such a heightened state of bliss for the past five weeks that I think we've both been fixated on each other so we could avoid thinking about the impending mediation.

But now, with just five days to go and a deadline looming, I'm starting to feel the pressure. I've been invested in showing Evelyn she can rely on me and let her guard down, but now I need her to open up completely. I'm hoping that tonight, after I show her my level of commitment with this permanent gesture, she'll be willing to do the same.

"You don't want any secrets between you two going into that meeting, Walker."

"I know."

"So as much as you may be afraid of pushing her too hard, you need to. Remember when Kelsea hid that photography program from me? It was brutal on us. You don't want to go through that if you can avoid it."

"You're right. I just . . . fuck, it's taken me so long to get here with her, Wyatt," I say, wincing through the pain of the needle as it passes over my pec.

"But does that mean you're just going to walk on eggshells with her forever?"

Fuck, he's right. I obviously don't want to scare her, but by avoiding the conversation, I'm not doing either of us any favors, either.

"Tonight. I'll try to have a conversation with her

tonight."

Wyatt nods. "I just want you to get what you want, Walker. You and Evelyn both deserve that. But your situation is delicate, and before you head into the final battle, you've got to be on the same page. Trust me. You don't want things to be any other way."

~

"There you two are!" Kelsea beams as she walks toward us, Wyatt hot on her heels. The crowd of people around us mill about as the seasonal bonfire-slash-barbecue at the Gibson Ranch bustles in full swing.

"Where's the moonshine?" Tim, one of the ranch hands, calls out over the music. He crosses in front of us toward a group of men passing around a mason jar full of the moonshine my father has been making since he was younger than Wyatt and me.

My eyes trail after Tim before landing back on Kelsea and my brother as they step in front of us. "Seems everyone is in the mood to celebrate tonight."

"Yeah. I still don't know why Mom and Dad insisted we have one earlier this year instead of at the end of the season like usual," Wyatt muses, sipping his beer.

"I know, me neither. But there's no arguing with those two when they set their mind to something."

"Agreed."

"Want me to take her?" Kelsea asks Evelyn, reaching for Kaydence.

"If you want to."

"Nope. That baby is mine." My mother waltzes up to us, arms outstretched, summarily stealing Kaydence from Kelsea's hands.

"Hey, baby hog!" Kelsea admonishes as she watches my mother dote on the baby.

My mother presses kisses to each of Kaydence's cheeks and then settles her on her hips. "That's right. This is my grandbaby, and we're about to dance so her mommy and daddy can have some fun tonight," she says, glancing over at me and Evelyn.

My heart doesn't miss that she referred to me as Kaydence's dad, and I don't think Evelyn missed that, either, based on the widening of her eyes.

"Well, at least let me help. I never get to see my niece anymore," Kelsea whines, trailing behind my mom as they walk away from us.

"I guess you're free for the evening, then?" Wyatt jokes, looking at us both.

"I guess. I didn't expect her to do that," Evelyn says.

"Don't sweat it, Ev. Momma is in heaven with that little girl. And if I have it my way, I'm gonna give her another baby to love on sooner rather than later," Wyatt says, smirking at his own plans.

"Jesus, now babies?" Forrest slides up to us, one of his hands buried in his pocket, the other holding a beer.

"Mine came as part of a package deal, Forrest. But I wouldn't have it any other way," I say, pulling Evelyn into my waist and kissing the top of her head.

"And Kelsea and I don't need to explain our life choices to you, fucker," Wyatt declares, glaring at our older brother.

"I'm gonna need more alcohol to get through this night," Forrest mutters, draining his beer before wiping his mouth with the back of his hand. "Fucking couples everywhere . . ."

"What crawled up your ass and died?" I ask. "Didn't you just get back from that convention in Vegas? Shouldn't you be well rested or at least less grumpy from the casual fuck I hope you had while you were out there?"

Forrest glares at me. "The convention was fine. It was . . ." He shakes his head, not finishing the sentence. "Let's just say the past has a funny way of popping up when you least expect it, and I was *not* expecting it at all."

"What happened?" Wyatt asks, pushing for more information. And I'm not gonna lie, I wanna fucking know, too. This is the most our brother has talked about his personal life in years, and we've heard two sentences in less than a minute.

He opens his mouth as if he's going to speak, and then he mumbles, "Fuck. Never mind. Beer's not gonna cut it tonight. I need some fucking moonshine." And then he walks off, leaving us baffled and concerned.

I look over at Wyatt. "What the fuck do you think happened?"

"I don't know. Who would he run into from his past in Vegas at a construction convention?" I reply.

Forrest went out there to network, talk to suppliers and contractors, and see if he could find some new project opportunities to expand work into other states.

And then it hits me. "Does Shauna still live in Vegas?"

Wyatt's eyes bug out. "I don't know, but that's where she went to college, right?"

"Yeah, she went to UNLV."

Evelyn steps forward, glancing between the two of us. "You think he saw her?"

"Saw who?" Kelsea asks, arriving back at our little circle sans Kaydence. I'm guessing she lost the battle of taking her back from my mom.

"We think Forrest ran into Shauna at that convention in Vegas," Wyatt explains, launching into a recap of our brief conversation for the girls.

Kelsea's eyes nearly fall out of her head when he's done. "Are you serious?"

"Who else could he be talking about?" I ask.

"Well, based on how he's acting, I'm gonna say it didn't go well." Evelyn shrugs.

"Do you think if we get him drunk, he'll talk about it more?" Kelsea suggests.

"Doubt it. He'll slip away and go pass out in his old

room. That's what he usually does at these things," Wyatt explains.

"Well, I'm not satisfied with the lack of answers to these questions." Kelsea takes a sip of her drink, smacking her lips together. "I think I might try to get him to open up." And then she takes off without giving any of us a backward glance.

"You might want to go with your wife in case Forrest turns into the big, bad wolf and tries to eat her," I say to my twin brother.

Wyatt sighs. "Yeah, you're right. Catch up with you two later?"

"Yup. We'll be here."

Wyatt strolls off, leaving me alone with Evelyn. She turns in my arms and gazes up at me. "Wanna grab a drink?"

"Sounds like a plan."

Music echoes into the night, coming from speakers situated within and outside of the event space on the property. Each season, our parents throw these parties for everyone who works here in celebration of their hard work and the success they help bring the ranch.

A dance floor has been set up in front of the barn, with strings of bulb lights hanging from a pole in the center of it. Cowboy boots scuff the wood tiles as couples two-step along to the playlist for the night. My dad always smokes brisket and tri-tip and barbecues enough chicken to feed an army, and Momma makes all the sides filling up everyone's plates.

The sun is almost set, and the moon is just beginning to light up the sky. It's a beautiful night, one I hope will only get better the later it gets.

I secure two drinks for me and Evelyn—beers from the Gibson Brewery that my brother donates each time for these events—and then we head for the food to grab a bite to eat. Once we find a table to sit at and start to stuff our faces, my father's voice cuts through the music, getting everyone's attention.

"How's everyone feeling tonight?" he asks, and the crowd of people hoots and hollers in response.

Evelyn turns to me from her seat on my right and smiles, prompting me to wrap my arm around her shoulders.

"I know everyone was surprised that we decided to have a bonfire a little earlier than normal, but the truth is, we have a reason for that." He clears his throat, and then his eyes find mine.

When he asked me if I would be okay with him announcing Evelyn and me as husband and wife in front of everyone, I didn't hesitate to agree. I know she'll be surprised, but I'm hoping she realizes just how much my family loves her and accepts her through this gesture.

Plus, it helps me show her that she's a part of my life now and I don't want that to change.

"Elaine and I have recently acquired two new members

of the Gibson family. Almost two months ago, our son, Walker, married a woman that he's loved for a very long time and vowed to love not only her, but also her daughter."

I turn to look at Evelyn. Her eyes are stretched open with shock, her lips parted with disbelief. I take her by the hand, help her stand, and then lead her over to where my father is standing.

I can hear murmurs around us, but I focus on nothing but her.

When we get closer to my dad, he turns to speak to us, even though he's still talking into the microphone. "Evelyn, you and your daughter are a part of this family now. You have helped our son become the man I raised him to be and given us a granddaughter to love. Elaine and I wish you two no less than a lifetime of happiness." Cheers ring out around us as Evelyn's eyes water and her cheeks turn pink. "Now, since you were in such a rush to get married . . ." He winks at her but then glares at me. "We thought you two might want to share your first dance as husband and wife in front of everyone. What do you say?"

Technically, it's not our first dance, but in other ways, it is. It's the first time we get to celebrate our marriage in front of other people.

"Will you dance with me, babe?" I ask her.

Evelyn nods, her hands shaking in mine. "Yes."

More applause and cheers ring out as I lead her to the center of the dance floor. The opening chords of "It's Your

Love" by Tim McGraw begin to play as I pull Evelyn into my body, wrapping one hand around her waist as I grab her hand with my other one and hold it out at our side. We sway along to the melody while I look into her eyes.

"Did you know your dad was going to do that?" she asks me as we move around with everyone's eyes on us.

"I did."

"That was sneaky," she whispers, but I can see a hint of a smile on her lips.

"Well, if I'd told you, would you have wanted to come? Or would you have been anxious about it all week?"

"No, and yes."

"Exactly."

I lean down and press my lips to hers. "I wanted to dance with my wife. Sue me."

"Your wife," she echoes my words, letting out a sigh of contentment. "I want to be mad, but I can't. Not when you're such a good dancer, Walker." She sighs again, closing her eyes. "I think I'd let you dance with me forever."

"That's what I want, Evelyn."

Her eyes pop open, and tunnel vision surrounds me because she's all I see. *My future.*

"I want forever with you."

The song ends, everyone claps, and I plant a passionate kiss on her lips for good measure. Then I take her by the hand, leading her away from the crowd to the main house, eager to find some place for us to be alone.

One of the guest rooms is free, so I pull her inside, slam

the door shut, push her up against it, and slant my mouth over hers.

Need races through me, from the tip of my toes through my heart to my brain. I need this woman right now. And nothing is going to stop me from telling her how I feel in this moment.

"God, why do you make me feel like I can't breathe?" she asks as my mouth travels up her neck to her ear, memorizing every inch of her flesh with my lips.

"You make me feel that way every day, Evelyn." I lift my head so I can meet her eyes. "But not because you steal my breath away. No. Your presence has shown me that I wasn't breathing without you in my life—without you being mine."

"Walker . . ." Her hands dig into my shoulders as I press my hips between hers, letting her feel what she does to me. And then I reach behind me, lift my shirt off my torso, and show her just how serious I am.

Evelyn gasps when she sees the ink on my chest. The skin is still inflamed, red and angry, but the picture is perfect, capturing my girls in a way that no one else will understand.

On the center of my left pec is a beautiful sketch of the moon, showing lines and shadows in the surface of the rock. And right in front of it is an angelic-looking owl with big eyes, just like the eyes of the little girl who has captured my heart. On the chest of the owl are also the letters J and S for John Schmitt. I wanted him to be a part of this piece as well—because he is, and he always will be.

The entire piece of art is done in black and white, but it's still stunning.

"When did you get this?" Evelyn asks, gently running her finger over the ink. I wince because the skin is still sensitive, but the way she's completely enraptured by the tattoo right now allows me to push through the pain.

"Today."

"Why?" Her eyes lift to meet mine.

"Isn't it obvious, Ev?" I ask, cupping her face with both of my hands and then let out the declaration I've been holding in for months. "I love you," I breathe out, letting those words come to life. It feels so *right* to set them free after weeks of having them live only in my mind, after weeks of telling myself that I shouldn't say them. But fuck it. This woman needs to know how I feel before we face the fork in our road to happiness.

"I love you and Kaydence, and I want to keep you both . . . forever." She opens her mouth to speak, but I place a finger over her lips, silencing her. "It's never been fake for me, Evelyn. In my mind, this entire marriage has never had an expiration date. I want it all, every good and bad day, every bump in the road and moment that takes our breath away. I want you. *I love you.* And it feels so good to finally say it." Blowing out a breath, letting my heart rate come back down, I continue, "You don't have to say it back, Evelyn. I know that you're not where I'm at, but I bet you're closer than you think."

"I care about you so much, Walker. I have such strong feelings for you, but . . ."

Fuck. I hate that word.

"But what happens after the mediation, Walker?" she finishes.

I swallow and then toy with her bottom lip with my thumb. "That's up to you. I'm in this. I have been from the beginning. But please don't think I suggested this marriage *anticipating* that you would fall for me." Her lips curl up in a soft smile. "Did I always hope that something could come from this? I'm not going to lie and say that I didn't. But my first thought from the beginning was saving Kaydence from growing up without you, and I will see that through as long as you need me to. But for us? After the past month or so? Can you honestly tell me that you don't see a future together, Evelyn?"

"I do. I'm just . . ."

I don't let her finish. Instead, I put my mouth on hers once more and try to swallow her doubts, her fears. Evelyn doesn't have to admit her feelings to me. I feel them every time we touch, every time she welcomes me home after a shift, every time she stares at me like she can't believe I'm still around. I want this life. Fuck, I want her and Kaydence until I leave this earth.

But does she want me back?

For right now, I have to settle for what I know because

at least she knows *my* truth. And hopefully that helps eliminate her doubts.

Our tongues meld and twist, and suddenly, desperation takes over. The need to connect with her, to remind her of what we have together is so overwhelming, that I'm unbuttoning my jeans and pushing them down my legs as Evelyn does the same to her shorts.

I strip her top over her head as well, leaving us both naked, and then walk us over to the bed. "Don't doubt this, Evelyn," I say as we lie down. Instantly, I slide inside her, and her moans fill the room as I do.

"I don't want to, Walker. I don't doubt *you*. I just doubt everything else . . ." she explains as I find a rhythm and seal my lips over hers to silence that fear.

I let my body do the talking as I grip her hips and ass, pulling her in as close as we can get. I seal my lips over her nipple, swirling around the bud with my tongue until she's writhing in ecstasy and clenching around me.

My heart is aching with the pain of both love and loss. With overwhelming, all-consuming love and pervasive, impending grief.

They say that grief is love with nowhere to go. I've experienced grief before, most recently from losing my best friend. But losing Evelyn? I don't think my heart would ever recover from that.

"Trust me, Evelyn," I say, fighting off my orgasm because I can feel that pressure building in my body. It feels like I can't get inside her deep enough to prove my love, my worth, my commitment. But every time I thrust into her, I try. "Trust me to love you, to be there for you, to stand by your side through everything."

Evelyn nods, slamming her mouth onto mine again as she falls apart, clawing at me desperately through her release. I make sure she's toward the end of her orgasm before I finally let myself have my own.

As we lie there, I consider how to bring us back to the topic at hand. But luckily, Evelyn finds her words first.

"I'm falling for you, Walker," she whispers, which has me lifting my head so I can see her face as she speaks.

"I fell a long time ago, Evelyn." Stroking my hand down her face, I say, "Fuck, you've ruined me, completely destroyed my desire to want anyone else. But I need you to let me in, babe," I say, placing my hand over her heart. "I need to know the real you—every flaw, secret, and bruise. I need to see your scars so I can show you that they aren't imperfections, Evelyn. They're your history. And the only thing we can do with history is learn from it."

She takes a deep breath, blows it out, and then bites her bottom lip. "Okay."

"Okay?"

"Yeah. I think it's time I told you a story . . ."

CHAPTER EIGHTEEN

Evelyn

"Your proposal is impressive," Seth Ferguson, my boss and mentor, clasps his hands over his chest as he stares at me across the desk. "But that doesn't surprise me."

"Really?" I practically bounce in the chair opposite his desk. I was so nervous to show him what I had been working on because I didn't want to let him down. He's spent years letting me shadow him in preparation to work at the firm. All of that time would have been for nothing if I couldn't produce what I knew he would expect.

Seth stands from his chair, circling the desk to sit on the edge of it in front of me. "I'm beyond impressed, Evelyn. I knew you were right for this job." He reaches out and tucks a strand of my hair behind my ear. My entire body goes on high alert.

Seth is old enough to be my father. I've known him my entire life, and he's never touched me like that.

Maybe I'm reading too much into it. Yeah, you're just being paranoid, Evelyn.

But then his fingers leave my face and trail down my arm.

"Um, Seth?"

"Don't act like you don't want this, Evelyn." He stands over me now, resting his hands on the arms of my chair, boxing me in with no way to escape.

"Want what?

"I've seen the way you look at me."

My brow furrows. "What are you talking about?"

He palms himself through his slacks. "You want this. And now that you're eighteen, you can have it."

Bile rises in my throat at the memory, which is part of the reason I don't talk about that night at all. It reminds me how naïve I was, how disappointed I felt when I realized that the man who had been grooming me for a job was also grooming me to be his mistress.

After Walker and I got dressed at the ranch, we grabbed Kaydence and decided to leave the bonfire early. Momma G wasn't happy that I took the baby from her, of course, but Walker and I needed to talk, especially since the mediation is only days away at this point.

And his confession completely rocked me tonight.

He loves me. He wants to stay married and be together. He got a tattoo of an owl and the moon, branding me and my daughter on his heart.

And I want that, too. I know I do. But I have to move past the fear holding me back, the fear that history will repeat itself.

I know that Walker isn't my parents or Seth Ferguson. But giving him that kind of emotional power over me is terrifying because there are people in this world who will use it as a weapon. I encountered that at a very young age, leaving me jaded to the idea of trusting anyone ever again.

Once Kaydence is tucked into her bed, I meet Walker on the porch. He already has a glass of wine poured for me. We sit on the loveseat out here this time so he can be near me.

And I just might need him when I begin to fall apart.

I told him I needed to tell him a story, and he already knows pieces of it. Now it's just about putting those pieces into place.

"I told you about my parents' friend, the one who allowed me to intern at his financial investment firm," I start, inhaling deeply to help regulate my blood pressure.

"Yes. Seth Ferguson, right?"

"Yeah." Staring down at my wine, I give myself a minute to pull my thoughts together. "After I graduated from high school, I started working at his firm full-time. I wasn't given any clients of my own right off the bat since I wasn't eighteen. But after my birthday at the end of July, Seth approached me with my first client. The catch was that I had to pitch my plan to him first before I could work with the client on my own." I stare out across the backyard. "I was so excited yet nervous. I wanted to prove myself so badly, to prove to Seth, too, that the time he had invested in me wasn't for nothing. I brought him my plan, and he loved it."

"Why do I feel like there is a 'but' coming?" Walker asks.

"Because there is." I give myself a minute to prepare to relive that night. "I met with him late at night in the office, per his request. I didn't think anything of it, considering he was a busy man and that might have been the only time that day he had to meet with me. We were the only ones in the building—no other witnesses." Walker clenches his jaw when I glance at him. He knows what's coming. "He made a pass at me. Proceeded to sexually harass me and force himself on me, Walker. He told me that now that I was eighteen, I could take what I always wanted, and that he was going to do the same."

"Jesus Christ, Evelyn." He leans forward in his seat, resting his arms on his knees, holding his beer in between. "Did he—"

"No. It never got that far. I kneed him in the crotch and ran out of the building as fast as I could." Thank God he never got the chance to touch me like that. I don't know how I would have survived that, too.

"Good." He swallows hard. "If he'd touched you . . . I'd have to murder him."

"Well, he wasn't happy that he didn't get what he wanted, and I didn't know what to do afterward. My entire world was upended." Shaking my head, I stare up at the sky. "So I did what any eighteen-year-old girl would do . . . I went to my parents. I knew Seth was their friend, but they would listen to me if I told them the truth. Or so I thought . . ."

"What did they say?"

My eyes focus on the trees in the distance. "I remember walking into the house, tears streaming down my face. But when they saw me, they had this look on their faces like they were angry. I was so confused. When I approached them, they said I didn't need to say a word. They already knew what happened."

Walker's brow pinches together. "What do you mean?"

"His wife came out of the kitchen of my parents' house with video footage of me and Seth together—laughing in meetings, me leaving his office while I was tucking my hair behind my ears, staring at the ground as if I was hiding a blush on my cheeks or some secret. And even footage of me storming out of his office that night before I raced home." I take another sip of my wine. "She was already at my parents' house, ready to tell them about what a whore I was because she'd been watching us. She accused me of having an affair with her husband, said that when he ended it tonight, I assaulted him and left the office in a rage, eager to accuse him of coming on to me instead of telling the truth. I'm guessing she called him after I left, and he told her his side of the story."

"What did your parents say?" he asks. But the lump in my throat has grown larger as I think back to the way they reacted. "Evelyn . . ." He reaches for my hand. "What did they say, babe?"

"They believed Seth and his wife," I whisper as the first tear cascades down my cheek. I bat it away and drain the rest of my wine glass, wishing I brought the bottle outside with me so I could fill it back up.

Walker practically jumps out of his seat. "Are you fucking kidding me?"

I grab his hand and pull him back down. "Yes, Walker. But you getting mad about this isn't going to solve anything. It happened so long ago . . ."

"Yeah, but it's not fucking right, Ev. Your parents believed them instead of you—their own daughter."

"I know. And that's not even the worst part."

Walker runs a hand through his hair. "Jesus, there's more?"

"Unfortunately." Sighing, I convince myself just to get it all out so I don't have to relive this again. "Seth's wife told everyone in our circle—all of the other couples my parents spent time with, everyone at the company, people around town. Anyone she could spew her lies to, she did."

"I've never wanted to go after someone so badly before, Ev."

I sigh again. "She's not worth it, Walker. I left, okay? I left that life behind, because honestly? For one, it wasn't what I really wanted. And two, there was nothing there for me anymore. Everyone thought I was a slut, someone who wanted to split up a marriage and sleep her way to the top. Even my own fucking parents. They looked at me with disgust, like they couldn't believe I would come on to a married man."

"God, it all makes so much fucking sense now," Walker mutters, staring up at the sky.

"What does?"

He drops his head, locking his eyes on mine. "Why you've been so uncertain. Why everyone's words and opinions about our marriage have been driving you so crazy." He closes the gap between us and frames my face in his hands. "I'm so fucking sorry for putting you through that again."

"You didn't know." Another tear streams down my face, but Walker kisses it away, licking his lips of the salt when he rears back again. "But like I said, at least you stood up for me. When you did that, I didn't know how to react. No one has ever done that for me, Walker. *No one.* Everyone turned against me when the thing with Seth went down."

"You never fucking deserved that."

"I know that now. I know that, but it doesn't change the fact that this experience scarred me."

"I told you. I want your scars. I want to know everything there is to know about you."

"Well, now you do."

He kisses me, his lips so soft that I melt into him. He just made love to me, and I want it again. I don't think I'll ever stop wanting him.

"Is this what you think John's parents found out?" he asks, bringing the point of this conversation full circle.

"It has to be. If I had to bet, I think Seth's wife probably saw this as an opportunity to smear my name through the mud again when they started digging and asking questions."

"Well, that's not going to happen. I'll make sure of it."

"How?"

He rests his forehead on mine. "Don't worry about it. Everything is going to be okay. This is my fight now, too—for you, for Kaydence. They won't win. I just won't fucking allow it."

I wish I could believe that he's right. But there's nothing like a last-minute test of a relationship to make a person see if actions can truly back up words.

My cellphone vibrates on the counter for the third time this morning, my mother's name flashing across the screen yet again.

After telling Walker everything about my past the other

night, the last thing I want to do is talk to her. She's been calling all week, which is very uncharacteristic of her, but she doesn't deserve my energy. She doesn't have the right to make me feel unworthy, like I'm a disappointment, which is what she does every time I speak with her. So I'm setting the boundary. I don't have to speak with her at all if I don't want to.

But it's hard to keep that boundary up when she walks through the door to my store and stares me dead in the eye.

Holy shit. What is she doing here?

"Mom?"

Her lips curl up in disgust as she glances around the store, taking one step at a time at a snail's pace toward where I'm standing behind the counter. Kaydence is napping in her Pack 'n Play, thank God, but if I start screaming in a second, she'll likely wake up.

"What are you doing here, Mom?" I'm frozen in place, watching her assess my store—my livelihood, the one thing I'm most proud of besides my daughter.

"Well, you would know why I'm here if you would answer my calls," she spits out, glaring at me now.

Staring at her is like looking into the future. I've always looked like my mother, taller than average, lean build—even though I'm not as lean after having Kaydence, but Walker doesn't complain—and blonde hair that you can't get from a bottle.

She's wearing a navy-blue skirt and matching blazer,

with a plain white blouse underneath. Her hair is smoothed back in a low bun, her signature look, and her makeup is flawless as always because she has someone do it for her every day.

My mother is *the* definition of high maintenance and put together. Not a hair out of place. No flaws. Flaws make you weak, and Trinity Sumner is *not* weak.

"I don't understand how you left nine years ago, and I'm still having to clean up your mess," she says, her eyes ice cold.

My head rears back on my neck. "Excuse me?"

"You're in a custody battle with your baby's father's parents, Evelyn. And they're trying to find out about your affair with Seth Ferguson."

I clench my teeth together. "I did not have an affair with Seth, Mother."

"Yes, I've heard that before." She rolls her eyes. "This is ludicrous, Evelyn. What kind of Podunk life are you living up here?" She fans her arms out to the side. The anger rolling off her is the one emotion she knows how to display. Not love, joy, or compassion. But anger? She has that one perfected.

"One you have no right to be a part of!" I shout, hoping I didn't wake up my daughter. "My mess is *my* mess, not yours, so why are you even here?"

She reaches into her purse, grabbing her checkbook. "How much will it take for this all to go away?"

"This can't be solved with money!"

"Then what am I supposed to do?" she yells back. "Your father is about to run for mayor." Wow, didn't know that. Shows how much I know about my parents' lives now. "We can't have this kind of scandal being dug up, history coming back out to play."

"Jesus, that's all you care about, don't you? Your precious name and reputation! Need I remind you that my last name isn't even yours anymore!"

Kaydence stirs behind me, but I keep my eyes locked on my mom. I don't want to give her the satisfaction of seeing my daughter, watching me break apart when I hold her—because I would *never* treat Kaydence this way. I can't imagine ever doubting her and abandoning her the way my parents have done with me.

"Well, at least there's that," she says, narrowing her eyes at me. "When is this mediation over?"

"Tomorrow! And then you don't have to worry about me ruining your life anymore, okay?"

"I should hope not. This trip ruined my schedule, Evelyn. You know how busy I am."

"Then leave. And don't come back. I'd hate to ruin your schedule anymore." Kaydence starts to cry behind me, but I stay rooted in place. My heart is pounding. I can feel sweat dripping down my back. And my stomach is twisted in knots. But I will not let her see what she does to me. I refuse.

My mother darts her eyes to my right, where Kaydence is shielded behind the counter. But she doesn't say anything. The last thing she'd want is to meet her granddaughter.

Nope. She just spins on her heels and heads for the door.

"I'd have thought you'd have grown out of this phase of chaos in your life by now, Evelyn. Guess I was wrong." Those are the last words my mother says to me over her shoulder before she exits my store.

I collapse into a ball on the floor, crying along with my daughter, because just when I thought my past was in the past, it forced its way into the present and made me feel like maybe I can't handle this life.

Maybe I need to run again, start over some place new. That's what I did last time. That's how I chose to deal with the lack of love and understanding in my life back then.

But there's so much more at stake now. I'm just not sure how much more of this I can take.

Walker finds me on the floor of my store thirty minutes later. "Evelyn?"

Kaydence is playing with her bottle between my legs, but I can't find the strength to lift us up off the carpet. I'm not sure how I look because I've been crying since my mother left, but as I stare up at him, another wave of tears hits me, and I lose it all over again.

What is he doing here?

"What happened? Are you hurt? Is everything okay?" He reaches down and picks up Kaydence then extends a hand to me, helping me stand.

I wipe my face on the back of my forearm and then walk away in search of tissue.

"Evelyn . . . talk to me, babe."

I blow my nose into a tissue and toss it into a trash can. "My mother just showed up here."

His entire body tenses. "What? Why?"

"To tell me what a piece of shit daughter and mother I am, apparently." Sniffling, I reach for another tissue and then walk to the mirror on the wall. Mascara is all over my face, my eyes are swollen, and I look like a wreck. Funny, I feel like one, too.

That's what a run-in with my mother does to me—leaves me in broken pieces. I haven't seen her in person in nine years, and now I remember why.

"John's parents are poking around, like I suspected, and my father is running for mayor of Dallas. Apparently, she's worried that my life is going to paint theirs in a negative light. She found out about the mediation."

Walker grows tense. "Why didn't you call me?"

"I didn't know she was coming! She completely blind-sided me!" I shout as I spin to face him.

"Fuck, Evelyn. What do you want me to do?" he asks as he bounces Kaydence in his arms.

"There's nothing you *can* do, Walker. She left, and hopefully she'll never come back." Fuming now, I clench my hands at my sides. "This is what they do, Walker. This is what my parents are like. They try to diffuse the situation by controlling it. She wanted to just throw money at the problem to make it go away." I toss my hands up in the air.

"Then don't let them try to control you. Who gives a fuck what they think? We've established that they're shitty people, Evelyn."

"God, why did she have to come up here?" I ask, staring at the ceiling. And then I drop my eyes to his. "This is my life, Walker. These people! This drama! The ridicule! Why on earth would you want to be a part of that?"

Walker looks like I slapped him across the face, but I'm serious. How could this man want to deal with this drama?

He grinds his teeth together before replying. "Because you don't deserve to have to deal with a family like that, and I want to be the family you *do* deserve, Evelyn." His legs carry him over to me as his hand reaches up and cradles my jaw. "I want to protect you from them and show you that you deserve to be loved. *I'm* the one who wants to prove that to you."

I bat his hand away, not allowing myself to hear him. "This is just all too much right now," I say as I begin to pace the carpet. "Those are the people who brought me into this world. I will always be connected to them. They will always try to control me, to make sure I know what a fucking disappointment I am. And you know what? Maybe I am!"

Walker crosses the distance between us again in a flash.

"Don't you dare fucking talk about yourself like that, Evelyn Gibson."

"It's Sumner!" I scream. "I haven't changed my name, Walker!"

"I don't give a shit. You're still mine!"

"Well, maybe I don't want to be. Maybe you don't need this. Maybe I need to leave again, start over somewhere new, somewhere far away . . ." I stare off into the distance, seeing nothing, debating how quickly I could get out of here.

I need this all to go away.

Walker shakes his head at me, fuming now. "So that's your solution to this problem: just run away? You want to take this girl away from the only life and family she has, Evelyn?"

I turn to face him again, throwing my hands above my head. "I don't know! But what if John's parents win tomorrow?"

"That's not going to fucking happen!"

"You don't know that! This could have all been for nothing." I close my eyes, take a deep breath, and let out what I need to say. "You don't deserve this. You don't need this stress in your life. I'm just going to tear you down right alongside me." Tears fall down my cheeks, but I don't try to fight them.

I'm so *tired*—tired of fighting. I've fought with John, his parents, my parents, and now Walker.

I just can't fight anymore.

Walker stares at me for so long, I think he's gone blind. But when he speaks, it slices right through my already broken heart. "You're making me pay for what your parents did to you, what Seth Ferguson did. But *I'm not them.*" He takes another step closer. "I'm in this, Evelyn. I want you forever. I've told you how I feel and that I would do anything in my power to help you. But something tells me you're not at the same point." And then I really start to bleed when he finishes with "and maybe you need some space to think about that."

He kisses Kaydence on the cheek, places her in her playpen, and then turns around and walks away from me, pulling on my heartstrings as he does.

I don't want him to leave. That's the last fucking thing I want.

I need him. I need him like I need air to breathe. I need his love, his loyalty, his strength. I need him to stay and fight with me, for me—*for us*. He's the only one who has the strength left to fight.

So then why did you just push him away?

CHAPTER NINETEEN

Walker

All I wanted was a stress-free evening the night before the mediation. I had groceries in the car, I was going to stop by the store and surprise the girls, and Melissa was on her way to finish out the day so Evelyn could leave early from Luna.

I thought it would be perfect. I thought we'd go into tomorrow with optimism and a united front.

But then it all crumbled and fell apart right in front of me, leaving me helpless, a feeling I fucking hate to have.

I've been on the road for five hours now, but the trip is almost over. The buildings of downtown Dallas loom in the distance, letting me know I've almost reached my destination.

When I left her store, I felt broken and utterly defeated. But I only allowed myself a few minutes of pity before I slipped right into fix-it mode. I had to do something to help the woman I love, and so I hightailed it over to Chase's office before he left for the day.

Now, with papers in hand, I close in on the Sumner residence, hoping to God that this plan of mine will work.

The house I pull up to on the outskirts of Dallas is three times as large as the ranch. This place probably has ten bathrooms. Who the fuck needs that many toilets?

But regardless of the difference in class and stature that Evelyn's parents possess compared to me, they're shitty people, and that's why they will never have the opportunity to contact their daughter ever again. I'm making sure of it.

I grab the manila envelope off the passenger seat of my truck and head for their front door. It's late, after midnight. Who knows if they'll answer the door. But if they don't, I'm sleeping in my truck until I can wake their asses up at the crack of dawn to hand them this no-contact order face-to-face. I want them to see the intent in my eyes when I tell them to stay the fuck away from Evelyn for the rest of our lives.

My wife will realize that last night was just her fear coming out. I know this isn't over, and I won't fucking let it be.

But one thing at a time, and right now this is something

I have to fix before we go into the mediation with John's parents tomorrow—or today, actually, given how early it is.

I ring the doorbell, peeking through the windows, and I notice there are still lights on in the house. I wait a few minutes for someone to answer the door, but no one comes. So I ring the bell again.

Ten seconds later, an older woman who could be the spitting image of Evelyn in thirty years answers, pulling a silk robe tightly around her waist. "Do you realize it's after midnight?" she barks as she answers the door.

"Excuse my language, but I don't give a flying fuck what time it is," I fire back at her as her head rears back on her neck.

"How dare you . . ."

I take a step closer to her, which forces her back a bit, her eyes widening in fear. I'm not going to assault the woman, but she sure as hell is going to realize how fucking mad I am.

"No. How dare *you* come up to Newberry Springs and verbally abuse your daughter, Trinity Sumner!"

An older man appears now behind Evelyn's mom, who I'm assuming is her dad. "Listen, young man . . ."

"No, you listen." I toss the manila envelope on the floor at their feet. Fuck handing the papers to them politely. They don't deserve the fucking kindness. "This is a no-contact order filed with the state of Texas prohibiting you from contacting your daughter for the remainder of her life." Her dad bends down to grab the envelope, opening it up to verify my assertion. "You are no longer allowed to see her, call her, talk to her, email her, or send a fucking carrier pigeon to deliver a message to her. She is no longer your concern. She is my responsibility, my fucking life, and I refuse to let you hurt her anymore."

"Who the hell are you to tell us that we can't call our daughter?" her mother spits out.

I take another step closer to her so I can see the flecks of gold in her eyes. "I'm her fucking *husband,* and you have made my *wife* cry for the last fucking time." I watch her swallow, so I keep going. "You will sign these papers, or I will contact every fucking tabloid and expose you for the horrendous parents that you are. Your little mayoral campaign will go up in flames, and I won't stop until it does. You don't deserve her love or energy anymore. She has done nothing wrong. You two are despicable human beings, and if you don't agree to this contract, I will make sure the whole fucking world knows it."

Her father glances at her mother, and I watch them have a silent conversation with their eyes. "Trinity, get a pen."

"But, Charles . . ."

"No. We can bury the contract in court records, Trinity. But we can't risk any more scandal. Just get a fucking pen," he seethes as she turns and walks deeper into the house. I stand there, crossing my arms over my chest, waiting until Trinity returns and signs the papers in front of me, passing them off to Charles Sumner to do the same. When he's finished, he puts them back in the envelope and hands it back to me. "There. It's done."

"Yes, it fucking is. I'm serious. Don't tempt me with exposing what scum you truly are. My wife and I are going to live our lives in bliss without the memory of you haunting her. You don't deserve to know the woman that you birthed but failed to raise. She's done that on her own. And she is an incredible, warm, compassionate mother, which is something you obviously didn't teach her," I say to Trinity before turning on my heel and walking away. "I hope you sleep like shit knowing you just lost the one person in your life you should want to know and love unconditionally," I call over my shoulder, firing one last insult at them for good measure.

Once I settle into my truck, I fight to get my breathing under control before I get back on the road.

Fuck, that felt good. But my heart is racing, my mind is a mess, and my stomach is growling because I didn't eat dinner. There wasn't time.

So I find the nearest drive-through, pick up something to eat, and then head back to the highway, eager to get back to Newberry Springs and my wife.

The sun peeks over the horizon just as I drive back into town limits, bathing the sky in yellow and light blue. Driving to Dallas last night was not on the agenda for the evening originally, but after Evelyn basically told me she didn't need me, I had to do something, and I'm glad that I did.

I know she didn't mean the words she spewed in the heat of the moment, but it still fucking killed me to hear them, especially after she opened up to me a few nights before. This woman is so fucking pure and good, and it kills me that people in her life would tear her down the way they have. So I helped put a stop to it. And I have no fucking regrets after seeing her parents' faces when they saw me on their doorstep.

The entire drive back, I kept replaying all of the things I should have said, which is pretty typical of any heated argument. Everyone always thinks of what words they could have chosen that would have hammered their point home after the fact. But I still feel confident that the trip and the contract will make our lives better moving forward.

So I have been in the car for nearly ten hours now, but I still can't go home. I don't want to wake Evelyn and Kaydence up in case they didn't get much sleep last night. I sent her a few text messages telling her how much I love her, but she never responded.

I didn't expect her to. I know my wife. She has to figure out what she wants alone, as much as it kills me. Because I want to reassure her face-to-face that I'm not going anywhere. But she'll figure it out.

At least, I hope she does—and before this mediation.

I have a few hours before I have to be at the courthouse, but right now, I really need a shower and a bed. And I know a place that can give me both, along with someone to talk to.

And what better person to listen to me than *my* mother.

I walk into the main house on the ranch just after six in the morning on a Wednesday. The day and time make my mother shocked to see me, as I expected. Her wide eyes tell me that.

"Walker?" She gapes at me as she sets her chef's knife on the counter.

"Hey, Momma." I stride across the kitchen and pull her into me, squeezing her so tight I know she can barely breathe. But fuck. I'm one lucky man to have this woman as my mother, especially after seeing what Evelyn has experienced.

"Son, you're scaring me."

"Don't be scared, Momma. I just want you to know how much I appreciate you, how much I love you."

"I love you, too, my boy." When I finally release her, she peers up at me, a wrinkle in her brow. "What's going on? Where's Evelyn? And the baby?" She turns back to the counter, picking the knife back up to resume her chopping.

"They're at home." At least that's what the location tracker on her phone says, the one I put on it when we got married because I'm overprotective and wanted to make sure they were safe at all times.

"And why aren't you there with them?"

I let out a sigh, fighting to keep my eyes open, and then take a seat at the island. "I just got back from Dallas."

"What on earth were you doing in Dallas?"

"I need to tell you something, Momma." The last thing I want to do is disappoint this woman, but it's going to be hard to explain what I've been through in the past twenty-four hours without admitting the truth.

She sets the knife back down on the counter and focuses all of her attention on me. "Walker . . . what's going on?"

"Evelyn and I weren't in love when we got married, Momma," I admit, waiting to see what she says. But my mother just stands there, staring at me like she's waiting for more, so I continue. "John's parents filed a custody contestation. They wanted to try to take Kaydence away from Evelyn, claiming she's an unfit mother based on some shit that happened in her past and the fact that she was single, raising that baby alone. So I offered to marry her, and I don't regret that for a second."

"Okay," she says, her eyebrows hitting her hairline.

"I'm sorry that I lied to you, to everyone. Well, except for Wyatt and Kelsea. They knew the truth since they were our witnesses."

"Walker, even a blind man could see you're in love with Evelyn."

I huff out a laugh. "I know."

"So you two getting married didn't really surprise me. It was the fact you didn't tell us that pissed me off."

"I'm sorry again for that. But it was a fast decision. Time was of the essence."

She nods. "I see. But honey, I saw how you felt about her before John ever died."

My eyes lift. "You did?"

"Yes. So I didn't question how you felt about her, if that's the point of your confession."

"Not really. It's more about her family, her parents and the crap they've put her through." I spend the next several minutes filling her in on Evelyn's mom and the visit yesterday that sent everything spiraling out of control, leading me to Dallas last night to make sure they could never hurt her again. Now *I'm* just hurting because the woman I love is convinced that she doesn't deserve *my* love.

"She told me that I'm better off without her." Hanging my head down, I hold back the tears I want to shed. I know this thing isn't over between us, but if that's what she really wants, I'd have no choice but to let her go.

"She's hurting, Walker." My mother rounds the island and places her hand on my shoulder, brushing my hair back from my face like she did when I was younger and sad about something.

"I just want her to want me, Momma. I need her to want me back."

"She does, honey. She just has to let herself accept it."

I pop my head up and look her in the eye. "What if she doesn't? What if I have to let her go? What if this was all for nothing? What if John's death continues to plague me? What if I can't handle the pain of losing him, his daughter, and Evelyn, too?"

My mother sheds a tear as she looks down at me. "That broken soul of yours that feels guilty for what happened with John, that part of you that you keep trying to put back together, can't even compare with the beautiful man that you are molding yourself into for Evelyn and Kaydence." She wipes under her eyes. "I'm so proud of you for what you've done for her. And Evelyn knows that, too. She needs time to catch up, that's all."

I wish my heart would believe my mother's words. "But the problem is, we're running out of time. And by the time she figures this out, it might be too late. The mediation is in five hours. We haven't spoken since I left the store last night."

"Well, do you plan on showing up for her?"

"Of course, Momma. There's no way I won't be there."

"Then that's all you have to do, honey. Show up. Actions speak louder than words. She knows how you feel, and perhaps her time alone has helped her realize how she feels, too."

God, I hope so.

"But you really need a shower. And some food."

"And some sleep," I add through a yawn.

"Yes. Go take care of yourself, grab a nap, and I'll call Wyatt to bring you a change of clothes."

Standing from the stool, I pull her in for a hug again. "Thank you, Momma."

"No, thank *you,* Walker, for being the man I raised you to be." She cups the side of my face. "There's no other way to make your mother more proud of you."

"Evelyn makes me want to be the man she needs, a man she can't live without. I want to be everything for them that John couldn't."

"And you are. You're honoring your friend by stepping up, but you're also honoring yourself by being true to your feelings. Everything is going to be okay. I firmly believe that."

I hope she's right. But then again, my mom is always right. She'd just better not break that winning streak with this.

CHAPTER TWENTY

Evelyn

When I wake up Wednesday morning, I can barely open my eyes. They're so swollen from crying that I know wearing makeup today is going to be a challenge, so I may as well just forgo it.

Kaydence's babbles come through the speaker on her baby monitor, so I know she's up. But she's not crying, so I take a moment to compose myself before I have to face the day.

Tears rise to the surface again.

Walker.

He should be here in bed with me, waking me up with his touch and gravelly morning voice. He should be pulling me into his chest, kissing my shoulders, and waking up my body in the way only he knows how.

But he's not. And I have no one to blame but myself.

I run my hand over the white sheets in the bed where he usually sleeps, inhaling the fabric, trying to get a whiff of his scent to help soothe the ache in my chest. But I can't smell him. It's as if he's drifted away and left me alone the way I thought I wanted.

God, I hate the way he left yesterday, the way I *made* him leave yesterday.

I was so distraught in the moment that I said things I truly didn't mean.

I don't want to run away. I don't want him to give up on me and Kaydence.

I want to love him forever, too.

I'm just scared. And scarred. And hurting—for so many reasons—and I took it out on him. But he has proven time and again that he loves me, is there for me, and won't give me any reason to doubt that. Yet, I did.

And now, it's the morning of the mediation, the day I have to face John's parents again and hopefully come to an agreement for visitations with their granddaughter. Or, if the worst possible thing happens, be told that I'm no longer the sole guardian of my child.

And I don't know if Walker will be there by my side

through it all. Why would he after what I said to him? Why would he want to fight with me any more about how he feels?

How long am I going to doubt that I can be happy with him, that things will work out despite the fact that they haven't been easy in any other aspect of my life?

I'll never know if I keep pushing him away.

Needing to know that I haven't lost him forever, I pick up my phone and reread the texts he sent me last night.

Walker: *I love you, Evelyn.*

Walker: *You can't push me away.*

Walker: *I'm going to love you forever.*

Walker: *I would fight every one of your demons just so you can feel like you can breathe, and that's what I'm doing right now.*

With a fresh batch of tears streaming down my face, I find his contact and tap his number.

I have to hear his voice. I have to make sure that we're okay, that I will see him this morning at the courthouse. But the line continues to ring and ring, and he doesn't pick up before his voicemail message starts to play.

I hang up and try calling again but still get no answer.

And then Kaydence starts to cry from her crib, so I don't have time to try again.

My mind goes to worst-case scenarios, wondering why he wouldn't be picking up—is he hurt? Did something happen last night?

He said he would fight my demons . . . what does that mean? What did he do?

If something happened to him and I never got to tell him that I love him, too, I won't survive it. I've already experienced that type of regret with John, stewing over my last words to him over and over, regretting what I *did* say.

I don't want to regret what I *didn't* say, too.

After I change Kaydence's diaper, get her dressed, and feed her breakfast, I attempt to distract myself with laundry and cleaning before I have to get us ready for court.

The distraction doesn't work, though. And after attempting to call Walker with no answer once more, the anxiety of today just builds and builds until I'm shaking as I drive us into town.

"Good morning," Chase greets us as I walk up to the front door of the courthouse. He's standing there alone on the steps, shielding the sun from his eyes. I was hoping Walker would be with him.

"Good morning."

"You ready for this?"

"As ready as I'm going to be," I reply as I reach the top step. My eyes search the parking lot, eager to find my husband striding up to us. "Um, have you heard from Walker?"

His brow furrows. "No. I thought he'd be with you."

"Oh. Well, he, uh . . . didn't come home last night."

"What?" Chase seems genuinely concerned, which is making me worry even more. "He should have."

"You saw him?"

"Yes. He stopped by my office yesterday afternoon."

"Why?" I ask, but Chase doesn't reply. Because before he can, Mr. and Mrs. Schmitt come walking up the steps to the courthouse.

They don't make eye contact with me this time like they did at the football game. Instead, they move right past us with their lawyer as if we don't even exist.

Chase waits until they go inside before speaking. "Have you tried calling him?"

"Yes, three times this morning with no reply."

He digs his phone out of his pocket, spinning away from me as he clicks a few buttons and brings it to his ear. The line must be ringing because he never addresses anyone on the other side, and then my supposition is confirmed as he leaves a message. "Hey, Walker. It's Chase. I'm here at the courthouse with Evelyn, and we're worried about you, man. The mediation starts in five minutes. Call us back." When he disconnects the phone, he turns back to me. "I'm sure he'll be here, Evelyn. He wouldn't miss this."

But what if he decided he's done?

I try not to let my mind convince my heart of that possibility, but I don't have a lot of time to do so.

"We should head inside." Chase smiles, clearly trying to reassure me, but it doesn't work.

Instead, I just nod and go through the motions, eager for this to just be over already. "Yeah. Okay."

Chase opens the door for me, allowing me to enter before him, and then he leads me and Kaydence down the same hall we used last time. When we stop in front of the large mahogany door, my knees shake, and I nearly collapse.

"It's going to be okay, Evelyn. I won't let them take this child from you, okay?" Chase whispers in my ear.

"Okay."

Chase opens this door for me as well, and I walk past him, keeping my head down to avoid looking at anyone else. I don't want them to see the emotional turmoil the last twenty-four hours have caused me, even though my puffy eyes and red face probably don't help disguise that. Without Walker here, I don't feel confident enough to face this. I need him here with me.

He's supposed to be here. We're supposed to be facing this together.

Well, whose fault is it that he's not, Evelyn?

"Good morning," Mr. Sullivan, the same mediating attorney from before, addresses everyone once Chase and I take our seats. "Are we ready to begin?"

Chase glances over at me, raising his eyebrows. He's asking me if I'm okay with getting started, and the truth is that I'm not. But what am I going to do about it? If Walker wanted to be here, he would be.

"Yes. Everyone is here," I say, my voice low and unsure.

"What about Mr. Gibson?" Mr. Sullivan asks. "I assumed he'd be joining us."

"Well, uh . . ." I can't form a sentence to explain why he's not here, because I don't know. But luckily, I don't have to, because Walker charges through the door at that very moment, stealing the breath from my lungs and making me choke back a sob.

"I'm here!" he yells, out of breath and hair in disarray. "I'm here," he says more calmly now as he rounds the table and pulls out the chair next to me. He sits down and reaches for my hand, bringing it to his lips as he kisses my skin. "Sorry I'm late."

He's blurry because my eyes are full of tears, but I can't help but fling myself at him, squishing Kaydence between us in the process. "You're here," I whisper in his ear through the lump in my throat.

"I'm here, baby. I'm here." His lips press against my temple, and for the first time since he walked out of Luna, I breathe.

"No problem. Let's get this underway," Mr. Sullivan declares, opening up his folder in front of him.

I wipe the tears from my face as Walker takes Kaydence from me, loving on her while we wait for Mr. Sullivan to assess the contents of his folder.

"Okay. Well, first, the report from Child Protective Services states that the safety of the child is not in question in her current home," he starts, which helps me breathe a little more easily. "The agent who visited the home felt confident that the child lacked for nothing and was receiving an abundance of love and adoration from her parents." Walker squeezes my hand under the table. "Mr. and Mrs. Schmitt have attended their grief counseling as well, as ordered." His eyes scan the page. "I'm still seeing mention of questionable behavior from Mrs. Gibson in her last job as grounds for contestation, though." He turns to the lawyer sitting beside Mr. and Mrs. Schmitt. "Care to explain?"

"May I say something?" Walker interjects, drawing everyone's attention to him.

"Mr. Gibson, you'll get a chance to speak," Mr. Sullivan declares, a warning in his voice.

"The information regarding Mrs. Gibson is not relevant to this case, particularly because it has nothing to do with her ability to mother a child," Walker says, ignoring Mr. Sullivan. "Besides, any information you gathered to use against her is not the truth, I assure you."

"That should have been taken out of the final paperwork," Mrs. Schmitt says, shocking both me and Walker. "We didn't want to bring that up again." She turns to her attorney. "I told you to take that out."

"My apologies. My paralegal must have missed it," he says, clearing his throat as his cheeks flush.

But then John's mom turns to face us both. "We owe you an apology, Evelyn. And you, Walker. I'm so sorry to have put you through this," she says through her tears. "I just . . . I miss my son."

She puts her hand on her chest, over her heart. "He was my whole world, and losing him has been the hardest thing I've ever gone through. I thought by taking in his daughter, I could hold onto a piece of him," she continues as John's dad rubs her shoulder, letting his tears fall as well. "But over the past few weeks, we've realized that grief has fueled many decisions, ones that not only impact us but you as well. We can see how happy she is, how in love the two of you are, and we don't want to break up your family. We just want to be a part of it."

As I stare at the woman across from me, I no longer see her as a villain but as a fellow mother with so much love for her child and nowhere for it to go. She lost her son. She lost the one person she loved more than life itself. And in that moment, I realize that I wouldn't wish that loss on anyone.

I've lost my mother. She never loved me the way I love my own daughter, the way John's mother loved him. Instead of fighting with one another, we should be helping each other through the pain.

So that's what I'm going to do.

"We would love for you to be in Kaydence's life," I say as a collective sigh resonates through the room. "Understand that this entire ordeal will take some time to move past, but . . ." I turn to Walker, seeing him looking back at me with love, adoration, and pride. He knows this is the right thing to do, too. So I turn back to face John's mom. "We would love to try, to let you get to know your granddaughter."

Margaret lets out a sob before nodding with a smile. "Thank you."

Mr. Sullivan clears his throat, gathering everyone's attention again. "All right. So we're agreeing to court-ordered visitation, then?" he asks, pen poised over the paper.

"Yes," Walker and I say at the same time. He leans over and kisses my temple as I let out the final breath I've been holding in.

"Great. I assume both parties have prepared scheduling requests?"

Chase slides a paper across the table to Mr. Sullivan as the Schmitts' lawyer does the same. "Fantastic. Then we will reconvene in two weeks to sign documents and file this with the court." He stands, closes the folder, and nods to both parties. "Nice work, everyone. See you in two weeks."

We watch him leave, and then Chase stands. "If you don't mind, I'd like to speak with my clients alone."

John's parents nod and stand along with their lawyer. "Of course." Then Margaret looks at me again. "Thank you."

"You're welcome," I reply, watching them leave before I remember there's so much more still to decide between me and the man sitting in the chair next to mine.

"Walker," Chase starts. "You had us going there for a minute."

Walker drags a hand through his hair, standing up with Kaydence still in his arms. "I'm so sorry. I got back from Dallas at like five this morning and stopped by the ranch to talk to my mom. I took a shower and then laid down because I was fucking exhausted. My mom woke me up fifteen minutes before I had to be here, so I rushed in a panic and didn't even grab my phone." He looks down at me. "I'm so sorry if I worried you."

But I don't care about that now. I need answers about something else he just said. "Why were you in Dallas last night?"

"I went to visit your parents."

I pop up from my seat. "What? Why?"

"I served them with a no-contact order, Evelyn." He kisses Kaydence's head before looking over at Chase. Chase just stands there, smirking, shoving his hands in his pockets.

"What does that mean?"

Walker closes the gap between us and reaches out to cup my jaw. "That means they can never contact you again, baby. They're out of our lives, legally."

"What?" I breathe out. "They signed it?"

"Yup. I told them that if they didn't, I would go to every tabloid and news outlet to expose them for the disgusting and abusive parents they are. You father practically forced your mother to sign it."

I cover my mouth with my hand. "Oh my God. I can't believe you did that . . ."

He smiles down at me. "When are you going to allow yourself to accept that I love you and would do anything for you, huh?"

Chase clears his throat. "I'm going to give you two some privacy. But I'll just say that I'm glad things worked out this morning. I'll be in contact this week with updates." He shakes Walker's hand, followed by mine, and then exits the room, leaving us alone.

I stare up into Walker's eyes, getting lost in his warm, brown orbs that I can't believe I ever thought I could live without.

I'm tired of living in fear. The fear I felt over the past twenty-four hours is enough to make me realize that I want him beside me forever. That I need him to help me learn to swim through the darkness and search for the moon when it feels like I won't ever find it.

"I feel like loving me is so fucking hard. I'm a difficult person to love, Walker," I admit when I finally find the courage to speak.

"No, Evelyn." He shakes his head, toying with my bottom lip. "Loving you is the easiest thing I've ever done. And that's because you're meant to be mine."

My heart is beating so hard that my entire body is shaking. "I can't lose anyone again, people I thought would be there for me. Losing you would mean losing Kelsea, your family . . . I can't go through that one more time in my life. I might not survive it."

"Then it's a good thing that I'm not going anywhere." His lips spread, and his smile lights up the room.

"I want to belong to somebody, Walker."

"And I want you to belong to me."

"I do. I'm yours." Wrapping my arms around his neck, I hold on as tightly as I can. Kaydence reaches for my face, grabbing my hair and inserting herself into our moment. But once I take her in my arms, kiss her a few times, and look back up at Walker, I know what I need to say.

But he beats me to the punch.

Pulling me into his chest again, he says, "I promise to give you everything you need in this world, Evelyn. I'll even give you the moon and stars if you ask for them."

God, this man. I don't deserve him, but I'm going to fight like hell every day to prove that I want him.

"Don't promise me the moon and the stars, Walker," I reply, resting my forehead against his. "Just promise me that you'll dance under them with me."

"I promise."

"You're the only man I've ever been able to depend on, and you're the only one I ever want to have to. I love you, Walker. And I want to stay married to you."

He takes my hand and places it over his heart, over the tattoo he got for me and my daughter. "Thank fuck." We both share a laugh. "Love is overwhelming, babe. But it's amazing, too. You are the love of my life, Evelyn Gibson.

And I'm going to love you as long as the moon circles the earth."

"Forever?"

"Forever, babe. You and me and this little owl here."

"Sounds like heaven," I say, smiling so hard that my cheeks start to burn.

"No, Evelyn. Heaven is here on earth with *you*. That's what heaven is to me, baby. And that's what I'll fight for until the end."

CHAPTER TWENTY-ONE

Walker

"Oh my gosh. She *does* look like John!" Evelyn looks up at me from over her shoulder. She's flipping through a photo album John's parents brought over to the ranch today, scanning through pictures and memories of his childhood that his mother wanted to share with her.

It's been three weeks since the mediation, and today is the first visit with Margaret and Robert.

I know that talking about him makes everyone emotional, but it's also a way for us to keep his memory alive—and I swear to do that just for Kaydence's sake. She deserves to hear about her father and how much he was loved.

"Definitely," I agree, squeezing her shoulder in support. It's surreal to look at baby pictures of my best friend knowing he's gone, but I feel a contentment about it, too. I'm sure he's here right now, happy to see everyone together.

"Look at you two!" Evelyn practically shrieks as she comes across a picture of me and John outside on a summer day, wearing our swim shorts next to a blow-up pool. We have to be around nine years old if memory serves me correctly.

"God, we were scrawny," I mutter mostly to myself, but Evelyn catches it.

"You're definitely not anymore." She looks up at me with that twinkle in her eyes, the one that tells me she's thinking about all the things I do to her when she's naked —things that require the muscles I now have and use to command her body.

"You know it, babe." I wink at her and then kiss the top of her head, glancing across the room to catch Margaret taking selfies with Kaydence. She's so enamored with that baby girl, which doesn't surprise me one bit. Everyone who meets her is.

Hell, I didn't stand a chance the first time she laid those big green eyes on me.

I was worried that today would be awkward, difficult even, for everyone. But when Momma insisted that John's parents join us for a barbecue at the ranch so the entire family could be together, I knew she had the right idea. Not only did she not want Evelyn to feel alone and nervous about starting this new relationship with John's parents, but it was important to her that Evelyn knows she has family now—*my* family.

We haven't heard from her parents, which doesn't surprise me. And if they know what's good for them, they'll adhere to that order and refrain from contacting her ever again.

Evelyn was still shocked that I went out of my way to do that for her, but once she accepted it, she was relieved. And I'm proud that I could take that stress away from her.

It's been an emotional rollercoaster since Evelyn and I decided to stay married. Things didn't go back to easy right away. I forced her to talk to me and made her see that she can't push me away like that again.

I know she was remorseful about it, but it still hurt me. I was fearful she would continue to face our problems that way. So we agreed, after a lot of talking, that the love we have will never go away as long as we communicate. She has to tell me when she's scared, when she needs space, and when she needs me to show her that she's not alone.

I promised to love her no matter what, and I meant it. She's mine, and there's no changing that, *ever*.

As I stare down at pictures of John, I have to remind myself, too, that he's watching over all of us, proud of what we've faced and solved together, and supportive of my relationship with Evelyn.

I don't know what would have happened if he would have survived that fire, but I can't live my life wondering. The only thing I can do is keep pushing forward, protecting those I love, and accepting both the good and the bad life brings.

And right now, there's so much fucking good that it makes my heart ache with love. It's a different kind of ache than the one I lived with for over a year, and this one I welcome with open arms.

Forrest storms through the door, slamming the screen against the outside of the house as he enters the living room, startling everyone and pulling me from my sappy recounting of the past three weeks.

"Jesus. You're going to scare Kaydence," I chastise him as he tears across the carpet like a grizzly bear that just came out of his cave. Kaydence's lip trembles as she fights off her desire to cry, but luckily, Margaret soothes her and prevents her from wailing.

My eyes trail my brother as he stomps along. His hair is a mess, he looks like he hasn't shaved in a week, and a permanent scowl is resting on his forehead.

"Sorry," he mutters, heading for the fridge to grab a beer. He doesn't even say anything to anyone in the house before opening the back door and heading toward the barn.

I glance at Wyatt, and we have one of those silent twin

conversations, the ones where we agree that something has to be said about his behavior without speaking a word.

Leaning down, I kiss the top of Evelyn's head. "I'll be right back, babe."

"Okay," she says, peering up at me. "I love you," she whispers, and hearing those words from her lips will never get old.

"I love you, too, Ev. So fucking much." I plant a chaste kiss on her lips and then follow Wyatt out the back door, heading over to the fence surrounding the horse pen. Forrest is resting his arms over the top rung, holding his beer between his hands.

"This can either go great or horribly wrong," Wyatt mutters as we get closer to our older brother.

"I agree, but I'm fucking tired of his surly ass. He's pissed about something, and it's time he fucking talks."

"Agreed."

As soon as we reach him, Wyatt and I take a spot on either side of him, caging him in.

"All right, Grumpy Gibson," Wyatt starts, calling him by the nickname we coined after he came home from college and this surly attitude of his started.

"Fuck off, Wyatt."

"No can do, big brother. Enough is enough." Wyatt crosses his arms over his chest, facing him straight on. "What the fuck is going on with you? You've been an asshole more than normal since you got back from Vegas, and you're scaring everyone."

"You frightened my kid," I add. "I'm not gonna pretend like that's okay."

Forrest growls, draining his beer and tossing the bottle into one of the cans stationed next to the horse pen. "I don't have to tell you two anything."

I shove him, which catches him off guard. He bounces into Wyatt's chest, which thankfully Wyatt's prepared for, but all it does is piss Forrest off even more. Once the initial shock has worn off, Forrest shoves me back, knocking me off-balance.

So I swing at him, which he dodges before trying to return the favor. His fist grazes my cheek, though, and now I'm fucking pissed, so I bend low, rush him, and tackle him to the ground.

"Am I supposed to just stand by and let this happen?" Wyatt asks as Forrest and I wrestle in the dirt.

I end up on top of him, pinning him beneath me, which is a feat in itself. Forrest has about thirty pounds on me, but based on the smell of alcohol pouring off of him, I'm going to say he's hungover, which, thankfully, is giving me an advantage.

"That depends on when Forrest starts talking," I say, holding his arms down.

"Get the fuck off me, Walker!" Forrest shouts.

"Not until you tell us what the fuck is going on!"

"Shauna is getting married tomorrow!" he screams, the last thing I expected him to say. But it also makes the most fucking sense as to why he's been acting this way for weeks.

"So you *did* see her in Vegas?" Wyatt asks, to clarify.

"Yes, and it was . . ." Forrest closes his eyes, huffing out air through his nose. "She's still—"

"—the love of your life," I finish for him.

All he does is nod, his eyes still closed.

"What did she say when you saw each other?"

Forrest breathes in deeply, finally opening his eyes again. "She hugged me, said it was good to see me. We shared an entire meal, and I swear, I was sixteen, falling in love all over again." He shoves me, knocking me off of him, but I don't fight. I can tell he's beating himself up enough.

Still sitting on the ground, my ass covered in dirt, I say, "So then . . ."

"I went to kiss her, just wanting one more taste of her, but she stopped me, and that's when her fiancé showed up. She didn't have a ring on her finger. It was in her pocket."

"Shit," Wyatt mutters, staring off into the distance. "So she's getting married tomorrow?"

"Yeah." Forrest hangs his head. "She's going to be someone else's wife—"

"Not if you stop her from marrying him," I say, cutting him off.

His head snaps over to me. "What?"

"Well, she's not married yet, right? Haven't you ever seen the episode of *Friends* where Rachel decides to crash

Ross's wedding? I believe her words were, 'it's not over until somebody says I do.'"

"What the fuck are you saying?" he asks, acting like he didn't just hear what I was implying.

"He's saying you go fight for her. You don't let her go without telling her that you're still in love with her," Wyatt clarifies for me.

"I can't fucking do that."

"Why not?" I shove his shoulder again, but this time he just glares at me. "If it were Evelyn, I'd be there on my fucking knees, begging her to see reason, to remember how good we were together."

"If it were Kelsea, I'd tattoo her name on my ass and drop my pants in front of her to show her that she's branded on me forever."

Rolling my eyes, I laugh at my brother. "That actually sounds like something *I* would do, asshat."

"Well, we both already have tattoos for our girls, so . . ." He shrugs. "Point made."

"You two have fucking tattoos for Kelsea and Evelyn?" Forrest asks, glancing between the two of us.

"Yup." I lift my shirt and show him the moon and owl on my pec.

"I got mine before Kelsea and I were ever together," Wyatt says as he lifts his shirt and shows Forrest the camera he has on his ribs for Kelsea.

"Jesus." Forrest drags a hand down his face and starts unbuckling his jeans.

"Uh, what the fuck are you doing?" I ask as I begin to scoot away from him, wondering if my brother is going crazy as he starts shoving his pants down. But then he pulls the leg of his briefs up so that Wyatt and I can both see the tattoo on his upper thigh of a girl on a horse, charging forward, her hair flung back as if she's racing into the wind.

"Holy shit," I say, leaning forward to get a closer look. "You got that for Shauna, didn't you?"

"In college," he replies, pulling his underwear and jeans back in place before straightening his legs out in front of him. "She's always been the one."

"We know," Wyatt and I say in unison.

"But now the question is: Are you going to let her get away, Forrest?" Wyatt pushes, kicking him in the ass while he's still on the ground.

"You'll always live with regrets if you don't try to tell her how you feel, how you've always felt," I add.

Our older brother stares down at the ground for so long, I wonder if he fell asleep sitting up. But then his head pops up, the scowl leaves his face, and instead of looking like his world is ending, determination fills his eyes.

He launches from the ground, not even bothering to wipe the dirt off his body. And then he starts to walk away.

I scramble to get up from the ground as well, desperate to follow him. Wyatt and I both race to catch up with him.

"Forrest?" He doesn't say a word, so I yell louder. "Forrest!"

When he spins around, Wyatt and I stop dead in our tracks. His eyes bounce back and forth between us before he finally says, "I have a fucking wedding to stop, boys. Wish me luck."

Wyatt and I just stand there, watching him walk away before looking at one another and then high-fiving in the air.

"Hell, yeah! Go get her, man!" I call after him.

It's time that our brother gets his happy ending, too. I just hope it works out that way, for all our sakes.

THE END

Thank you SO much for reading Walker and Evelyn's story! If you enjoyed it, PLEASE consider leaving a rating/review on Amazon and/or Goodreads 😊

And if you would like a glimpse into Walker and Evelyn's future, click here for an exclusive BONUS EPILOGUE!

Forrest and Shauna's book, *Everything But You,* is coming December 2023!

Looking for more smalltown romance? Did you know that Javi and Sydney, the couple from the fire station fundraiser, have a book? Read their story in *Guilty as Charged,* a sexy, smalltown standalone between the construction worker and the sassy lawyer, full of sexual awakening 😉

Or if series are your thing, start my other smalltown romance series next with *Tangled,* a one-night-stand turned co-worker romance with a surprise twist you won't see coming!

Or if you're in the mood for a Sex In the City inspired rom-com series, pick up *Never Say Never,* the first book in my Ladies Who Brunch series, a childhood enemies to lovers, fake relationship romantic comedy here!

MORE BOOKS BY HARLOW JAMES

The Ladies Who Brunch (rom-coms with a ton of spice)

Never Say Never (Charlotte and Damien)

No One Else (Amelia and Ethan)

Now's The Time (Penelope and Maddox)

Not As Planned (Noelle and Grant)

Nice Guys Still Finish (Jeffrey and Ariel)

The California Billionaires Series (rom coms with heart and heat)

My Unexpected Serenity (Wes and Shayla)

My Unexpected Vow (Hayes and Waverly)

My Unexpected Family (Silas and Chloe)

Newberry Springs Series (smalltown, brothers)

Everything to Lose (Wyatt and Kelsea)

Everything He Couldn't (Walker and Evelyn)

Everything But You (Forrest and Shauna)

The Emerson Falls Series (smalltown romance with a found family friend group)

Tangled (Kane & Olivia)
Enticed (Cooper & Clara)
Captivated (Cash and Piper)
Revived (Luke and Rachel)
Devoted (Brooks and Jess)

Lost and Found in Copper Ridge

A holiday romance in which two people book a stay in a cabin for the same amount of time thanks to a serendipitous $5 bill.

Guilty as Charged (Javier and Sydney)

An intense opposites attract standalone that will melt your kindle. He's an ex-con construction worker. She's a lawyer looking for passion.

McKenzie's Turn to Fall

A holiday romance where a romance author falls for her neighborhood butcher.

ACKNOWLEDGMENTS

Walker and Evelyn are no longer in fictional limbo! LOL

Poor Walker! He was left on the cliffy in Everything to Lose for TWO YEARS, so when I finally sat down to write his book, his story just poured out of me. I wrote this book in four weeks because I was so obsessed.

I LOVED writing these two! In fact, when I was done, I told my beta readers that this might be my favorite book I've ever written. There were so many layers, I loved how fiercely protective of her he was, and add in a baby and meddling family, and I just had the most fun writing this story!

This series has been in my mind for SO long, it feels surreal to let it out finally, and I hope you fall in love with these brothers as much as I did. I can't wait to bring you Forrest and Shauna's book. At this moment, their story is already written, and will be hitting your kindles on December 1st.

Stay tuned for alerts and news related to my next releases!

To my husband: Thank you for cheering me on and

celebrating my success with me as I release each book. Thank you for understanding how much joy this hobby brings me. Thank you for listening to me vent when I'm struggling, and helping me turn this into a business now, including being my "book bitch." 😉 Here's to our adventures this next year doing signings and staying in many hotel rooms with no kids. And thank you for being my real life book husband and giving me my own true love story to brag about.

To Lizzy: I remember sitting on the beach, plotting this series, and now it's finally come to life. You were right. It just wasn't the right time back then, but now, the Gibson brothers are done. I love you and couldn't do this without all of your support along the way.

To Emily: I'm convinced that I wrote this book so fast just for you 😉 I tortured you with that cliff hanger, and you still haven't let me forget it. Thank you for being my sounding board with this series. I appreciate your friendship and support more than you know, and our friendship means the world to me.

To Melissa, my editor: I am SO grateful for our working relationship. I always know that my book is in great hands with you. Thank you for your dedication to my stories and I look forward to working together for a long time.

To Abigail, my cover designer: For three years now, you have brought every vision of mine to life, and this book was no exception. I LOVE working with you. Thank you for putting in so much time and love to my books. I think these might be my favorite covers yet!

And to my beta readers, ARC readers, and every reader (both old and new): Thank you for taking a chance on a self-published author. Thank you for sharing my books with others. Thank you for allowing me to share my creativity with people who love the romance genre as much as I do.

And thank you for supporting a wife and mom who found a hobby that she loves.

ABOUT THE AUTHOR

Harlow James is a wife and mom who fell in love with romance novels, so she decided to write her own. Her books are the perfect blend of emotional, addictive, and steamy romance. If you love stories with a guaranteed Happily Ever After, then Harlow is your new best friend. When she's not writing, she can be found working her day job, reading every romance novel she can find time for, laughing with her husband and kids, watching re-runs of FRIENDS, and spending time cooking for her friends and family while drinking White Claws and Margaritas.

facebook.com/HarlowJamesAuthor
instagram.com/harlowjamesauthor

Made in the USA
Middletown, DE
06 March 2025

72139410R00233